Maid For The Maestro

Diana Rock

Published by Diana Rock, 2025.

SECOND EDITION
Digital ISBN: 9798990323230
Paperback ISBN: 9798990323247
Audiobook ISBN: 9798990323254
Editor: Lynne Pearson, All that Editing
Cover Designer: Gemma Rakia
This is a work of fiction.

Dedication

To my favorite conductor for fanning the flames of this story for 20+ years.

WELCOME BACK

THE DOOR HITS MY BACK as I struggle through the entrance of the building. My breath comes hard and fast as my eyes follow the stairwell up four flights to the shared apartment. Having spent the last two days emptying my house, I'm tired and drained. My nerves tingle like a lit fuse as fatigue and tamped-down emotions get the better of me. Emotions I have held in check for the last two days.

My pocket snags on the door handle. I pull hard to free myself. With a tearing sound, I break free, my heart sinking further at the damage to my only winter coat. A single tear streaks down my cheek before I can brush it away with my lapel. I am already very late. *Pull it together, woman.* Squaring my shoulders, I start up the stairs.

On the third-floor landing, I pause to catch my breath again. My heavy wool coat and the exertion have made me overheated. I set down my overnight bag. This is not something I like to do...allow my body or personal items to touch any part of this filthy stairwell. It reeks with a mixture of trash, stale beer and piss. Smeared handprints, grease, graffiti, and God only knows what else pepper the walls. There is no such thing as a five-second rule here. It can't be helped. I need this break to muster enough energy for the last flight.

My knees and back ache from all the boxing, lifting, and moving activity over the weekend. Bending over to rub my knees, my vision halos, stars swirling in the black periphery. Flailing, I reach out for the banister, and my sweaty palms grasp the sticky handrail. Who knows what infectious diseases linger on the wooden banister. Its polyurethane coating has long since been rubbed away by decades of tenants. I wipe my palms on my jeans and lean my back against the wall.

A wave of memories from before everything went wrong, from before Brannon's death, chokes my thoughts. I try not to think about how much my circumstances have changed since then. From living

1

in a cute cape in the town of Crabtree with my husband, to this dingy and unhygienic building. It's temporary, I tell myself for the thousandth time. I just need time to get the house sold and use whatever is left to find a better living arrangement. If there is any money left once the medical liens are paid off.

Shrill laughter bursts from above, making me wince. I know that cackle's owner. My hopes of getting into my room unaccosted are dashed, and I slump further. "Great," I mumble, picking up my bag to tackle the remaining flight of stairs. Girding myself for the coming encounter, I pray I can keep my emotions in check until I reach the tiny but safe confines of my private room.

The apartment door flies open as I reach the landing. I jolt backward, teetering unsteadily, and flailing to grasp the banister. The cackler, Veronica, sashays out, takes one look at my struggles, and bursts out laughing again. Standing on the landing, she yells through the open doorway, "Abigail's back!" A chortle and shriek come from inside, and my other two roommates peek out the doorway.

"Look at you! We thought maybe you decided to leave us for good," Jenna says, her face flushed bright as if she's just finished a marathon. The fuchsia color of her cheeks matches the dyed ends of her short, spiked blonde hair.

If only I could. Can I sidestep around Veronica without getting shoved down the stairwell? I size up the space and Veronica's stance. Her bulk makes it impossible to bypass her.

"Yeah, where have you been? You missed our big party last night." Meghan flings her arm out as if showing me the way in, nearly hitting Jenna in the face.

Jenna grabs Meghan's arm and wrenches it out of her way. All three of them disintegrate into convulsions of alcohol-infused chortling.

I fume. I'm in no mood for their noise and nonsense. All I want to do is get into my room, take a shower, and get into my dress. Clare is taking me to a symphony concert to celebrate my birthday. It's bad enough I had to cancel our dinner reservations because of the monstrously slow tram ride back into the city. There's no way I'm going to miss the concert focused on one of my favorite composers.

I advance toward the door, Veronica stepping out of my way. Living with college students who do more partying than studying is less than ideal, but it's all that I can afford.

As it always does, the stench of the place hits me like a slap. Remnants of stale beer, unwashed dishes, rotting trash, and marijuana assault my nostrils, making me hold my breath as I make a beeline for my room.

I grind to a halt, my bag dropping off my slumping shoulder to the floor with a thud. My nerves start pinging loose like bobby pins in a badly secured up-do. "What happened to my lock?" I shriek.

The door to my private room is open. The remains of the hasp that had been there dangle, only semi-attached to the doorframe. It hangs in midair, my lock still attached. The top corner of the door is splintered from whatever force pried the metal from the wood. Blood surges through my body, my face burning like a hot iron. My three roommates stare back at me; Meghan stifling her laughter with a hand, Jenna smiling smugly and shrugging one shoulder, and Veronica grinning ear to ear as she steps forward.

"We had a little party last night." She shrugs. "A few people were going at it hot and heavy, and we told them to get a room. All the rooms except yours were already in use." Veronica giggles and wiggles her eyebrows, as if her proclamation is funny.

"So, you let them break into mine?" I squeal, my entire body trembling with pent-up fury. "That's not coming out of my security deposit," I spit through clenched teeth.

Veronica snorts. "Planning to leave so soon?"

Forgetting my palm is tacky, I slap it to my forehead and look into my room in disbelief. I ignore Veronica's question as something

3

lying on my bedside rug catches my eye. I step into the walk-in closet-sized room and stare down at the neon green condom, sticky with semen. I shudder and stumble backward. "A used condom, on my rug? Somebody better pick that up." I'm used to dealing with body fluids in my part-time job, but this, in my own room, from a strange guy, is beyond my ability to deal with, especially today.

Veronica chortles again. "It won't hurt you." Jenna and Meghan join the chorus.

Hands fisted, I whirl on Veronica and advance so swiftly that she stumbles backward as if afraid to be struck. Nearly out of control, I shake my finger inches from her nose. "You. Pick. It. Up."

"Why me? It's not mine," Veronica huffs, glaring back at me.

"Maybe not. But you were here when it happened, and as the apartment's leaseholder, you are responsible for damages. Even ones you didn't cause." I plant my feet firmly and point at the condom. "Well, Miss Leasee, pick it up."

The other two women watch, their eyes as large as dessert plates as Veronica's mouth opens as if to protest. But she stops and closes it without uttering a word. She glares back at me, her arms crossed over her breasts. Her mouth opens as if she wants to reply, but it slams shut again. Seconds later, she stalks into my room and picks up the offending item. Holding it between her thumb and index finger, she saunters to the kitchen's overflowing trash can and drops it on top of the pile. It tumbles off, creating an avalanche of debris. Everything hits the sticky floor.

No one dares to laugh as Veronica's eyes narrow and darken.

I pick up my overnight bag and enter my room, shutting the door behind me. I pause inside for a minute, my eyes running over everything. Nothing seems taken. There wasn't much in the way of personal items anyway. Just some clothes, an ancient clock radio, and stacks of books on the floor.

Gathering my wits, I glance around the room one last time for more ick, and my anger ebbs slightly. No more condoms in sight. Nothing seems out of order except my bed. The neatly made air mattress I'd left behind is a tangled lump of sheets, the pillows tossed awry. I won't be sleeping in that tonight. With only one set of sheets, I don't have time to wash and dry them before leaving for the concert. Where I'm going to sleep tonight, I don't know, but it won't be here. Perhaps my best friend and former college roommate, Clare, could put me up until the morning?

My phone alarm sounds, reminding me I have one hour to meet her downtown. With two fingers, I fold the rug in half and shove it under the bureau to get rid of its offending sight and smell. I drop my bag on the bureau top, pull out the dress I will wear tonight, and hang it on the hook on the back of the door. It's time to start prepping for my evening out.

I strip off my clothes, wrap myself in a beach towel, and grab my shower caddy. When I emerge from my room, the apartment is empty. I can use the bathroom without interruption.

A quick rinse-off shower later, I slip on the dress. It's a plain, black sheath with a white Peter Pan collar. I have not worn it since my husband's funeral ten months ago. I pull my hair up into a loose bun, toe on kitten-heeled black pumps, and grab my purse. I'll put on lipstick in the taxi. With one last look around the room, I wrestle into my ripped coat and bolt out of the apartment.

THE STARE

THE CAB DROPS ME OFF at the entrance to Symphony Hall, and I sprint up the staircase as best I can in my clacking heels, spotting Clare at the outer doors. The hem of her coral colored sheath dress is visible beneath her coat, glowing in the fading shafts of daylight. I collapse into her arms, out of breath. "Made it," I hiss.

"What happened?" Clare glances over her shoulder. "Never mind, tell me later. They're flickering the lights. Good thing I got the tickets at the will-call window already." She pulls me by my upper arm into the vestibule and on into the orchestra seating area.

As we settle into our front row, left of center seats, the concertmaster, first violinist Haruka Satō, strolls along the stage front, her elegant black gown flowing behind her petite frame. She begins the customary tuning sequence with the oboe player, making sure every musician is in their place and ready. Ten seconds after she sits down, Maestro Kendrick Grant strides from the left side curtain, igniting thunderous applause. He shakes the concertmaster's hand, then acknowledges the crowd's adoration. Raising one arm overhead, he gives the audience a wave and a huge smile.

Like in every photo I have ever seen, his black tuxedo fits him like cling wrap. How can he move while conducting? I don't have a clue. He is gorgeous with strong, chiseled features and not an ounce of discernible body fat. His distinctive red plaid cummerbund is a nod to his Scottish heritage, and a red bow tie finishes the outfit. Though he stands close, his blue-green eyes are dark in the flood of spotlights centered on him. Bowing to the audience, the piercing stare he gives me sends a shiver down my spine. It holds for only a few seconds before his gaze scans the expansive auditorium and sold-out crowd.

Clare leans closer to my ear. "Wow, did you get checked out!"

I shake my head at the absurdity of Clare's take on the moment. "Nonsense. He was just feeding the frenzy. You know what a ladies' man he is." Still, I fan myself with the program booklet to disperse the heat racing through my body. My pounding pulse slowly subsides from the intimacy of his heated stare. What is happening? It's been less than a year since my husband died. Pressure builds, as does guilt following my reaction.

Maestro Grant steps on the riser, his back to the audience, his strong, sturdy legs spread apart. When he raises his baton, the crowd falls silent, caught in suspended animation. The moment it moves, the music begins.

The soft, peaceful notes of the opening movement start, reminding me of dawn's light slowly inching across the earth. My eyes follow Maestro Grant's hands as they make slow, hypnotic gestures. My pulse slows, and weariness filters deeper through my body. I close my eyes and let the music wrap around me like a warm blanket, easing my troubles and the tensions of the weekend.

Something jars my shoulder hard. I jolt up in the seat, my eyes springing open. The audience is clapping. "Wake up," Clare whispers, giving my arm a nudge as she resumes clapping. "He's staring at you again."

Maestro Grant is bowing to the audience, yet his fierce stare remains on me. When he walks by, leaving the stage for intermission, his eyes remain fixed on me, a scowl on his face. After he disappears into a stage wing, the audience lights come up.

No wonder he's angry. I've slept through the entire forty-five-minute piece. I catch Clare's arm. "Please tell me I didn't snore."

Her face screws up into a smirk. "Well, just once. It was more a snort than a snore." She presses her lips together, merriment flashing in her eyes. "It was during the adagio part. I don't think many people heard it."

My face grows hot. I don't know whether to be mortified that it happened or glad I was unconscious and can't remember it. I let go of Clare's arm and bury my face in my hands.

"I don't think he liked that you were asleep." Clare stands and stretches. "Let's get some exercise before the next half starts." She pulls me to my feet and then leads me out to the foyer, where refreshments can be purchased. "Want something? Coffee, maybe?"

I shake my head. "Thanks, but no. Although I could really use one, apparently. It's probably served so hot you can't even sip it before intermission is over."

Inside the ornate intermission room, the overhead chandeliers' brilliance blinds after the long auditorium's darkness. The intricate wood paneling, cornices, and crown moldings glow warmly, reminders of the Gilded Age, when the symphony house was built. A gas fireplace tops off the elegance of the room. "You went out like a light bulb not two minutes into the piece," Clare quips as we stroll arm in arm. "I thought you said you liked Aaron Copland's works."

"I did, I do. It's been a difficult Sunday to end a horrific weekend. Between the traffic and my roommates..." I gasp, remembering what I need to ask her. "I can't sleep there tonight. Can I stay at your place?"

Her eyes widen in surprise. "Yes, of course, but you'll have to tell me all about your weekend later, over a couple of drinks."

"It's a deal."

The massive chandeliers' lights flicker overhead, and the foyer empties as everyone, including Clare and me, reclaim their seats.

"Do you think you can stay awake during *Appalachian Spring*?" Clare teases.

I whisper back as the concertmaster returns to the stage, "It's my favorite. I'll try."

Maestro Grant strides onto the stage. Bowing to the audience, it doesn't escape me that his eyes linger over me. There's no scowl this time, and I endeavor to not give him another chance to do so again.

I manage to stay awake for the remainder of the evening's program. The music is lively, folksy, and simpler than the previously played Third Symphony. The flitting notes and sweet melodies lift my spirits. Concentrating on staring at Maestro's back, I'm able to stay awake.

He's a majestic conductor. All the rigidness in his frame disappears with the music, like starch washed out of a stiff shirt. The fluidity of his movements is electric and mesmerizing. His lean, animated frame dances on the dais, weaving, twisting, and bending, his arms and hands, along with his baton, so expressive. Even his legs, like oak trunks, get into the movement. At the end, I fear he might fall backward off the riser as he jumps on a downbeat to accentuate the final note. Thunderous applause and shouts of "bravo" reverberate through the acoustic hall.

This time, when Maestro Grant turns around, I notice how the music has loosened not only his body, but also his expression. For only the second time this evening, he smiles as he bows to the audience's enthusiasm. Spreading his arms wide to acknowledge the entire orchestra, he joins the crowd, clapping his appreciation for his fellow musicians. He looks straight at me, our gazes meet and hold. It might have been only for seconds, but a fluttering explodes in my stomach and my pulse quickens when he gives me a nearly imperceptible nod before striding off for the wings. I try to harness my reactions. It's way too early to be feeling aroused by another man, I chastise myself.

"He did it again," Clare says out loud, as we stand to leave. "Do you know him?"

"No. We've never met. This is the first time I've been at a symphonic concert in a very long time."

We leave Symphony Hall, walking a couple of blocks to the Elliott Hotel. Everything is dark in the lounge area, with dim lighting from opaque ivory sconces on the black walls and black furniture. Faint light reflects off the buffed tin bar top and the mirrors behind the rows of liquor bottles. It's crowded and noisy. The smell of seafood strikes my nostrils hard, making my stomach growl. Settling at a table for two, we slip off our coats and order cocktails. When our drinks arrive, Clare raises her glass. "To my bestie, happy thirtieth birthday."

I clink my martini glass with Clare's and take a deep sip of the cold fluid. "I'm going to order some appies. I can't drink on an empty stomach."

Clare reaches out her hand for my arm. "You didn't get any dinner before the concert?"

I shrug. "Didn't have time. What with the long commute back to the city and the fiasco at the apartment, I barely made it as it was."

"Tell me everything." Clare's eyes narrow with concern. "How did it go at the house?"

"Okay. I got everything out and stuffed it into three storage units with the help of the college guys and the truck I hired." I gulp my drink and reach for the fried calamari as soon as the waiter sets the heaping plate between us. Once again, my nerves start snapping, though not as sharply this time. Telling the tale is much like being immersed in it again. The antics might get a smile out of me, but the full impact is muted. "The trams couldn't go any faster than about twenty miles per hour because of the falling snow. The trip took two and a half hours instead of the usual one and a half. Plus, the heat wasn't working, and every car was crammed full of under-dressed students heading back to the city for classes after the MLK holiday."

"Maybe you should get another car?" Clare suggests. "No, scratch that idea. I know it would just add to your expenses."

My mouth full of chewy calamari and marinara sauce, I nod, my hand ready to catch anything falling before it can soil my dress. A dry cleaning bill is not in my budget this month.

"When is your real estate agent going to start showing the house?"

"She's been showing it, despite the boxes and furniture. There's an offer on the table, and I've accepted it."

Her eyes widen. "That was fast. But I guess there really is a shortage of single-family homes available."

"No doubt. She showed it to two couples, and an offer came in almost immediately," I reply before biting into more calamari.

"What about the apartment? What happened?" Clare daintily bites a crispy fried ring.

"Ugh, the girls were inebriated when I got there. Not sure if it was left over from the party they had last night, or they started up again on awakening—hair of the dog style." I pop another golden ring in my mouth and munch. "The hasp lock on my room door was broken by somebody during the party." Clare's eyebrows shoot up. I hold up my palm. "Wait—it gets better. A couple decided they needed my bed for sex. The door was damaged, my bed a mess, and they left a slimy, used condom on the floor as a thank-you gift."

Clare chokes on her drink. "You've *got* to be kidding? You've got to get out of there. I can't believe you're living there. They're so immature, even at twenty!" What she doesn't say is that there are ten years between me and my roommates. A recipe for disaster from the beginning.

As the waiter passes us, Clare holds up her empty glass for a refill and cocks her head toward me. I shake mine.

"You know I can't leave. Not yet. I just emptied out my own house for the sale." This entire weekend felt like a month. The last ten months have felt like an eternity as I waited for Probate. "The apartment is only a fifteen-minute walk to the hospital. I can't afford my own place right now, not at four thousand dollars for a studio. Bad enough I have to put all my furniture and personal belongings into expensive storage units. Maybe when my research lab position becomes full-time..." My words falter with my spirit.

"When's that supposed to happen?" Clare takes the drink from the waiter and orders some sushi.

I hedge. "In another month or so." Truth is, it should have happened by now. The researcher assured me during my interview that his grant would go through any time now.

The waiter sets down the plate of sushi. Clare snatches up a piece of uramaki, the gears in her brain almost visibly churning. After a minute, she says, "You know, there's another option. I heard on Friday that a new partner at work hired a live-in maid. She works from eight to three, gets a stipend, plus free room and board for doing the shopping, cooking, laundry, and basic housecleaning. Plus, the woman works a part-time second shift job at a radio station. It's all arranged by a household help company called McAuliffe Agency." She dips her next maki roll in wasabi. "You should look into it." She gobbles the roll, immediately wipes tears from her eyes, and grasps at her drink. "Spicy salmon roll..." she croaks.

"Hmm." I contemplate the option. Granted, the new law partner at Malcom, Fitzgerald and Hennessey could easily afford such a luxury. However, if I didn't have to pay for my room and had a stipend, and I continued to work at the hospital lab part-time, I would save more money for my own apartment. In the meantime, if the job turned full-time, I could find someplace more suitable than a college dorm-style building. "I'll look them up. See if it's a possibility."

Clare flips her credit card onto the table, and the waiter swipes it. "Let's get a cab and get you settled on my couch. My brother shouldn't need it tonight."

The mention of Clare's brother reminds me that he had been staying on his sister's and brother-in-law's couch until classes resumed and the dormitories re-opened at Baymont University.

"You sure?" I ask, not wanting to put her brother out or force Clare to make a choice between him and me.

"I'm sure. Though if he does show up, it might be interesting. You know he has a crush on you." Clare winks, grabbing my arm and leading me out to the sidewalk.

My insides cringe at the possibility. "You know I'm not ready for that." Brannon still has a strong hold on my heart, even from the grave. I am beginning to think he always will.

• • • •

I CLENCH MY BACK TEETH while changing into street clothes for the livery ride home. I twist and tug at the bow tie at my neck, seeing it in the dressing room's mirror. Rage steams and bubbles over in my chest, and I fumble to get rid of it. At least that little minx in the front row managed to stay awake during the second part of the performance. She'd smiled and clapped at the end, the weary expression apparently unrelieved by her extended nap during the first part of the concert. *Serves her right.*

I have no idea why she caught my eye. Perhaps her large, round, doe-like eyes that were colored a bright apple green. As the stage lights reflected in them, they glowed like the neon glow sticks kids used at Halloween. Her appearance was understated like a high-society matron, even if she didn't look quite twenty-five years old. Light-brown hair pulled into a chignon, the black sheath with a demure white collar and a natural look. Either the woman wore minimal makeup or none at all. And no bling. Not around her neck or dangling from her earlobes. Only a simple gold wedding band. *How unlike Cynthia.*

A knock jerks my thoughts away. "Enter!" I yell, giving up on the bow tie for the time being.

Malcolm Trier enters. "Wonderful performance, Maestro," says the president of the Baymont Symphony Board of Directors.

My entire body tenses, preparing for the impending attack. "Thank you, sir," I say, shaking his hand.

"I've been meaning to tell you, the board will be discussing your contract renewal at our next meeting." Malcolm slips his hands into his pockets, a tight-lipped smile on his ancient face.

I raise an eyebrow. "Oh? Should I be in attendance?" I want to be there, but I know Malcolm won't allow it. Fair enough. No doubt my contract will be stripped down even more than it was three years ago. A thinly veiled retribution. As if I were to blame for the incident.

Malcolm shakes his head too rapidly. "No need. It's just a preliminary discussion amongst the board." Malcolm rubs the tip of his chin between his thumb and index finger. "Speaking of attendance, this concert didn't bring in our usual numbers. Can you hazard a guess why that is?"

I scowl, delighted that Malcolm left himself open for negative comments. "Perhaps the reduction in advertising the board recently enacted has something to do with it? If the public doesn't know it's happening, they can't buy tickets." Sweat forms again on my already cold, sweat-soaked tuxedo shirt. I turn to the mirror and undo my cummerbund, my eyes never leaving his reflection in the mirror.

"Hmm," Malcolm mutters, grimacing. "Numbers have been sliding for the entire fall season."

"The Christmas season saw record numbers of attendees." Freed of the band, I toss it into the laundry basket like a basketball. "The economy hasn't been great since the pandemic, but it's getting better. I think people are being a little more parsimonious with their money."

"Perhaps." Malcolm rocks on the balls of his feet as he glances around the room.

It is the best of the dressing rooms, such as it is. The chipped linoleum countertop in front of the mirror, the lumpy stuffed armchair in the corner, and a loveseat along one wall. A three-foot-long clothes rack holds my street clothes, and a side table, under which is tucked a mini fridge, completes the scant furnishings.

The board promised to renovate and redecorate my dressing room in the first contract. Ten years later, I'm still waiting and will continue to wait into infinity, as the promise has been absent from all subsequent contracts. I toe off my black shoes. It's getting overheated in here. "If you'll excuse me, my livery ride should arrive any minute, and I need to change."

"Ah, the livery ride. Do we still provide that?" Malcolm smiles broadly, his spirits visibly perking up. "No matter. We'll talk again soon." Malcolm begins humming a tune from the performance as he leaves the room.

When the door clicks, my shoulders slump. I can read Malcolm's words well enough to know they are more promise than threat. The new contract won't provide the livery service that takes me from my townhouse to official symphony business, and back again. A pang in my gut warns me that's likely the least of my worries.

I resume struggling with the bow tie that's choking me. After several frustrating minutes, I grab a pair of scissors, cut the offending tie off, and slam it into the trash can.

A NEW OPTION

I ARRIVE AT WORK THE next day, having borrowed a T-shirt and jeans from Clare. After changing into scrubs, I set to work on my share of today's cases. My boss, the researcher, doesn't have his shit together, so my services are sloughed off to the main lab again. I don't mind doing diagnostic cases. It isn't what I was hired for, though, and I'm tired of being a Ping-Pong ball between the research and testing labs.

My break and lunch times are spent finding and checking out the McAuliffe Agency. I like what I read, and the reviews are positive. Different scenarios fill my head with the possibility of escaping that hideous apartment and being able to get my own place in time. I won't need to be in servitude for more than a year. I square my shoulders for more confidence and dial to inquire about available positions.

"I'm sorry, we thoroughly investigate people asking for help, as well as people offering their services. If you can come for an interview, we'll see if you're a good fit for any of our clients," Mrs. Wainwright says.

My heart sinks. Of course applicants are heavily vetted. How long will this process take? A pang in my chest has me wondering if all this will be worth it. Can this really work out for me? I let out a heavy sigh. What do I have to lose?

"What's your earliest appointment?"

"I have a cancellation today. It's at four this afternoon if that's convenient," the woman says.

I accept the appointment and go back to work testing tissue samples for cancer and other diseases.

Two days later, my coworker yells from the office, "Abigail, your telephone."

The tray of microscope slides I hold rattles precariously as my hand shakes. "Coming," I shout, gently setting the tray on the black soapstone counter and stripping off my nitrile gloves as I rush to answer the call. The only phone calls I ever get are from the lawyer, the real estate agent, or Clare. What remains of my family, immediate or otherwise, never calls me. Ever.

The office is tiny. Even smaller than my room, which had been a pantry closet. Three coworkers and I share desk space around the rectangular room's countertops. I grab my phone off the wall shelf and check the caller ID.

The screen indicates it's the McAuliffe Agency. What is Mrs. Wainwright doing calling me so soon? Didn't she say it would take a few days to complete the background check and drug tests? Plus, it might be a while before the kind of position I want presents itself? Maybe my background check went badly? I slump into the nearest chair, steeling myself for bad news. "Hello?"

"Hello, this is Emily Wainwright, at McAuliffe Professional Personnel Agency. We have a client with a position very similar to the one you are seeking. He would like to meet you for an interview this afternoon, if that's possible. I've sent an email with the specifics for your review. You'll be meeting Evelyn Farthing first."

My fingers fumble as I search for the email. "I see it." Opening it, I scan the document, my eyes flitting over the keywords...musician, male, thirty-eight years old. Visions of wild, alcohol and drug-filled parties, lots of noise and messes make me wary of this "gentleman." No name is given, but the locale is perfect. The Newfane Avenue residence would be closer and likely only a ten-minute walk to the hospital. He's in search of a live-in maid/cook. "I got it. Any idea about the hours?"

"Limited hours that should fit into your plan nicely, provided you both accept the terms."

The call ends, and I keep repeating Mrs. Wainwright's words...four o'clock, 16 Treble Street. Evelyn Farthing. I can't remember saying yes, but I know I accepted. What do I have to lose? I glance up at the wall clock. I have six hours. Just enough time to finish my work and get there.

My nerves jittering, I go back to the cramped laboratory area filled floor to ceiling with shelves of glass flasks, bottles of chemicals, supplies, and boxes of personal protective equipment. The slide tray with yesterday's work goes into the to-be-filed pile before I focus on the samples already in testing. Coworkers are doing the same thing on surrounding workbenches.

My hands move through the repetitive motions as my mind strays. Emily Wainwright didn't provide any information about Evelyn Farthing. Images of a graying, middle-aged woman form. Maybe this woman is his secretary or personal assistant. He, on the other hand, could be of any nationality. The city of Baymont has a large contingent of professionals from all over the world. Not that I mind. Having worked in the medical field for over seven years, I am used to working with people from different cultures, walks of life, religions, and languages. Still, an uneasy twinge in my gut has me wondering if I can do this with a musician who lives life on the edge.

As I grab my purse to leave, I glance at my scrubs. *What will Evelyn Farthing think of me showing up in work attire?* Maybe it's a good thing. I want a position with responsibility, and this uniform-like appearance might help. Hopefully, whoever it is won't be put off by them. I scurry into the locker room to change into fresh scrubs. They will have to do. There isn't time to go back to my room to change. I catch a cab to 16 Treble Street, my fingers crossed I won't be delayed by traffic and thus late, making a terrible first impression.

Everything becomes clearer when the taxi pulls up to the curb in front of 16 Treble Street. It's the Baymont Symphony Orchestra's concert hall. The very same concert hall that Clare and I attended Sunday night.

A dry lump grows in my throat with each step up the marble stairs to the enormous, embossed brass doors. A banner hangs above the center doorway, announcing the tenth season of the orchestra's conductor. His blue-green eyes beam down from a handsome face framed by neatly combed dark brown hair. He wears his signature crisp red tuxedo bow tie below a wide, perfect smile. The close-up shot shows a hint of crow's feet wrinkles at the corners of his eyes and a clean-shaven face.

My breath pauses again, while my pulse kicks up a notch. *Maybe it's Maestro Grant?* The fluttering in my chest increases at the thought of staring directly into those eyes.

When Maestro Kendrick Grant initially took the Baymont podium, he did so as the youngest conductor in the symphony's one hundred and two year history. I read the articles and heard the controversy that ensued during his first year. They didn't like his arrogance, his sternness, and his insistence on excellence. His critics were silenced within weeks of the start of the season, thanks to his brilliant execution at the podium. To the symphony staff and musicians, he is said to be curt and exacting. Yet, his warm and friendly interactions with audiences bring them back again and again. Ticket sales, especially subscriptions, surged, particularly among the city's women who were titillated to have such a sexy, virile, accomplished professional bachelor in their city. His good looks and trim physique make him appear ten years younger than he is, broadening the range of feminine appeal. An appeal that doesn't escape my notice. Everything about him, even his haughtiness, starts a fluttering in my stomach.

If it is him, will he remember seeing me, scowling at me, just days ago at the Copland concert? I finger the hem of my scrub top as apprehension floods through me. How humiliating it would be if it were him and he threw me out of the interview after recognizing me.

TERMS AND CONDITIONS

CALM DOWN. IT'S NOT likely to be him. I walk through the brass doors and approach a woman sitting behind the ticket window in the vestibule. "I'm here to see Evelyn Farthing."

"One minute, please," the woman says and phones someone. Less than a minute later, she tells me, "She'll be right with you. Pass through into the lobby." The woman gestures toward a set of thick wooden doors.

Pushing through the solid oak doors, my eyes sweep the ornate area. Marble tiles echo my steps under the vaulted ceiling. Massive chandeliers hang overhead, unlit but glittering as wall sconces illuminate the vast space with muted light. The tapping of footsteps approaching draws my attention to the impressive marble staircase. A tall, sturdy woman with a stiff carriage descends the steps from the upper echelons of the building.

"Mrs. Davitt, follow me please," the woman says, not bothering to introduce herself before leading me up two flights of stairs, through an unmarked door, and down a well-lit corridor. Music-oriented artwork and posters of various symphony conductors line the walls, along with oil portraits. I spot one I recognize as Beethoven.

Evelyn Farthing stops at the end of the hall. Opening the door, she steps aside to let me pass. The first thing I notice is the sterile soft gray of the walls and carpet. My gaze lowers, and my jaw drops open at the sight of *the* man seated in the cold, glass and chrome modern office.

Maestro Kendrick Grant sits rod straight in a large black leather office chair, intensely studying one of three computer screens spread across his desk. A pristine white dress shirt, complete with a red bow tie and silver cuff links in the French cuffs, fits snugly to his torso, accentuating his ripped, hard chest. Sheathed in black pants, his long, lean limbs are visible under the glass-topped chrome desk. His legs crossed at the ankles, his pair of highly buffed black wing tips rest on the steel-gray carpet.

"Abigail Davitt to see you, Mr. Grant," Evelyn Farthing says over my shoulder.

His gaze doesn't lift. His focus remains intent on the computer monitor as the door closes with a click behind me. Stunned by the sight of this man who stared me down at the Copland concert, my step falters. He is the last person I expect to need a maid. A stage or sound manager, perhaps, but not one of the most prestigious conductors in North America. Will he recognize me? Will he throw me out for having slept during the Third Symphony? Will this job possibility sink with one look?

My knees wobble while I wait to be acknowledged and invited to sit. Perspiration starts dampening my armpits and under my breasts. It is unbearable to stand here, waiting for him to glance up and recognize me. I want this job, and I need it desperately for more reasons than I can elucidate. Thinking fast, I make up my mind about how much information I am willing to divulge. Nothing about the lien on the house. Nothing at all about the house if I can avoid it. I glance down at my wedding ring. Should I have removed it temporarily? Or does wearing it serve me better? Will it give him the impression that I'm still married, and thus not interested in having anything to do with him relationship-wise? I will say nothing about my husband, though it's sure to come up. Can I get away with saying that it's personal information he doesn't need to know?

Looking up, Maestro Grant locks me with those stunning blue-green eyes. My breath catches in my throat. On his feet in one regal motion, he stalks around his desk and extends his hand. It feels massive in my extra-small hand. His mesmerizing yet fleeting smile sends my butterflies into a frenzy of fear. There is no hint of recognition in his eyes. I finally breathe and give him as genial a smile as I can.

"Hello, Mrs. Davitt. Thank you for coming," he says, turning his back to me as he returns to his desk.

"It's no problem, I was down the street about a mile when I got the call from the agency," I reply without thinking, not moving.

"Yes, I was just re-reading the referral notice from the agency. So, you are working at Baymont General Hospital?" he asks, seating himself. Motioning me to a set of armchairs in front of his desk, he says, "Forgive me, please have a seat." Not waiting for me to accept, he focuses again on the computer screen.

I watch as he continues to read while I sit in the nearest chair. His brisk manner cools my enthusiasm the longer he ignores my presence. I take in the rest of the room. Walls filled with proclamations, Maestro Grant's diplomas from undergrad studies at Berklee College of Music, and graduate studies at Carnegie-Mellon University, pictures of him with various high-profile composers and conductors. A black leather couch is along the back wall, and beside it is a full-sized refrigerator. A dozen or more awards fill a bookcase, one of which appears to be a gold-plated Grammy Award gramophone trophy. In a back corner sits a baby grand Steinway, the closed lid covered in sheet music. Two black metal music stands are tucked out of the way at the far end of the piano.

Mr. Grant asks, "In the pathology laboratory?"

My head snaps forward to meet his eyes. "Yes."

A soft ticking sound fills the silence as he scrolls the mouse. "So, you're seeking a live-in maid position?" He cocks his head to the side and glances at me again.

"Yes, sir."

His eyes harden as he scrutinizes me. He folds his hands together on the glass desktop. "Why?" he scowls as he did during the concert.

"There's no way I can afford my own apartment within city limits. So, I brainstormed and came up with this idea." My voice trails off, trying to ignore the dampness gathering in other, more personal places on my body. Whatever feelings of attraction I might have evaporate with his rigid countenance.

He raises an eyebrow at my statement but says nothing. Under Maestro Grant's hard glare, I squirm in my chair. His frown speaks of disapproval, but for what reason, I can't tell. Is it recognition or my impertinence?

Maestro Grant rocks back and forth in his chair, his fingers interlaced, one elbow resting on the chair's arm. His piercing stare remains focused intently on me. In the silence, I hear someone practicing scales on an instrument somewhere outside this stifling room. Perhaps a trumpet? "Have we met before, Mrs. Davitt?"

There it is. He is remembering me from the concert. "Not officially, sir." The lump in my throat gets larger by the second.

His eyebrows knit together. "Not officially? Where or how then?"

I swallow hard. "You might recognize me from the Copland concert last Sunday night."

He studies my face intently as his eyes darken, and his forehead creases. "You fell asleep." His jaw tightens, an irregular tic in his cheek as his lips purse.

Although I'm sitting, my knees feel like they're rattling together. "For the first piece, yes, I'm afraid so. It was a difficult day. The soothing opening lulled me to sleep." I opt to say no more. The urge to bolt from the chair, the office, the building grows stronger with each heartbeat spent under his stare.

His eyes narrow further. "Do you routinely fall asleep with music playing?"

"Not usually, sir. I do like music, especially piano and cello." I pray that he grasps the change of subject. The tension in my chest eases when he does.

"Do you play an instrument?" Again, his hard, almost penetrating stare pins me to my seat, my insides quaking like gelatin.

"Yes, I used to play the flute and took private lessons throughout high school."

"You know how to read music?" Mr. Grant asks wryly.

"Yes, I can read music," I reply in a serious tone, not rising to his bait. Of course I can. Before I can hold my tongue, I blurt, "Is that a requirement?"

He gives me a thoughtful look, like he's trying to decide how to answer my question. "I never gave consideration to it as a job requirement, but it is a leg-up on the other contenders." Maestro Grant picks up a stylish black and gold fountain pen and scrawls something on a notepad beside his keyboard.

I give him a half smile, then press my lips together to stifle it. Perhaps he won't throw me out on my ear. At least those lessons will have served some purpose after all.

"What makes you qualified to run a household? Can we assume that you know how to clean a house?" One corner of his mouth quirks up slightly, his smug reaction shooting down any fluttering butterflies in my stomach. His question is filled with sarcasm and disdain, like it's a running joke. Abruptly, he leans forward in his chair, his index finger tapping a steady rhythm on the desk like a metronome. "Well?" he says, impatient for my reply.

My shoulders and spine stiffen. Should I tell him what I'd hoped to keep hidden? I decide to tell him a fragment of the truth. "I've managed my own house in Crabtree. It made sense to see if there might be a position available that would give me a quiet place to live in exchange for housekeeping duties."

"Why not commute from Crabtree?" he demands, leaning forward in a scrutinizing manner. If he were a judge, he would be peering over the edge of his bench, staring me down.

I inhale sharply and huff it out, my ire spiking. Biting back a sharp retort, I explain, "It takes over an hour and a half on the tram. I don't own a car. There isn't any other choice except to live here in the city, somewhere close to the hospital." *And I needed to escape what has been and will never be again.* Since it worked once already, I attempt to redirect the conversation away from me. "What exactly do you expect from your maid?"

He sits back, his body suddenly stiff and formal. "I need someone to handle minor cleaning, organizing things like dry cleaning and laundry, which by the way is sent out, grocery shopping, taking care of the mail, packages, and minding the premises while I'm away. Occasionally cooking for me and some of my friends. It will take someone with good organizational skills and attention to detail, but not a lot of time overall."

My nerves simmer. While it sounds like a lot of work, I guess it wouldn't be too overwhelming with my hospital job. "I assume the financial dealings with the different vendors have been or will be arranged."

His expression hardens again. "Of course. You are to contact Evelyn Farthing in cases of emergencies or problems."

I nod. *Does this mean I have the job?* After the manner in which he's behaved, a better question is...do I really want this job? There might be others with more congenial people.

"I moved into the townhouse about eight months ago, and it's still pretty sparse. You may need to procure items that I haven't had time to obtain. In most cases, you won't get much direction from me, except on special occasions or for big purchases. I need someone who's capable of working independently and gets the job done without coddling. Your work experience suggests you can handle that. What else do you need to know?"

"Compensation?"

That's the sticky point. Whatever is offered must be sufficient to justify leaving the cheap apartment. I cross my fingers in my lap. When I see Maestro Grant look down, I remember the desk is glass and he can see my gesture. It occurs to me that as long as the compensation is adequate for my plan to succeed, I will take it. I can always continue searching for a better post.

"There's a small suite in the townhouse. That's free of charge, as are all the utilities except your own cellphone. Food is included, although you'll be cooking it yourself. I don't have an extra vehicle, so if I'm using my car, you will have to use cabs, buses, Uber, Lyft, or the tram. However, I can arrange for monthly public transportation passes to be purchased for your convenience.

"What else should I tell you?" Maestro Grant asks himself, tapping his jaw with his index finger. His eyes widen in an eureka moment. "I'm pretty much home except during symphony touring season, or guest events. For three weeks in June, there's the summer season in Sutton Lake. I have a condo out there, but you don't have to worry about that. My days are usually from nine a.m. to eleven p.m. or midnight. Even if I'm not conducting, I'm often at meetings or evening functions, especially fundraising events for the symphony. Sometimes, I'm rarely home for more than sixty minutes at a time, unless I'm sleeping."

I note the hard edges of his words regarding his erratic schedule. "So, I'd pretty much just manage the place and the comings and goings of laundry, groceries, and workmen, while you pop in and out like The Flash?" I ask with as serious a face as I can muster.

"In a nutshell, yes." His jaw softens ever so slightly before his features return to their haughty expression. Like he's trying to retain control, despite finding my comment humorous.

I give him a genuine smile. The fluttering in my belly starts up again. I wish they'd stop. It's terribly distracting.

"This job keeps me going to more and more functions and fundraisers than I care to count. Anyway, the compensation is minimal, one thousand dollars a week, no benefits other than three weeks' vacation, not all at once, and subject to my schedule, and one day off a week." He pauses, then adds, "I'm flexible if you should get sick. Holidays are a little tough for me, what with the symphony season and all, especially Christmas," he says, but then stammers on, "I mean, I'm sure you'll want Christmas off and Thanksgiving and such."

Little does he know that is precisely what I don't want. Without close family, and Brannon deceased, I'd prefer working or volunteering at a soup kitchen for the holiday instead of wallowing in my sorrow alone.

"I like to give dinner parties for symphony guest performers on occasion. We can hire a chef and serving staff for those events."

My mind races through the dozens of celebrities who have starred with him in the past. This could really be fascinating. He gets some very famous people to perform with the symphony.

He rubs his palms together. "Well, if that is acceptable to you, when can you start?"

The shock of the sudden offer halts my breath. "Seriously?"

Maestro Grant stands up behind his desk. "Yes. I've been searching for weeks. Other agencies sent over candidates who were rather lackluster, and some had no experience. Or no personality."

"Is next Thursday, okay?" I ask, feeling a little giddy now that the deal is coming to fruition.

He walks me to the door. "Evelyn will call the agency to let them know to have a temporary contract signed. This is for a thirty-day trial. Your continued employment is contingent upon your ability to manage everything successfully. If everything works out, you're hired."

"Sounds easy enough." I stop at the door. "I'll see you next week, then. Thank you, sir," I say, extending my hand to shake his.

"Excellent. Oh, um, one thing. From now on, call me Mr. Grant instead of sir or Maestro." He gives me a nod as he shakes my hand. It is large, warm, and smooth, and it raises goosebumps on my arms. This is going to be interesting.

• • • •

I WATCH MRS. DAVITT walk away, heading for the exit. There is something about her, something that draws me to her. Her manner is pleasant enough. She even showed a sense of humor with her Flash comment. Unable to put my finger on it exactly, I go back to my desk and check the day planner. There is nothing else official to do this afternoon. Thoughts of the interview and Abigail Davitt return.

Is it a coincidence she caught my eye at the concert? Is it fate?

When I'd walked out onto the stage that evening, I'd noticed her immediately, sitting all prim and proper in the front row. The color of spring clover, her bright green eyes sparkled. Those eyes were maddeningly closed when I turned around after the first portion of the concert ended. Was that snort I'd heard halfway through the piece, in the adagio section, from her? It fired up my indignation to think she'd conked out like a child up past their bedtime. The orchestra and I performed the piece brilliantly. And she'd missed it.

Now, here she was seeking the maid's job. I return to studying the confidential information the agency supplied. Something puzzles me, which is why I stared at it so intently when she arrived. I wasn't able to figure out what it was. Now, I see it. She is listed as widowed in the report, yet she still wears her wedding band. Mrs. Davitt? She seems rather young to be a widow. Thirty as of three days ago; the night of the concert, I notice.

I replay much of our conversation. She didn't mention being widowed...didn't mention anything about being married either, now that I think about it. Between her circumstances and this bit of omission, my interest stirs. Her background check was stellar, and her drug test was clean. What's the truth about this Mrs. Davitt? I close down my computer and decide to call it a day. During the drive home, my mind re-runs the interview, looking for answers to the enigma that is Abigail Davitt.

• • • •

"CLARE!" I YELL INTO the phone.

"Can you hold, please?" She clicks off the line, probably due to an incoming call. I'm surprised she's still working since it's nearly five-thirty. Although she knew I'd applied at the agency, I hadn't had a chance to call her about the last-minute interview appointment. With a click, she's back on her cellphone. "Abigail? What? What is it?"

"I got a job!" My enthusiasm explodes.

"What job? You didn't tell me you had an interview," she whispers. She must be held over at work.

"The agency called me earlier today and sent me for a four o'clock appointment. And you're never going to guess who it is!" The news so astounds me that I want to giggle like a child. She's never going to get it.

"Mayor Wynn?" she guesses, not sounding all that enthralled with our Q&A session.

"Nope. It's the guy who put me to sleep Sunday night."

There's a silent pause, then she asks, "Maestro Grant?" Her voice rises an octave in question.

"Yes, can you believe it?"

"Did he recognize you?" She lowers her voice to a whisper.

My enthusiasm ebbs. "Yes, eventually he did. But he didn't say anything against it. I was afraid he would, but he didn't."

"Wow. I can't believe it. When do you start?"

"A week from Thursday. I start a thirty-day trial period." I continue, explaining the duties and the benefits of the position, "I'm already praying everything goes smoothly. It's a Godsend, really. Though I do have a few misgivings."

"Why? What makes you think it won't end well?"

I struggle to articulate my reservations. "He's sort of a real stuffed shirt. He seemed very full of himself, though I did manage to see hints of amusement during our discussion."

"Maybe it's all an act? You know, the diva Maestro." She laughs. "Can males be divas? Or are they divos?"

"Not sure, but he seems like one nonetheless."

THE START

MRS. WAINWRIGHT CALLS me two days later. She assures me that the thirty-day trial period would be entirely paid by the agency, provided I don't quit and no untoward actions or events create a breakdown in the contract. However, I must first stop by the office to sign a non-disclosure agreement, a requirement of the position. I agree. During our brief meeting, I wonder if I should mention I've already told Clare about the job. Since I told her before I signed the agreement, I opt to keep it quiet. Working in a legal office, Clare knows how to maintain discretion.

Not many hours later, Evelyn Farthing calls to say Maestro Grant will take me over to the house on Thursday at nine a.m. I am to meet him at his office at eight thirty. Picking up my phone, I call my boss and arrange to be out that Thursday and Friday. Fortunately, the researcher doesn't ask why. If I had to guess, he sounded pleased I'd be out for those two days. He's used to me being out periodically to handle issues related to Brannon's death. He must think it has something to do with that.

When I arrive at the Baymont Symphony offices at the agreed-upon time, Mrs. Farthing tells me Maestro Grant is not available to take me to the townhouse as he had wished. Instead, she will take me to the residence and give me the preliminary tour.

"Have a seat." She gestures to the chair in front of her desk as she clears a space on the desktop. "There's something that needs to be done first." I sit down opposite her. While she digs a folder out from her desk drawer, I check out the room. One wall holds family photos, while another features a huge corkboard filled with concert program cover designs at various stages of mockup.

Mrs. Farthing spreads two separate, three-page documents before me. "These are NDA contracts. You must sign both."

My mouth goes dry as my confusion rises. "I already signed one with the McAuliffe Agency."

Mrs. Farthing holds out a pen. "Yes, we know that. However, this one is meant to protect Maestro Grant as well as the Baymont Symphony from—well—disclosures of any kind, whether good or bad. It's required for this position."

I pick up the sheets and begin reading silently. I'm not to disclose that I work for Maestro Grant, or reveal who he sees, dates, socializes with, or where he goes. I can't even mention what he eats. Weird.

The second wad of papers is for the symphony. I am not to disclose anything I overhear about the symphony orchestra, its board of directors, and its foundation. All standard terms I have already promised in the agency's NDA. Everything seems innocuous until I get to the last page of each. One clause, identical on both documents, makes my heart sink.

I catch Mrs. Farthing's attention. "It says I would have to pay for any required publicity to fix any difficulties resulting from a disclosure of information." I drop the papers on the desk, my hands trembling so hard I fist them together to try to control them.

Mrs. Farthing's cheeks redden. "Yes. I know. It's highly unlikely that a major upset would occur from a disclosure, but it's possible. Every symphony employee must sign these NDAs. The attorneys are covering all their bases."

My gut clenches tighter, and I stand. My wobbly knees have me clutching the edge of her desk. "I can't afford such a penalty."

Her palms planted on the desktop, Mrs. Farthing says in a huff, "Then don't create one."

We glare at each other. Mrs. Farthing's stance softens. "Look, Maestro Grant and the symphony have a reputation to uphold. They don't want it besmirched."

"I have no intention of besmirching either of them."

DIANA ROCK

"What's your hesitation then? If you don't intend to create PR damage, what's to keep you from signing?" she asks, a quizzical expression on her face.

How can I tell her I'm financially broke and have already broken the NDA? That I'm so tangled in money issues I can't risk the possibility. But I might have to explain why, or I'll have to drag my suitcase and overnight bag back to that filthy place. Much like the agency's document, the start date of the NDA is today. Again, I reason I can't be held responsible for a disclosure outside that time frame. Fingers-crossed.

Mrs. Farthing must notice I'm wavering, because she rearranges the papers on her desk and holds out the pen again. I move forward with hesitant steps and take it. She points to the line on each document. Holding my breath and saying a prayer, I sign them all. "I want a photocopy of each," I demand. "Please."

"Certainly." Mrs. Farthing makes copies and hands them over after storing the originals in a desk drawer. "Well then, let's go to Maestro Grant's townhouse."

Ten minutes later, we arrive at Newfane Avenue, a wide cobblestone street lined with three and four-story townhouses for the entire quarter mile length of the street. Each townhouse's walkway to the front door is sided with landscaping.

Mrs. Farthing pulls up to the curb in front of a four-story unit. Being mid-January, the small trees and shrubs are bare except for the evergreen rhododendrons. Other flowers are unidentifiable from their dried-out state. Wrought iron fences enclose the withered gardens lining the edge of the sidewalks. Beside the front door is a brass plaque with the house number 1425. We climb the steps. There must be a boxwood shrub somewhere close. I can smell the urine-like odor it gives off.

"I have a key for you. It's to this front door only." Mrs. Farthing unlocks the door and steps inside a couple of feet. She gestures toward a keypad on the wall. "The current code is 1425, same as the house number. You have thirty seconds to disengage the alarm system when you get in the door." She punches in the numbers, and the incessant beeping of the keypad stops. "It's disarmed."

I nod, the tension in my backbone easing. Nobody mentioned the alarm system, but I am pleased to hear about it. The idea of being in this new environment all alone while Mr. Grant is at work or on tour seems less menacing.

Mrs. Farthing walks down the short hall into an open area that must serve as a living room to the left, while a long, twelve-seat dining table occupies the space to the right. "The living room and dining room." She sets the key down on the dining table and points beyond the table to a doorway. "The kitchen is through there." She continues through the area to a stairway. Pointing down a hallway that bypasses the stairs, she says, "Down that hall is Maestro Grant's music room and office."

Instead of leading down that way, she climbs the stairs up one half flight. A door off the landing is closed. "Maestro Grant's suite is here." Trying to keep my bearings, I realize that in relation to the front door, he must have a view of the back of the house.

Mrs. Farthing heads up another half flight of stairs, so we are at the front of the house. Two closed doors are nearly side by side. "These are the guest bedrooms, each with its own bath." She turns to me. "Up those stairs," she points up to the next landing, "is your room." Realizing it's on the fourth floor of the building, I am begrudgingly grateful I've been trudging up four flights of stairs for the last five-plus months. The cardio exercise has done wonders for my stamina, which will come in handy here.

We trudge up to the door and open it.

A "wow" flies out under my breath as I wander in and set my bags down. It's like another suite. A small sitting area holds a love seat, a TV, and a rocking chair. A small kitchen table sits by a huge window overlooking a fenced backyard. I'm already in love with this place. My tiny apartment room doesn't have any windows. Being claustrophobic, it's horrendous living there.

To the left is the bedroom with a full-sized bed. Attached to the bedroom is a complete bath including a shower and a bathtub. A glorious trembling starts in the center of my chest. This place is entirely more than I'd imagined. I had visions of an attic garret, like those in a historical romance novel. Dusty, dirty, mouse-infested, minimal furniture, and cold...always cold. This is so far from being a maid's room, I can't believe it. This entire suite is larger than Veronica's apartment. The bathroom alone is bigger than my former closet room.

"You should be comfortable here." Mrs. Farthing glances around and smiles after seeing my face. I can only guess it exposes my astonishment. "Get yourself settled in. Mr. Grant will be dining out this evening. He doesn't expect to be back before midnight, so you're on your own for dinner." She heads back down the stairs.

Abandoning my suitcase, overnight bag, and coat, I follow her. "I should set the alarm after you leave, right?" I'm unsure. It makes sense, but not being familiar with alarm systems, I have no understanding.

"Yes, of course. Maestro Grant will disarm and rearm the system when he returns. Poke around a little bit so you know where everything is. But stay out of his bedroom suite and the music room for now. Tomorrow morning, he'll probably give you another tour."

The mention of morning jolts me. Is there any food in the kitchen? "What does he like for breakfast? Does he drink coffee or something else?"

She pauses in the living room. "He does drink coffee. Come to think of it, after ten years working for him, I don't think I've ever seen him eat breakfast. Not at the office anyway. You'll have to figure that out." She heads toward the door. "Oh, and I typed something up for you." She digs into her handbag and pulls out a couple of pages. Holding them out, she says, "It's about ordering food, where and when the laundry and dry cleaning get done, and when it's picked up and delivered, how to answer the phone, etc." Opening the front door, she steps out onto the landing. "My office and cellphone numbers are on there also, in case you have any questions or problems."

"Thanks, Mrs. Farthing," I say, fisting the papers tightly as I watch her get in her car and drive away. I shut the door, lean against it, and close my eyes. My head spins with questions, directions, so much so that I have to sink into a dining chair to get my head lower than my heart. This is happening. It's really happening, and the accommodations are far better than I expected. Laughter bubbles up, bursting from me like a bark. I can't help dancing down the hallway, wishing I had some celebratory music.

For the rest of the day, I will be alone to unpack my few belongings plus explore the premises. Especially in the kitchen. Back in my suite, I drop the papers on the table. Curiosity overtakes me at all the space I now have to live in. There's a proper table, so no more eating on my bed. Recalling Maestro Grant's words about some things missing, I dig a spiral notebook out of my suitcase and head down to the first floor.

Realizing I didn't arm the system, I return to the keypad, my finger poised to enter the number. But I can't remember what it is. I remember that it's the same as the townhouse's street number.

I unlock the door and step out to look at the brass number plate on the right side of the door. The doorknob slips out of my hand as I angle myself to see it...number 1425. When I turn the doorknob to let myself back in, I learn lesson numbers one, two and three.

The door automatically locks when it closes.

Lesson number two is to keep the house key in my pocket.

And lesson number three is to never leave the house without my cellphone.

What to do? Maestro Grant isn't expected back until midnight. I have no way to get into the house and no phone to call anyone, even if I had a telephone number. Hailing a cab at the street corner where it meets the heavily trafficked Ackerman Avenue is also not an option. Any cash I have is in my purse up in the suite. The symphony building isn't terribly far away, about ten blocks or so. I could walk there but I don't have my coat either.

Tears spring to my eyes at my dilemma. With them comes overwhelming indecision. I crumple onto the top step and bury my head in my hands. Yet another problem to solve. The constant rollercoaster ride of events and my emotions dredges up more misgivings about this job, about my life, and about my future. Will I ever feel stable again?

Above all else, I want to scream at my incompetence. It's like some silly pun or joke. It's my first day, for crying out loud, and I did a stupid, stupid thing. The urge to flee surges in my chest, my limbs tingling to jump up and leave. Maestro will come home after midnight to find his new maid nearly frozen and sitting on the stoop, locked out of the townhouse. I'll be fired on the spot.

I surge up and pace the sidewalk. What I need is to distract myself. Get away from the indecision and calm down. Only then can I decide on a plan.

I walk to one end of Newfane Avenue, where it intersects with Sarte Street. A corner convenience store is located on the ground level of a five-story walk-up. Beside it is another similar building, which holds a laundromat, a liquor store, and a nail salon. The idea of going to one of the shops and asking to use the phone to call Mrs. Farthing at Baymont Symphony occurs to me. Lacking her telephone number, I could try calling the box office. I'll use that tactic as a last resort.

Heading back, I go all the way to the other end of Newfane Avenue, passing townhouse after townhouse. My attention is drawn to the different designs of the little garden spaces between the building fronts and the sidewalk. At my own house, I'd entirely planted around the house's foundation. Getting garden soil under my fingers is a pleasant and relaxing pastime. I linger far too long at each garden, a wave of nostalgia dragging my mood lower than it has been in days.

The street noise increases as I approach the corner of Newfane Avenue, where it intersects Ackerman Avenue. Cars fly by going east on the one-way, three-lane street. On the opposite side of the street, there's a dry cleaners, another convenience store, a florist, and a doughnut shop. What I wouldn't give to have a cup of tea right now, and something to eat. I neglected to have breakfast this morning, afraid my walk to the symphony might be delayed.

My stomach growls. I spin on my heels and walk back to Maestro's townhouse, where I resume sitting on the stoop. My eyes close against the bright sunlight. At least the unusual warmth today, together with the sunlight, and the black sweater I'm wearing, keep me warm enough. But as the sun sets and darkness falls, I will be cold. I have to make a decision.

The sound of a door opening behind my back startles me. I scurry to my feet.

"Mrs. Davitt?" Maestro Grant demands, standing at the open door, his face thunderous.

My heart pounds against my chest wall. I cannot meet his eyes. "Yes, Mr. Grant?"

"What on earth are you doing out here?" He opens the door farther and pokes his head out, scanning the area as if to ascertain I am alone.

I swallow that hard lump in my throat again. "I got locked out." My compulsion to flee urges me, but it would do no good now.

"Without my key or cellphone." My voice sounds as weak and embarrassed as a child caught shoplifting a candy.

"No coat, I see." His scowl says all that needs to be said as he steps back, his face frozen hard, opening the door wide to let me in.

"I'm so sorry, Mr. Grant. Please forgive me," I say as I slip past him into the townhouse.

With a curt nod, he walks back to the living room. "Consider yourself lucky I forgot something."

I nod, though he can't see it. Not knowing what to say, I blurt out, "Thank you for saving me."

Maestro disappears into his bedroom suite as I remain in the living room, unsure of what to do next. Waiting to be fired and sent away, I wring my hands, my teeth clenched tight. He surely is going to fire me.

He returns, having changed into jeans, a T-shirt, and sneakers. His smoking hot visage knocks me off balance. Those jeans fit his ass and legs perfectly. "I couldn't imagine why the alarm system was off."

Here it comes. Shuffling my weight back and forth between my feet, I decide to apologize again in the hope he will take pity and not send me packing on my first day. "I'm very sorry. It won't happen again."

He scowls as he looks me up and down. "Is it safe to leave you until I return later this evening, Mrs. Davitt?"

The bite of his words stings my ego. "Yes, sir." Again, I cannot, will not, meet his eyes.

Briskly, he replies, "See that you do." He heads out a door I haven't explored yet.

Following him, I peer through the door. A black Porsche Carrera sits in the one-car garage. Maestro Grant gets into the vehicle and reverses out of the garage onto a lengthy asphalt driveway leading to an alley. He gives me another scowl. He must have pushed a button because the overhead garage door descends with a clattering sound.

I shut the door and arm the system, vowing not to step foot outside the brick confines of the building for the remainder of the night.

With nothing left to do, I go back to my room and settle into the rocking chair. As I contemplate my current scenario, the rocker gyrates swiftly.

None of my roommates were home at the time I packed up most of my things. I left no messages about my whereabouts either. When I don't return, they might guess I've gone back to my house, which is fine.

My personal business, especially this new job, is a secret. I am paid up for my room in hell until February 20th, three weeks from now. This should give me enough time to go through most of the trial period. Within that timeframe, I'll determine whether it works for me or if Maestro Grant is too difficult. The six-month lease I signed back in August never mentioned any required notice for leaving. My twenty-six-hundred-dollar security deposit should be fully returned.

It will be one drop in a ten-gallon pail compared to the tens of thousands of dollars I owe. If I'm lucky, the equity in the house will cover all the liens and leave me a little money. If there is nothing left for me, I will throw my room security into my minuscule savings account. If this trial period doesn't work out, I'll need to find a new place to live. I will not willingly go back to that apartment.

It seems incredible that this should happen exactly as I wished. If the contract extends beyond the trial period, it will be better than my wildest dream. A thousand times better than living in that derelict space with juveniles masquerading as adults. This is a terrific gig, despite the inauspicious start. Between two jobs, I know I will be far too busy to even consider the past, let alone grieve over it. Even if I do have to put up with a grumpy, starched shirt of a man.

SETTLING IN

A CARDINAL CHIRPING incessantly outside the window rouses me from sleep. It is almost sunrise, that much I can tell. Faint, glowing streaks of peachy-pink grow visibly above the rooftops against the dark, blue-gray eastern sky as I watch out the window.

Other than the bird chatter, the house is completely silent. If I get up to make coffee this early, will I awaken the house's only other occupant? I decide against it and snuggle down into the warm, comfortable bed for a little while longer.

The evening before, I had unpacked my suitcase of clothing, an extra pair of shoes, and toiletries. With little else to do, I roamed through each room, examining everything and trying to memorize the placement of objects. My last stop was the kitchen, which I found beautifully designed but not well stocked with cooking utensils or food. The light-brown birch cabinets and drawers held flatware, a set of dishes for four, and a French press coffee maker. The light beige speckled marble countertop was spotless and free of clutter except for the toaster. No decorations, nothing hanging on the walls, or the white subway-tiled backsplash.

I made a list of items I would need: a colander, food prep knives, a few good, sturdy skillets, and some roasting and baking pans.

Likewise, the massive stainless steel side-by-side refrigerator-freezer was poorly stocked. A box of granola, a half-gallon of organic whole milk, a half-dozen organic eggs past their use-by date, a bag of French roast coffee, a half stick of butter, a jar of orange marmalade, and a loaf of whole grain bread were the only inhabitants of the refrigerator. A bin full of ice cubes was the freezer's only occupant.

When I finished taking inventory of the foodstuffs, I made a list of basic supplies. I hoped to develop a weekly menu to go over with

Maestro at the earliest convenience. From there, I'd finalize my food purchase list and call in the order as soon as possible.

Perusing the list reminded me I hadn't eaten anything all day. It was tempting to walk to the convenience store, but I don't want to tempt fate with the front door again. Instead, I found a takeout menu on top of the fridge for an Italian restaurant. If Mr. Grant used them, it was probably good food.

I placed an order online for home delivery. An hour later, chicken parmesan with linguini and a tossed salad arrived. Returning to the kitchen, I ate every bite. It was delicious and sated my appetite. With nothing else to do, I double-checked the alarm system and retreated to my suite to surf the cable channels. Sometime later, I'd fallen asleep sitting up in bed.

My six a.m. phone alarm startles me out of my reverie. I ready myself for the day and descend to the kitchen to make coffee, bringing my electric kettle with me.

The press pot of French roast coffee is finished steeping when Mr. Grant strides into the kitchen carrying a newspaper. Dark shadows surround his puffy, bloodshot eyes.

"Coffee," he growls, dropping heavily into the chair facing me.

My fingers tightly curl around my mug. "Milk and sugar?" I ask, even though Mrs. Farthing told me how he likes his coffee prepared. Turning my back to him, I fill a mug with the rich-smelling, dark-roast brew. Behind me, I hear the crinkle of the newspaper being spread open.

"Milk."

I lean against the refrigerator after placing his cup on the table. He ignores my presence. When his hand blindly grips the mug, unease blossoms in my gut. Should I exit the kitchen and leave him be? Or stay and be ignored as though I'm not here? Will he bark an order for breakfast when he's ready, or should I interrupt his reading to ask? The icy silence continues except for the rustling of the newspaper pages flipping every few minutes.

I open the refrigerator as if seeking something, my toe tapping on the tile floor. The paper rustles again, breaking my indecision. "Would you like breakfast?" I turn to find his cold, bloodshot eyes staring at me over the top of the paper.

"Two slices of toast. Bring the marmalade," he barks, then focuses his attention on the paper, his head disappearing behind it.

It is an order, and not an order in the way of a restaurant order. More like a dictator's or general's order to a soldier. My ire rises, but he did answer my question, and I now have something to do besides stand here uncomfortably waiting.

"Butter?"

"If I wanted butter, I'd have asked for it," he says sternly, not bothering to lower the newspaper between us.

What an insufferable, arrogant coot! I bite my tongue to keep an angry retort from spilling out. When I set the hot toast and marmalade down on the table, he closes the newspaper, folds it in half twice, and sets it aside.

"I suppose I should give you a tour of the house." He scoops a blob of orange marmalade onto his toast with a spoon and spreads it evenly with the back of it. A small bit falls over the edge onto the tabletop. He swipes it up with his index finger and licks it off. The look on his face, at the sweetness or tartness of the jam, the licking tongue, sends tingles through my lower abdomen. He must hear me inhale sharply because he catches my eyes in a hot, almost surprised glance, before he looks away.

I glance away too. "I—I did look into every room, but I didn't enter them. Perhaps you can tell me what you expect me to do in each room." My words aren't eloquent, his continence upsetting my sense of self. Watching him eat, his tongue darting out to catch stray jam-coated crumbs, unsettles me. I have to turn my back on him and busy myself wiping the countertop.

"Good, we'll start in twenty minutes. Meet me back here."

Unceremoniously dismissed, I retreat to my room for twenty minutes of pacing. Is this the way it is to be? Is this *really* better than my current situation? While my mind screams yes, my heart isn't so sure. I hoped it would be amicable. But the knot of tension quivering in my gut from our morning encounter keeps telling me this trial is doomed. Am I better off sticking with what I already know, even if it has significant disadvantages? Is it always better to stay with the familiar, as much as it is despised? Will this arrangement become better over time? Less stiff and formal? Less unsettling?

The more I ruminate over the situation, the more I think back to my marriage. Brannon and I had been friends for a long time before we got married. Our home life was never uncomfortable, except in the final year of his life. I guess my heart ached for just such camaraderie, however wrong for the arrangement.

Mr. Grant and I aren't friends. We haven't spent years getting to know each other. It's ridiculous to expect a rapport to develop so quickly. He is the landlord and master of the house. I am the paid servant. I need to rearrange my thoughts to reality and ignore my body's response to his every move.

Twenty minutes later, I'm back in the kitchen as directed, this time with a notepad to write down specific instructions.

Mr. Grant arrives moments later. "Follow me," he says briskly and strides out the kitchen door into the dining area. He keeps walking as he gestures to the twelve-seat table. "I don't use this except for dinners with special guests. It hasn't been used since I moved in. The table has five additional leaves, expanding to hold thirty people. Extra chairs are in the basement."

I glance around, unsure whether the area can accommodate that size of a table, but I say nothing.

Striding into the living area, he sweeps his whole arm, indicating the room. "The living area, as you can see." He adds, "with a fireplace." The entire room is plain, with little to catch the eye, except for a Colts stein on the mantel. The room is sparsely furnished with mission-style furniture. Despite the mahogany-colored leather sofa, I've seen better-appointed consignment furniture shops. The bookshelves are the room's only saving grace.

"Do you use the fireplace much?" I ask, wondering if I will need to secure tinder and firewood.

"No." He heads for the music room. To my surprise, he opens the door on the left instead. Descending the steps, he leaves me to trail behind him. At the landing, there is another door. He unlocks the door with a key he pulls out of his pocket. Opening it wide, he proclaims reverently, "The wine cellar."

My mouth hangs open. I step past him into a large room filled with special holding racks. Shelving against one side holds liquor bottles with all the remaining shelving full of wine bottles tipped on their sides. "I'll select the wines as needed, especially for events," he says behind me. "I might need you to accept deliveries and put things down here."

"Should I shelve them too?" I shiver. The climate control unit shows the ambient temperature is fifty-five degrees.

His shoulders stiffen. "No. A business installed the shelving and organized the bottles. I haven't studied the layout yet. Let's go upstairs."

He steps back toward the doorway, forcing me to sidestep by him. Our torsos brush lightly in passing. His chest to my breasts. A tiny zing surges through me at the touch. Goosebumps erupt on my arms and my face grows hot. I quickly turn my back and ascend. Mr. Grant follows.

Back in the first-floor hallway, he opens the door to the music room.

Morning sunlight streams through the vast room, which features a wall of windows. At the near end of the room is a gorgeous, shiny, black grand piano.

His voice softens, becomes almost languid. "This is my baby." His palm caresses the glossy closed top. "You'll need to take good care of her. Wipe her down daily with a fresh microfiber cloth."

He gestures toward the wall behind us. Elaborate shelving is filled with modern electronic equipment, and four long rows of CDs, as well as another of vinyl record albums. "You can dust as needed, but don't disturb the order. I know where everything is."

An extra-large music stand is full of sheet music, sticky notes attached all over the place. Bending down, I pick up one that had fallen to the carpeted floor. "Don't touch anything on the music stand," he barks, returning to his ogre self. He holds out his hand and I drop the paper into it. He shoves it into his pants pocket.

Another order from the general to the cannon fodder. My irreverent humor begs me to salute and say, "Aye, aye, Captain." Since I'm not sure how he'll take it, I hold my tongue.

A haphazard pile of compact discs is stacked on the piano top. "I have a terrible habit of taking CDs out of the cases and not putting them back."

"I'm sure I can match them up," I say, adding, "If you want me to."

"You should probably ask before you tidy up, just in case it's something I've been working with. Don't ever try to re-file them on the shelves. I'll do it." The curt tone makes me wince.

"Understood." I clench my hands, lacing my fingers together to prevent saluting.

Starting to leave the room, he stops abruptly. "There's a bathroom off to the side here. You can keep this tidy, as needed."

Without waiting for a reply, he marches out of the room and up the stairs. At his bedroom door, he pauses, his stilled hand on the knob. "My room," he pronounces with solemnity, as if it's some kind of throne room. "I keep it rather sparse, minimalist."

He opens the door dramatically. A richly dressed mahogany bed, topped by a navy, lightweight down comforter, dominates the space. Unusually centered in the room, it faces the uncurtained windows. Like the music room directly one floor down, the room is bathed in morning sunlight. A chest on chest and double dresser with a mirror are the only other pieces of furniture. A group portrait in a silver frame rests on the double dresser. No pictures hang on the stark white walls.

I nod, not saying a word. My fingers fidget in my lightly clasped hands. One look at his unmade bed and my face blushes hot. I force myself to study the dresser across the room. *What the heck is wrong with me?*

"Back behind here is the bathroom," he says, clearing his throat lightly. He gestures but does not move. As if he expects me to check it out.

Does the bed unnerve him too? Or did he see my reaction to it? Moving on, I poke my head into the bathroom to see piles of towels on the floor, beside the luxurious walk-in shower with multiple waterspouts. I almost grunt my disapproval. Why is it so hard to fling them over the shower door? "I'll come back for those after the tour."

He gives me a sharp nod, his eyes not meeting mine, then he strides out of the room.

We head up the short flight of stairs to the two guest bedrooms. Mr. Grant swings open the doors, allowing me to peer inside. I checked them out yesterday, so I give them a cursory glance. I also know each has a full bathroom attached.

"I don't anticipate having overnight guests very often. Keep one room ready. In case a family member decides to show up." He closes the door and pauses.

"Ah, your room is just up there." He gestures up the next flight of stairs, but makes no move to ascend. "There's actually another room up in the attic above the guest rooms. It's meant to be a maid's room, but it doesn't make sense to put you there. It's rather tiny and doesn't have a bathroom."

"Thank you," I say with genuine appreciation for the thoughtfulness. I'm glad to hear he isn't a stickler about space.

His composure goes rigid again as his cheeks actually flush pink. "Well…" he clears his throat again. "Let's go to the basement."

Mr. Grant leads me back to the garage door. "The door to the other half of the basement is here." He opens the door and flicks on the light switch. "There's some furniture down there, and the extra dining chairs. Not much else besides the furnace, on-demand water heaters, etc." He glares at me as if daring me. "Do you want to go down?"

"No, I don't think it's necessary. I'll check it out later."

He nods and leads me back to the kitchen.

I have to address the food inventory. "I took stock of the kitchen shelves. There are some things I'd like to purchase. Also, I would like to know about your eating schedules. For example, what would you like for lunch and dinner today?" I add, "Assuming you will be here for either."

"My schedule is pretty erratic day to day, week to week. For the most part, it's planned ahead with Evelyn's help. We'll have to sit down together every week to discuss it, so you can plan ahead." He glances at his watch. The Rolex gleams gold in the few rays of sunlight penetrating the kitchen. "Tonight, I'll be out with friends. Now, I'm due at the rehearsal hall. I don't expect to be back again until after ten tonight."

"Thank you for telling me," I say. "I'll order some routine staples using the information Mrs. Farthing gave me."

He nods, and disappears into the garage.

DIANA ROCK

I stand by the window watching him back out of the narrow driveway into the alley. I notice the enclosed lawn, edged with palisade-style fencing behind shrubs and a hint of garden edging. I'll have to check it out later. First, I need to get the towels off the bathroom floor and order groceries.

FIRST DINNER

A RAY OF SUNLIGHT STREAMING on my face pulls me from sleep the next morning. The sound of music seeping into the room alerts me. I sit up in bed, trying to remember where I am and where it might be coming from. It is probably from the music room. If he's awake, he'll be wanting coffee. I get up and check the time. Ugh, six-ten in the morning. I throw on my jeans and a long-sleeved sweater and slip down to the kitchen. I start brewing the coffee before going back to my room for a quick shower.

Back in the kitchen half an hour later, I consider bringing him a cup, but don't know if food and beverages are allowed in the music room. Erring on the side of caution, I wait for him to come to the kitchen. Besides, it gives me time to see if the food delivery is still scheduled for this afternoon. I pour myself a cup, settle into a chair, and check my emails.

Mr. Grant stalks into the kitchen, giving me a nod without smiling. He's dressed in what I've already come to define as his work clothes, black dress pants, black wing tip shoes, long-sleeved button-down shirt, and a bow tie. Only the color of the shirt changes. Today, it's light beige.

"Good morning. Don't get up." I stand to pour his coffee, but he waves me to remain seated and retrieves a cup himself.

"Refill?" Mr. Grant asks, not glancing over his shoulder, the French press in his hand.

"Not yet, thanks," I say, trying to stay relaxed and calm. This morning is already better than yesterday. I don't want to push my luck.

Mr. Grant sits across from me. No smile on his handsome face, but also no scowl this morning...yet anyway. There's a short silence as if neither of us knows what to say. "Did you sleep well?"

His question throws me off. "Uh, great. The bed is perfectly comfortable." A burst of heat floods my cheeks. I stare at my hands wrapped around the mug. Why is it awkward to say the word bed?

"Excellent," he replies, as a sudden strangeness settles over the table like fog rising over winter snow after a warm rain shower. "I'll be at the office all day, but I expect to be back by six tonight."

"What would you like for dinner this evening?" I ask, hoping to get the menu settled for today.

"Eggplant parmesan." His reply is swift, almost as if he didn't need to think about it. Did he decide beforehand, or is this his favorite meal? I decline to interrogate.

I didn't order an eggplant with the groceries, but perhaps I can add it to the order at the last minute. "Yes, of course. Breakfast? What would you like?"

"A couple eggs over-easy with toast."

I nod. Good thing I picked up a dozen eggs yesterday at the convenience store. His tone is still a little curt, but I am pleased that he doesn't bark the order like he did yesterday. Perhaps yesterday, like me, he'd felt uncomfortable and anxious. Today, he is slightly more pleasant. I get to work and set the plate on the table along with the marmalade jar, and then refill his mug.

He gestures for me to sit down.

"You go back to work at the hospital on Monday?" he asks, digging into his food.

"Yes, all next week. Nine to two pm."

Nothing more is said while he eats his eggs and his toast with huge dollops of marmalade. Finishing, he brushes crumbs from his placemat onto the table. Mr. Grant leans back in his chair with a satisfied sigh. "Good breakfast."

"Thanks." The heat of a blush rushes up my neck. My chest lightens at the compliment. Today is definitely going much better than yesterday. I don't want to ruin the mood, but I need to ask.

"There are some kitchen utensils and supplies that would be good to have here."

"Didn't we discuss this yesterday?" Mr. Grant's words cut the good vibe to shreds. "Order them online, or hit the stores. I assume Evelyn gave you the particulars about those kinds of purchases."

"She did. Would you like to see the list? It's quite extensive."

"No." He stares me down. "Don't bother me with mundane questions. I have far more important things to address."

I'm stunned into silence as his eyes narrow and his glare bores into me. Beneath the table, my knees tremble as steam gathers in my chest, ready to explode. How dare he! I'm trying to get information about his desires and needs, and he's going to act like that? Pinching the bridge of my nose, the backs of my legs shove my chair along the tile floor as I stand. With my teeth clenched so hard I fear breaking them, I give him a nod and retire to my room to quiet my inner ranting.

After he leaves, I spend the remainder of the day browsing online cookware shops and high-end stores. I review my list, ticking off each item as I check out my online cart. Everything is ordered express delivery, costing a small fortune in fees.

At one o'clock, the food delivery arrives. I'd forgotten to add the eggplant, so after tucking the food away and eating a quick lunch of PB&J, I head back out.

Later in the afternoon, with a few more items and the eggplant in tow, I'm back at the townhouse to settle everything in and start dinner.

That's when my lawyer calls.

"Mrs. Davitt, the closing for your house has been scheduled for next Saturday morning at my office, ten o'clock."

Tears flood my eyes as a falling sensation fills my body. It is happening. The final step to ending this financial mess. Cutting off the last connection to my previous life. I'm not ready to say goodbye to the house that Brannon and I shared. I don't know whether to be relieved or bereft. A thousand thoughts zigzag through my mind. I picture the bathroom we'd refinished together, arguing over the tiles. What changes would the new owners make?

"Mrs. Davitt?" my lawyer repeats, his tone a little softer this time.

"Yes," I reply and nod, though he can't see it. "I'll be there."

"Good. The buyer's agent will be taking them through the house for the final walk-through early that morning. If there are any problems, I'll let you know."

Please, God, no more problems, I pray. "Fine. See you at ten." I hang up just before I lose my composure. In my room, I let my heart wring itself out for what I hope will be the last time. My mind questions the need to sell the house again as I prep the dinner. Perhaps I could find another professional couple to rent it? A couple who didn't mind the minor problems and inconveniences? Who wouldn't call me about every little thing that disappointed them?

Mr. Grant arrives home by six-thirty. Without stopping or acknowledging me, he walks from the garage door to his bedroom without a word. He returns to the kitchen dressed in jeans and a light blue Henley, and stocking feet. Everything is ready for tonight's dinner. The eggplant parmesan is in the oven, staying warm. The entire townhouse smells of garlic and tomato sauce.

Realizing this is the first time I'm serving him dinner at his home, I'm stumped. "I neglected to ask you if you prefer dinner here in the kitchen or at the dining table." I ask after placing a basket of warm Italian bread on the table along with a dish of herb-infused olive oil for dipping. Beside it, I set a tossed Romaine salad with a lemon wedge.

He gives me a hard stare. "The kitchen. Always in the kitchen, unless there are guests coming for dinner. I thought I mentioned that during the tour."

My gut tightens as I remember he did say something about it. I didn't write it down on my notepad. Actually, I didn't write anything down. He stands behind his chair and watches as I set the placemat for him at the table.

"Where's your place setting?" he asks, his hands resting on the back of his chair.

It wasn't a question I expected. "I, um, thought you might prefer to eat dinner alone, in quiet."

"Nonsense. We have things to discuss." He points to my chair and makes curt gestures for me to sit.

"Okay." I set my place while he watches. The idea of eating with him prickles my neck. I'd much rather eat by myself, as much as I hate eating alone. Far better for my digestion to not have to make small talk. "What do we need to discuss?"

He sits after I place the baking dish along with additional bowls of linguini and extra sauce on the table. "Smells good," he says as if he is surprised. "I shall be hosting a dinner party a few months hence."

Hence? Did this guy read Shakespeare? Or Donne, Marlowe, perhaps Tennyson? It is an unusual word to hear spoken in the twenty-first century. As a fan of British prose and poetry, I am familiar with the word and stunned to hear it spoken aloud in everyday conversation. My interest piques. There may be more to discover about Mr. Grant. Perhaps the books on the living room shelves can give me some hints.

As we eat, Mr. Grant explains, "This is how it's going to work. Evelyn will be in contact with the guests' agents. She'll send the invitations and gather information on food preferences, likes, dislikes, and food allergies, that sort of thing. Then she'll write up a memo and forward it to both of us so we know our parameters. We'll collaborate on a menu and wine list." He goes on to tell me it's a night near the end of the spring concert season. "Don't worry about anything right now. We'll discuss it more in the coming months once all the information is gathered."

I nod, not sure how to deliver my question. I don't want to make it sound like I prefer to pass the reins. "Would you like a first-rate chef to do the cooking in-house, and a professional wait staff?"

"I'd rather not, if at all possible. My goal is to give them a quiet, stress-free, and informal home-cooked meal. I want them to feel comfortable within these walls." He lifts his hands, indicating the townhouse. "As I said, we'll discuss this again in a few weeks."

We continue to eat in relative silence. I push pieces of eggplant around my plate, but don't eat many of them.

He picks up the wedge on his salad plate and glares at me, one eyebrow raised. "Lemon?"

I draw my salad plate toward me, pick up the fresh lemon wedge, and squeeze the juice onto the parmesan and romaine lettuce. "It's the way the Italians eat it." I start to rise. "If you'd rather an oil and vinegar dressing—"

He cuts me off. "No, I'll give this a try." He squeezes the lemon over his salad and then tastes it. He cocks an eyebrow at me as if in surprise. "Not bad."

Small miracle. I smile on the inside at teaching Maestro Grant something new.

"Dinner is great. You are a good cook. Thank you for that," he admits after cleaning his plate.

"Thank you." The compliment suggests he didn't believe I could cook anything beyond breakfast. Since we are both in a congenial mood, I decide to push a little for more information on the guest events. "You've held these dinners before?"

"Yes, but not here. When I was engaged, I did so at my old house. I've not entertained here since moving in."

Engaged? I hadn't heard he'd been engaged. Obviously, it didn't end with a wedding. I make a mental note to check online for any information about his fiancée and when the breakup occurred.

Mr. Grant rubs the back of his neck before getting up. "I forgot the Rangers have their last game on TV tonight. I'll catch you in the morning." He turns back, adding, "Thanks for your help today. I appreciate your organizational skills."

His comment is so totally unexpected that my heart skitters in my chest. "That's what I'm here for." I smile, then clear the table and hasten upstairs after the dishes are washed. I, too, need an entertainment escape after this arduous day. My concentration drifts sharply, though, as I recount the encounters with Mr. Grant. In some ways, he's as rigid and unmoving as a telephone pole. In other ways, he surprises me. In time, I hope to get to know the man behind the stoic demeanor who uses the word hence.

THE QUESTION

I CONFESS THAT MY FIRST week was a struggle. Getting to work for nine a.m. becomes my rush hour. Up by six, I get myself ready before going down to the kitchen to make coffee and be there when Mr. Grant appears for breakfast around seven. Fortunately, he is cognizant of my time crunch, so he immediately has breakfast, rather than read his newspaper first. Once he's eaten, I clear his plate, pop everything into the dishwasher, and leave. The walk to work is short, and if I reach the bus stop on Ackerman Avenue on time, I catch the bus for the final few blocks to the hospital.

I breathe easier once I'm there. As frequently happens, there isn't any research to do, so I help with the diagnostic lab workload. Much of it is performed on a machine. This means I have one hour to put the final touches on the testing and distribute the slides to the pathologists for interpretation.

After leaving the hospital, I get back to the townhouse to wait for any deliveries after three pm. Groceries are delivered on Tuesday. On Wednesday, the dry cleaning van arrives to pick up and drop off. The laundry service comes on Thursday, picking up and dropping off as well. If I need to run errands, hit the post office, or specialty stores, that will happen on Mondays and Fridays.

My paycheck from McAuliffe is directly deposited into my bank account on Wednesday. Like a greedy fool, I check my account online to make sure it arrives.

I stop at the apartment on Thursday after work to pick up a few things. While I never told them where I would be, I leave a note taped to the fridge saying I was there, so sorry I missed seeing them, and I'll be back in a few days. I'm not sorry I missed them. Since I know their course schedules, I deliberately arrive when I know they're gone. It saves me from a lot of questions and dealing with their immaturity and shenanigans. The hasp on my room door still hasn't been fixed, leaving my belongings, however few, at the mercy of someone's conscience.

Veronica has left me a note reminding me that the rent is due in two weeks, and if I want out of the arrangement, I should give notice immediately. The note causes a stir in my gut. I still have three weeks left in the thirty-day trial period. Everything is going well as far as I can tell, but Mr. Grant hasn't mentioned his intentions to keep me on or not. I need to ask him outright.

As the first week comes to a close, I broach the subject. I wait until the end of a dinner he'd earlier expressed as one of his favorites. Mr. Grant sits back in his chair after finishing a plate of meatloaf and roasted winter vegetables. I set my utensils down and clear my throat of the lump threatening to impede my practiced delivery. "Um, I'd like to know what your thoughts are about this arrangement. Are there any duties I've neglected to perform or performed unsatisfactorily?"

Mr. Grant shakes his head. "Not that I have seen."

"Do you have any idea if you'll be extending my trial into a permanent contract?"

He picks up his napkin and dabs his lips as he appears to be deciding how to answer. His eyes darken and narrow. "Do you need to know now?" His voice is hard.

I nod, though my hands shake and my fork clatters onto the stoneware plate. "It would be helpful. My rented room either needs to be emptied, or I need to pay for another month." My lip quivers as a surge of emotion threatens to escape my tight hold. "Are you unhappy with anything that's happened over the last week?" My hands clench and unclench in my lap.

"No, but we still have three weeks left in our arrangement. Can I tell you later?"

Tears sting my eyes. What have I done or not done to warrant his indecision? He ate the meals I prepared each night with gusto, giving me grudging compliments. Other than eating with him, I've stayed out of his way as much as possible. "If something is not to your liking, I would appreciate it if you could tell me." What is it? I can't fix anything if he doesn't tell me.

An uneasy silence fills the air between us.

He sets down his napkin beside his plate. "It's been fine." Leaning back, he examines me. "I intend to invite friends over tomorrow night. We're going to watch the Colts game. Can you provide refreshments, munchies, and such?"

Is this a test? "Sure. Are these male friends, or mixed company? It would help to know about the items on the menu. Unless you have suggestions." There's a tremor in my voice, and I hope Mr. Grant doesn't pick up on it. As a musician, his ears are highly attuned to sounds, and he might catch it.

"Men only. The usual pub type fare—wings, sliders, nachos, dips, that sort of thing." He stands. "Unless you have any additional questions, I'll be in the music room."

I huff, drawing breath from deep in my chest as I watch him leave. I'll have to wait for an answer. Meaning, I might end up having to pay for another month's rent. Or pay late. Jenna is always late paying her rent. Veronica never says anything.

Veronica, being her money-hungry self, could refuse to return my security deposit, even though my contract makes no mention of such a penalty for leaving at the last minute. I wouldn't put it past her to do it anyway. She knows I don't have any money to take her to court. Still, losing my deposit would hurt.

While clearing the dishes, I ruminate over the possibility. Veronica said something odd when I moved in that puzzled me at the time, but now, an explanation springs to mind. She said that if her parents ever came to the door, I was to say only that I was a friend spending the night there. I wasn't supposed to tell them I rented a room. Before now, I didn't have a reason to question the odd request. I need to investigate.

My thoughts are interrupted by the jingling of keys in Mr. Grant's hand.

In a gruff voice, he says, "I'm going out for a few hours. See you in the morning." He pulls on a supple leather bomber jacket and heads for the garage. His black jeans are a snug fit. I have to blink several times to break eye contact with his ass. The overhead garage door sounds like a coffee grinder as it opens, letting me know he's driving the Carrera instead of taking a livery or taxi.

I'm alone. Again. Did my questions bother him? Did they drive him out of the house to keep from being under the same roof as me? It's futile to worry. I put away the remaining food and clean up, then retreat to my room. Not mine, but a room that has been temporarily assigned for my use, I remind myself. Perhaps only for the next few weeks.

. . . .

I DON'T HAVE ANY PLACE to go when I leave the townhouse in my Porsche. No visits to make or appointments to keep. Mrs. Davitt's questions threw me into a mild panic. How can I tell her I'm unsure about having her remain after the trial period? Not because her performance isn't up to snuff. But because she is getting under my skin. Simple conversations about menus and household tasks over our meals together are keeping me sane in one way while driving me crazy in others. Her quiet, calm presence mocks what I once had.

I focus hard on my job, squeezing every ounce I can out of the orchestra musicians and the symphony staff because it's all I have left.

Returning to the townhouse every night makes me dwell on the events of the last nine months. The day I arrived home to surprise Cynthia with an afternoon off on her birthday. Little did I know the surprise was for me, not her. I found my fiancée naked and bent over the edge of our bed, locked together in a carnal moment with Malcolm Trier.

She opened her eyes, actually grinned at me while the president of the symphony's board of directors, still oblivious to my presence, thrust away like he was rowing a scull. I walked out of that house, a three million-dollar home I had bought because she wanted it. My attorneys and accountant determined that I'd also given her more than $ 2.1 million over the course of our relationship. It hadn't been enough for her. Nothing was ever enough.

During our two years together, you'd think you would know someone. Why was I so blinded by her manners, her beauty, and her sophisticated friends? After the breakup, I vowed to pay more attention to the women I interacted with. My trust and loyalty would not be so freely given only to be trampled on again.

I realize Mrs. Davitt is nothing like my former fiancée. Cynthia never once greeted me with a home-cooked meal. Never once made an effort to learn my favorite foods. I'm aware that Mrs. Davitt is simply doing her job. My insistence that she eat her meals with me is because it makes more sense than for her to have them in her room. That would leave me alone. And I've had more than enough of that.

THE CLOSING

SATURDAY MORNING, I make the coffee and get Mr. Grant's breakfast together. Today, it's bacon with a veggie omelet. As soon as he leaves the table, I clean up and head out for the errand I'm not looking forward to. Oh, how I wish I could continue renting out the house. Doing so had worked for six months. In the end, the hospitals and doctors were insistent about getting their money faster. Today, I'm having to say goodbye to the place I call home.

The cab arrives at the law firm's office just before ten o'clock. Sitting down at the conference table full of people makes my knees rubbery. The buyers and their lawyer, my own lawyer, and the hospital's lawyers are all waiting for me. Here to witness the last vestige of my former life disappears.

A mixture of emotions clusters in my chest. The loss of Brannon and of Kendall, and all our dreams of a long and happy future together. The trip plans we will never make, the national parks we will never visit, the European cities we will never see again. Bitterness fills me. If only Brannon had taken a corporate accounting job, I wouldn't be stuck cleaning up this financial mess. A hard pressure in my chest threatens to erupt like an air bubble under water. I hold fast, keeping it in check, stuffing it down. For my dignity, I need to get through this hour as unemotionally as possible.

I sign contract after contract as my lawyer slides them in front of me. He starts telling me what each is for, until I ask him to stop. It doesn't matter what they are for. It needs to be done. I focus on my penmanship instead of what they say. It is better than facing the reality raining down with each stroke of my pen.

When the papers stop coming, I slump in my chair. My eyes focus on the tiny scratch in the polished wood tabletop. Around me, the lawyers shake hands with the buyers and with one another.

One hand enters my peripheral vision. I don't shake it. It finally withdraws, as do all the other people except my lawyer.

"Mrs. Davitt?" He returns to my side, his hand lightly resting on my shoulder. "Are you all right?"

No. No, I'm not all right, and I don't think I ever will be again. I'm treading water in the middle of an ocean, bereft of a life jacket, a boat, a goal, a husband, a dog, and now, a home. "Fine," My voice is flat.

I stand and slip the strap of my purse over my shoulder. "How long before everything is settled?" My attorney mentions the various checks and payments that will need to be made. I will get anything remaining. If there is such a thing.

"A few weeks. It should be straightforward. We'll send a residual check to your post office box."

I leave. Rather than hail a cab, I wander down the street seeking a quiet and private place to burst. A local park bench holds me up when the bubble pops. I slump, sobbing uncontrollably while people walk by...couples, individual men and women, bicyclists and skateboarders, people walking dogs, and mothers and nannies pushing strollers through the cloud-dappled sunshine of this winter day. When my tears run out, I notice lovers strolling the wide sidewalks hand in hand. It's time to leave.

I make a quick stop at my post office box. A wad of letters and circulars clogs it, requiring some effort to remove them all. Stuffing it all in my purse, I walk all twenty-three city blocks back to Mr. Grant's home. There is nowhere else I have to go.

He's not alone in the townhouse.

Voices travel from the music room, as do snippets of musical phrases from a violin. The door is propped open. Wanting to let Mr. Grant know I'm back, I go to the open doorway and knock on the frame.

Mr. Grant and Haruka Satō look up, both poised at the music stand as if reading the score together. "Yes, Mrs. Davitt?" Mr. Grant asks, one eyebrow quirked up, a dark scowl on his handsome face.

"My apologies for interrupting. Is there anything I can get for you or Miss Satō?" Something doesn't feel quite right, but I can't tell what. There's tension in this room.

The maestro questions the concertmaster. "Haruka? Anything?"

The woman flings back her long, straight, black hair, shaking her head. "No, thank you." Her thin, soft voice is barely audible across the room.

"Nothing for me. Thank you, Mrs. Davitt." He turns away, pointing at the sheet music for Miss Satō to notice something.

I nod, though neither of them sees it. My emotions are upended again. I want to growl, miffed inexplicably by Miss Satō's flirtatious hair gesture. Is she out to snare Mr. Grant? He is incredibly handsome and very single. Does she have designs on him as a husband?

Unneeded, I retreat to the kitchen and begin preparations for this evening's party. Half an hour later, I hear the front door open, polite salutations between the maestro and Miss Satō, and the door click closed.

Mr. Grant walks into the kitchen. "Thank you for being hospitable."

"No problem," I say, wiping my hands on a dishtowel and eyeing him as he leans against the door frame with an expression I define as apologetic. A bubble of emotions well up from deep inside me. Threatening to explode into sounds and words I will regret. I swallow hard. Brannon used to stand like that too.

He pauses, examining me with concern in his eyes. His lips part slightly as if waiting to say something. He inhales and then asks, "Are you all right? Has something happened?"

After a few seconds, I tell him, "The closing on my house was this morning."

"You sold it? Why?" His gaze deepens as he examines my face. "What are you going to do if this situation doesn't pan out?"

Explaining why I sold it would expose my vulnerability. I settle for, "Selling it is my best option. I have a friend here in town who can put me up temporarily if needed."

His lips flatten, and his shoulders slump. "I'm sorry."

"Thank you." I untangle my hands from the dishtowel, fold it neatly, and place it on the counter. I don't want to say anymore. I can't talk about it. I need to shut down any further discussion on the topic. "Do you need anything else?"

Mr. Grant inhales deeply. "No." He walks closer to the counter and glances at all the preparations. "Is there anything I can do to help you?"

I get the impression he's not speaking of party preparations. I shake my head.

"It looks like you have everything well in hand. But I'm here if you need me." He pauses, our eyes holding for a few seconds before he breaks contact, an odd expression on his face. "I'll be in the music room."

While I put together the sliders I'll serve tonight, I put my phone on speaker and call Clare.

"How did it go?" Clare asks tentatively.

"Okay. It's done except for the accounting," I reply, as I add stone-ground mustard to the corned beef sliders. "I'll have to wait to see about the outcome." I silently pray I make something out of the sale.

"You should. It's a beautiful house and property. Do you want to come over and hang out with me tonight?" Clare says, "Hold on for a second." She must be talking to Louis.

When she comes back, I answer her question. "Can't come over tonight, but soon, I hope. Maestro Grant is having friends over to watch the game. I'm serving the food." The words are out of my mouth before I remember the three NDAs I signed. While I'm speaking with someone whom I know I can trust not to repeat the information, it gives me pause to consider any other conversations.

"Huh. That's why I'm alone tonight. Louis is going to a football party too."

I know Clare well enough to know she hates being alone. "Lucky you. Get yourself a good book and a glass of wine. You won't miss me."

"More like a bottle. I'll miss you more without your help drinking it."

"Another time, girlfriend."

Clare starts talking to Louis in the background. When she returns, I say, "Hey, I've got to go too. Talk to you again soon. We'll do lunch or something."

"Yes! Absolutely."

Mr. Grant's friends begin arriving at about seven. Some toting bottles of liquor or six-packs or growlers of craft beer. I set out a tray of chips and dip and crudités with a garlic-chive cream cheese spread for dipping. Mr. Grant takes over the role of butler, answering the door and taking coats to hang in the closet.

I'm grateful for his help. Even more grateful he does it without being asked.

Our plan is to bring in a platter of something new every half hour. Before kick-off, I bring a tray of Reuben sliders and meatloaf with cheddar cheese sliders.

"Who is this lovely lady and why is she not in here with us?" an equally handsome auburn-haired man asks. His freckled cheeks are chubby on his otherwise slim face.

Mr. Grant stands. "Gentlemen, this is my housekeeper, Mrs. Davitt. She's prepared a feast for tonight's game." His hand slaps the man's shoulder. "This is Rick Weatherby, assistant conductor."

"Pleasure," I say, nodding to each of the other five men seated around the living room's giant screen television. "Pace yourselves, gentlemen. It's a long game, and I have a lot more coming."

A round of laughter ensues. Rick opens a bottle of beer and holds it out to me. "Join us."

I glance over at Mr. Grant. Both of us know I can't watch the game and continue with the food prep. He takes the bottle and hands it to me. "Enjoy. Keep the food coming. I'm starving."

His pals raise another ruckus at this; comments about his tighter clothing, his gaining weight, and speculation that I have something to do with it echo in my ears. Their friendly banter buoys my spirits far more than their compliments. "Thanks," I say with a smile, returning to the kitchen to get the next platters: buffalo wings and nachos with cheese and jalapenos ready for half-time.

• • • •

I TRY TO KEEP MY MIND on the game, but the look on Mrs. Davitt's face is hauntingly sad. There wasn't any indication she was selling her house. I assumed it was being rented out, either as short-stay housing or a long-term lease. Berating myself for not taking a more personal interest in Mrs. Davitt's life, I try to think of ways to get to know her better. The agency didn't provide much information, perhaps at her request. She calls herself "missus," as though she is married, and she wears a wedding band. Yet, there isn't any mention of a husband, by name or reference, and certainly no mention of children.

Do I have the right to know more? As long as she doesn't let her personal life interfere with her work, it won't matter in our employer/employee relationship. Or will it? I'm not sure. I prefer a gruff, cantankerous exterior at work, but something a little softer with her feels more appropriate.

Having never had to deal with a maid before, I'm not quite sure what the extent of our relationship should be. My only real exposure to anything resembling this situation is based on Cynthia's dealings with the maid and cook at our house. She was firm with them to the point of forcing some to quit. Otherwise, I've seen this situation in movies and TV shows, including *Downton Abbey*. But they weren't real, were they? I have no idea. Perhaps over time, Mrs. Davitt and I will become better acquainted.

The guys whoop loudly and cheer. The Colts scored again.

THE SCARE

AT ELEVEN IN THE MORNING on Tuesday, my cellphone rang with Mr. Grant's ringtone: the bagpipe tattoo most people don't know is named "Scotland the Brave." He's never called me during my hospital hours.

"I'm sorry, but I need some personal advice." Mr. Grant's tone is deep and serious, his voice wavering over the phone. "My mother just called. She found a lump in her breast, and her primary care doctor is advising a biopsy with a breast surgeon. What do you think?"

I'm more than a little amazed he's asking me for an opinion on a medical issue. "Whoa. It's not that simple. First of all, I'm not a doctor. Secondly, there are about twenty different factors to consider. All of them unknown to me so my guess would be just that, a crap shoot." I don't like being put on the spot with no information, not that I'd give him any specific medical advice anyway.

"But you deal with this every day," he protests.

"I can get a referral to a doctor here if she wants a second opinion, which is always a good idea. Doctors are only human," I add. "Don't tell them that, but they are."

"Get me that name today," he growls.

His demand is understandable even if unnecessary. "I will. Calm down. I know it's scary. I've been there. It sucks. But fear isn't the answer right now. Your mom needs your steadiness. I'll call you in a couple hours."

"Can't you get it faster?"

"I can, if you let me get off the phone now," I snip.

"Bye."

Twenty-three minutes later, I'm on the phone giving him a doctor's name.

"I suggest getting her an appointment right away if she is amenable to it."

After I hang up, I try to push away the memories associated with Brannon's initial consultations about his unexpected blood test result. My knee-jerk reaction is to warn Mr. Grant about the rollercoaster of emotions he will experience. Having been there, I know his mother and his entire family will need as much support as I can provide. So long as I don't cross the line that might get me fired from either the hospital or the agency.

Mr. Grant's mother, Marcie, arrives at the townhouse with her entourage of daughters, Orlaith and Fiona. Marcie's three children escort her to her consult appointment with Dr. Crawford Greene. Dr. Greene advised a stereotactic biopsy, which was hastily scheduled for the following day. Celebrity does have its advantages.

I stay clear of the diagnostic area Thursday morning. Luckily, I've been assigned research work for a change, so I'm in another area of the lab. I'm grateful for the physical separation today. The less I know, the better. Hours later, Mr. Grant calls with news. "The biopsy showed cancer, but they want to excise the entire thing tomorrow. Whatever that means."

"It means the breast surgeon will remove the lump." I try to calm him. "A pathologist will examine it and decide what to do next." While I can't tell them the diagnosis, I can provide them with a generalized explanation of the process. They've been informed that the final and full diagnosis is 48-96 hours away. Nonetheless, I expect to dodge questions, however innocently asked.

That evening, I serve a light dinner, cognizant that Marcie Grant needs to have nothing to eat after seven that night. Wishing to give them privacy, I eat alone in my room after cleaning up the kitchen and dining room. Since Marcie is first in the OR in the morning, Mr. Grant already told me they would have breakfast at the hospital cafeteria early the next morning.

I arrive at the hospital at eight-thirty and pop down to the surgical waiting room to see how everyone is holding up.

The three siblings surround me. "How's it look?" Mr. Grant asks as soon as he sees me, concern etched into every minute crease in his handsome face.

I lie. "I haven't seen it." Fresh from the operating room, I did see it, and it didn't look good. It definitely looks like cancer. But that is only the beginning of the story. How bad or good a cancer it is and how it will be treated has yet to be determined. Rather than try to explain all that just now, I fib.

"She comes home tonight?" Fiona asks.

"That's what the surgeon said," Mr. Grant replies.

I'm glad I gave up my room to Marcie, settling myself in the attic room so the sisters can take the two guest bedrooms. When they return to the townhouse, the daughters help their mother get into her nightgown and tuck her into bed.

Later that night, while Marcie is resting upstairs, the siblings gather in the living room. Mr. Grant had me order pizzas, which they eat while trying to keep a conversation flowing amid a sea of worry. I refill glasses of soda and wine as needed, but otherwise stay out of sight. They need to discuss family matters. And I need to avoid any potential interrogations.

Walking as quietly as possible to deaden the sounds of my slippered footsteps, I go room to room on the upper floors, checking on the guestrooms. I flip down the fresh linens, fluff the pillows, and place fresh towels in the bathroom. It's a house full, but Mr. Grant won't have it any other way. They are in this together for their mom and I admire that. If only Brannon's family had rallied around him like them.

I appreciate this opportunity to see the Grant family dynamics. More importantly, it reveals a side of Mr. Grant that I have yet to experience. There is a soft heart beneath that gruff, commanding exterior. He is affectionate with all three women, making sure they are as comfortable as possible under the circumstances. Perhaps someday he will warm to me enough to treat me in the same manner. The very thought makes me shiver.

As I return to the kitchen, Orlaith calls out from the living room. I cringe, sorry to be caught. I stick my head around the corner of the kitchen doorway. "Yes?"

"Mrs. Davitt, what happens now? I mean, I know she's going to see the doctor tomorrow to check if the wound is okay, but what's happening? Why does the final diagnosis take up to four more days?"

I sit on the arm of the sofa. They silently wait for me to answer. How can I explain in layman's terms? How to say something that will give them some calm in the storm of the unknown, and yet not divulge specific information. "Right now, the mass is being processed overnight. Very early tomorrow morning, thin slices will be placed on glass microscope slides. About nine a.m., laboratory technologists will start to run tests on them."

Fiona cups her hand over her mouth to muffle a sob.

I quickly add, "There are several different types of breast cancer. And not all of them are treated with the same drugs. The outcome of those tests will allow the oncologist to treat your mother with the best drug treatment, chemotherapy, or radiation needed."

Each of their faces sag, but they seem to understand. Fiona sniffles, wiping her eyes with a tissue.

"Are some types better to have than others?" Mr. Grant asks.

"Theoretically, yes. Some are more responsive to treatment than others." I don't want to sugar-coat my answer. It would be a disservice to give them incorrect information. Better that they know up front that treatment doesn't necessarily always end in a cure.

"So, if it must be cancer, we should hope for a treatable type?" Fiona asks.

"Yes, you want one that has a good prognosis, a good outcome, and a long survival rate."

Orlaith starts to ask something else, but Mr. Grant stands up. He holds up his palms toward both sisters. "Okay, we get it. We won't hold your feet to the fire." He sends a weary smile in my direction after giving his sisters a stern look.

I nod, grateful for his interruption, and leave them to discuss the issues without my presence.

I'm at work early again the next day. As I feared, with no research samples to test, I am sent to the diagnostic lab as one of the other technologists is out sick. The remaining tech and I split the workload equally. I'm not sure I have Marcie Grant's samples. As I usually do, I set up the samples for testing slowly and methodically. The testing sequence is finished without incident or problem, and the pathologists have the slides for review by one p.m.

I go back to the laboratory to clean up my bench. The pathologist will call the surgeon, who will contact Marcie Grant about the diagnosis.

I promise myself to stay away from them until after they receive the results. Mr. Grant said he'd contact me with any news.

Rather than leave the hospital area, I dally at the nearest doughnut shop. Reading and re-reading the same few pages on my app. My impatience is finally broken with his phone call.

"It's a treatable cancer. She should have a full recovery."

I hear the tremor in his voice. No doubt he and his sisters are overcome with relief. "That's wonderful news! I'm so happy to hear that."

"Did you already know?" he asks.

I roll my eyes. "Mr. Grant—I told you I can't—"

"Okay. Never mind. Whether you were involved or not, thank you...just...thank you." He sounds so relieved that it makes my heart feel lighter.

With help from the hospital staff, Mr. Grant manages to get his mother's outpatient treatments set up at the hospital closest to her hometown of Greenville. Wishing to be in her own home to recuperate, the encampment leaves on Saturday afternoon. The house settles into an eerie quiet after the last five days.

I go up to strip the beds and remake them. But the beds have already been stripped and remade. The used sheets and towels are piled neatly by the doors. Who did that? I doubt it was Orlaith or Fiona. They don't strike me as helpful. Certainly, it wasn't Marcie. There's only one other person under this roof. As I recall, he went up to these rooms to make sure nothing was left behind. Did he do it? My heart squeezes and warms to think that Mr. Grant did this to help me after such a harrowing week. I return to my suite, more than a little grateful for his kindness.

• • • •

I THANKED ABIGAIL FOR all she did to keep us calm during the storm. Her technical expertise in the area of biopsy testing has been a Godsend for my mom, my sisters, and me. Just being able to explain things in regular English put all of us somewhat at ease. I'm beyond grateful she knew exactly what we were feeling and handled it brilliantly. It's almost as if she has experienced this herself.

For the hundredth time, I wonder about her past while lying on my bed. Mental and physical exhaustion settled into my body the moment my mother and sisters leave, yet I'm unable to sleep. I listen to Abigail checking the guest rooms and returning to her suite. I can't help but grin. Was she surprised to see what I did? Might she think Fiona or Orlaith did it? Perhaps. I know I did it, and that's enough for me.

She doesn't know it, but I often track her whereabouts in the house by simply listening. I don't understand why it feels so important to follow her movements. It's almost like snooping or spying. I chalk it up to loneliness. I find it comforting to have someone else in the house. I hadn't realized how lonely I've been here until this woman with a firm grip on things entered the house and promptly locked herself out. I can't help chuckling, remembering the expression on her face when I opened the front door. She'd been placidly sitting on the stoop, looking this way and that as if totally unperturbed by the situation.

Her presence here feels like a gentle spring breeze through an open window. It's so very different from my ex-fiancée's and every other woman I've dated. Her presence is good for me, calming my soul.

DAY OFF

SUNDAY IS MY DAY OFF, although I haven't used it yet. Today, I am. I need to be alone. It feels luxurious to rise at seven-thirty. Mr. Grant is also sleeping in this morning. I make the coffee. He can reheat a cup later when he wakes up. He's on his own for breakfast today, though there's plenty of leftovers in the fridge if he decides to go that route. I leave him a note saying I will be gone all day.

I head to the nearest bakery on Sarte Avenue for a relaxing French press pot and a croissant with fresh butter and jam. Each table, except mine, is occupied by a couple. A man and a woman, two women, or two men. A burning rises in my chest as I watch the seemingly happy couples relax and enjoy their breakfast and comradery. Memories of Brannon flood me. Of all the times we did the same in Paris. Missing him is as hard now as it was a year ago, this very day.

I chastise myself for not remembering to think of him as often as I should. Surely, a widow should think of her deceased husband every day, at least once. With all the turmoil of the job, the trial period, dealing with the financial ramifications of his illness and death, and my new job, I haven't. Being a maid and laboratory technologist keeps me busy. Too busy to grieve as a normal widow should. My appetite wanes. I leave the remains of my breakfast and walk the downtown city streets.

I consider going to the apartment, but all three are surely there, likely unconscious after a night of carousing. If I run into Veronica, I will have to tap-dance around the topic of renewing my rent for another month. My brain still puzzles over what she told me about her parents. What does it mean? I set the thoughts aside and look up and down the street. Should I visit the Museum of Art, the public library, or the aquarium?

I decide on the Museum of Art for a stroll through the galleries. Art will distract me, though it is one of the things Brannon and I did at least once a year.

The time disappears. About three o'clock, I stop to enjoy tea and finger sandwiches at the museum's cafe. It's expensive, but I feel the need to pamper myself today. Just a little. Just this once.

The soft murmur of light conversation surrounds me. I distract myself by admiring the fountain, the sound of the water trickling, and the tropical plants shading my table on the patio. Once again, thoughts of my husband interrupt my pleasant, relaxing afternoon. He always enjoyed coming to this museum. For one reason or another, we never found the chance after his diagnosis. My stomach twists in a knot at this memory. Abruptly, I rise, drop two twenties on the table, and leave, not waiting for a doggie bag or my change. Tears threaten to spill, and I don't want to mar this beautiful setting and the other guests' afternoons by sobbing uncontrollably at my table.

I hide on a shaded bench in the park beside the museum. Barking draws my eyes to the right. The bench is a mere hundred feet from the city's dog park. Reflexively, my tears come harder as memories of my dog—no, our dog, Kendall, come to mind. While Kendall survived longer than my husband, he succumbed to cancer only a few months later, leaving me completely alone and with no reason to get up in the morning. He'd been such a great dog. A Christmas present from my husband when we were engaged. Adopted from a local shelter, he made our life feel whole, and his unconditional love made us a family. My grief for both of them nearly drops me to the ground. I let the tears flow, hoping they will release me from my sorrow.

Sometime later, having run out of tears and my face and eyes swollen, I retreat to the townhouse in a cab, my heart still throbbing with grief that will not ease.

When I arrive, Mr. Grant calls to me from the music room.

"Sorry for the late notice, but I have a free ticket for you if you'd like to go to the concert tonight."

"I am...not sure I can go tonight."

Our eyes lock. "Tough day? Maybe this will cap the day off on a good note?" he asks. His grin widens, "No pun intended."

I force a smile. "Thank you, but no."

"The box seats are part of my contract and are excellent. You should take the ticket."

"Perhaps another time," I say, edging toward the stairs.

He steps closer. "We're playing Satie. I insist you go."

"Not tonight," I snap.

His eyes narrow. "Why not?"

I am barely holding it together. Answering that question will put me over the edge. "Is my continued employment dependent on attending the symphony tonight?"

Stiffening, his eyes narrow further. "No."

"Then I will accept your offer another time. Is there anything else?"

He gives me a searching glance but shakes his head.

I nod and retreat up the stairs.

DISLOCATION

I WORRY THAT MY EMOTIONAL outburst will cost me my job, but I eventually fall asleep.

What feels like hours later, I awake to hear the growl of his car as he pulls into the driveway.

The house remains quiet. Closing my eyes, I go back to sleep intermittently until five a.m., when I give up. I enjoy the peaceful morning before sitting at my table and watching the sunrise. The pastels of the morning sky change into a brilliant, cloudless blue that is forecast to be a spectacularly warm day for February.

Ending my reverie, I relocate to the kitchen to make coffee. I pour myself a cup and wait for Mr. Grant to arrive. He is usually punctual about his breakfast. It is already half an hour past that time, and there are no signs or sounds of him in the house. I peek into the garage to assure myself I did hear him return last night. His car is there. Perhaps he is sleeping in?

My hands twist together as I try to decide whether to knock on his bedroom door. What if he brought someone home? What if there's a lover in his bed? He won't take kindly to my snooping, and I wouldn't blame him. We have always tried to maintain a respectful physical and emotional distance between us. No sharing of secrets, no gossip, and few hints of our respective pasts. Only if he asks something outright do I answer him with the truth.

I tiptoe to his bedroom door and pause to listen for any sound that might indicate his presence. A moan makes my hair stand on end. He does have someone in there. Visions of opening the door and finding him with someone in a sexual encounter make me back away. But what if he's injured or sick and needs help? That's also possible. He could have slipped in the bathroom and struck his head, and fallen unconscious. Another moan comes from inside the room. If I were to guess, it's not a pleasurable moan, but one of pain.

I lean close to the door jamb and loudly call out, "Mr. Grant? Are you all right?"

"No," he calls out, the thick wood door muffling the word.

I fling open the door to find him on the floor beside his bed. "Do you need an ambulance?" I ask, kneeling at his side. "Where does it hurt?"

He glares at me, pain contorting his face. "My left knee." He winces as he tries to move it. "It's been dislocated before." Through his grinding teeth, he adds, "Old injury."

"Don't move. Let me check for any abnormalities," I say. "I have some emergency medical training."

I shimmy the leg of his pajama pants up as gently as I can. His lower leg appears fine. The muscles are firm, and the dark hair on his leg tickles my hand. My fingers explore up to his knee with a featherlight touch, without moving the joint or the rest of his leg. I nod. "It feels dislocated. I'll call for an ambulance."

"Don't," he cries, his hand gripping my forearm tightly. "Help me get to my car."

"That's down two flights of stairs!" I exclaim, standing to pull my phone from my jeans back pocket. "Absolutely not. You could worsen your injury if it's not splinted. Let's get the professionals to assist you."

"Call Evelyn first," he grunts. "Tell her to cancel my appointments today."

Ignoring his demand, I dial 911 first and give the dispatcher the information. When I disconnect the call, I hasten for the door. "Stay still, right where you are. I'm going to shut off the alarm and meet the paramedics at the door."

"Call Evelyn," he yells as I head for the door.

I call Mrs. Farthing as I wait for emergency services to arrive. Standing at the open door, my knees feel like jelly, and yet I can't stand still.

"Not again," she groans.

I'm stunned. "Does this happen often?"

"Once or twice a year. Usually at the worst times." She grumbles, "like today. Tell him I'll handle everything."

As I disconnect, the ambulance siren grows louder as it gets closer. I wave them in, then direct them to his bedroom while I shut the door.

They start assessing his injury. I linger in the doorway, trying to give them enough room to work, when a police officer comes up behind me. "Are you the one who called 911?" he asks.

I nod and he begins asking what seem like unnecessary questions. My gaze focuses on the action as Mr. Grant's vital signs are taken and his leg is stabilized for transport to the hospital emergency department. Several firefighters arrive, the gurney in tow. As I continue to answer only the relevant questions, they move him to the cot and wheel him out to the ambulance.

"Where are you taking him?" I ask as the paramedics trail the stretcher.

"Baymont General Hospital Emergency. Are you coming with us?"

What should I say? No thanks, I'm just the maid. I'm not Mr. Grant's significant other, who would have a right to stay by his side. If I ride in the ambulance, we'll have to get an Uber or such back home. Do I dare take his car, even if I can find his keys? Without further decision, I blurt, "Yes."

The ride is short, as the emergency department in the hospital where I work is just minutes away. Mr. Grant is immediately triaged then wheeled through the double doors that separate the waiting room from the treatment areas. Not sure what to do, I step back and sit with two dozen other people in the waiting area. My fingers fiddle with my purse strap. Within half an hour, an aide calls my name and escorts me to Mr. Grant's side.

He's on a stretcher and appears exhausted and tense. His hair is messy, his stubbled jawline tight, yet his eyes have dark circles. He must have fallen sometime during the night. The pain must have been excruciating. Why didn't he call me on his cellphone?

"Did you call Evelyn?" he demands.

"Yes, of course." I approach his stretcher. "She's taking care of everything."

His scowl deepens as he grumbles, "I have a concert tonight." He bellows for the nurse, his commanding voice no doubt heard as far as the waiting room.

A male nurse pokes his head in the doorway, his expression one of controlled anger. "What do you need, Mr. Grant?"

"I need to get this reduced immediately. I have a concert tonight." He barks, "And some pain medication."

"You know we do an X-ray first, then Dr. Edleman will do what's necessary." He disappears.

He grumbles louder, muttering to himself, and drops his head back against the stretcher mattress. With his eyes closed, he snarls, "Get me a pillow, for God's sake."

I recognize his snarl as a result of his pain and his impatience, and don't take it seriously.

My experience in emergency departments, both as a volunteer EMT and with Brannon, is extensive. I know pillows are rare, if ever available. "I'll look for one," I say, grateful for an excuse to leave him alone to deal with his anger and frustration.

Retreating from the room, I ask the first person I see, "Can Mr. Grant please have a pillow?"

The young woman examines me. "We don't have pillows in the E.D."

I linger in the hallway, not wishing to elevate his wrath by returning too swiftly. In the mood he's in, he'll accuse me of not trying hard enough to find one.

After five minutes, I return to his side empty-handed. He gives me a fierce glare. "They don't use pillows in the ED," I report and watch his face contort through rage, ebb to anger, and finally, resignation.

He sighs heavily. "Damn place. Who doesn't provide pillows for patients?" he mutters under his breath. Dropping his head back, he closes his eyes again. Over the next few minutes, his breathing eases. He must have been given something for the pain before they adjust the joint.

While I'm sure the pain of a dislocation is substantial, Mr. Grant is making an ass of himself. Brannon acted in this manner, only harsher. His treatments were extensive and painful, twenty-four hours a day for weeks. He complained bitterly to the staff, berating their help and insinuating their incompetence. I had cringed every time he went off on his tirades. In the same way I'm cringing over Mr. Grant's behavior.

As I watch, his breath becomes deeper and more regular, and the tension in his face and jaw slackens. He's my employer and is going through something he's unable to control. No wonder he's irate. However, as his employee, I'm not enjoying having to deal with his temper tantrums.

Three hours later, after a closed reduction of his knee, I call Mrs. Farthing and ask her to arrange a livery car to pick us up.

Back home, with my help and the use of the crutches, he slowly enters the townhouse and settles on the living room couch. As he struggles to swing his injured leg up, I assist, placing my hands under the brace and guiding it safely. Settled, he flings his arm over his eyes. "I need a quick rest before I get ready for the concert."

"Y—You can't conduct like this."

"If I don't, the entire event will be canceled," he growls.

"Rest, I'll wake you in half an hour." He eases his head back and closes his eyes, and I flee to my room where I call Mrs. Farthing. "What about tonight's concert? He's insisting he can conduct it."

"Sounds like him. We have contingency plans for such an issue. The conductor at the Bright Water Conservatory, Eric Jarvis, is stepping in for him tonight. Tell him the announcements have already gone out."

They have a substitute ready to step in? "I take it this happens often?"

"Usually it's not on a concert night, but yes. Often enough for a contingency." She sighs. "He's not going to like it, he can't possibly conduct on one leg while holding on to crutches."

I wake him when I hear him groaning in his sleep. Whatever painkiller the nurse gave him started to wear off.

"I need to get ready," he says, reaching for the crutches leaning against the back of the couch.

"No, you don't. Mrs. Farthing said the contingency plans have been activated, and Eric Jarvis is stepping in tonight. Everything is settled."

If his glare was harsh before, it's nothing compared to his expression now. His features contort, his eyebrows pulling into one long black line over his murderous glower. His face, which was initially drained of color, is now flushing a deep red. Despite my protestations, his efforts to stand resume.

I let him fumble to get the crutches in position and then try to stand on his good leg. He wobbles dangerously, his white-knuckled grip on the hand rests tenuous at best. I cringe as he tries to take a step, despite the doctor's orders.

As soon as he puts weight on the leg, his face blanches, and he cries out. His cursing makes me flush red hot as my ears burn. I reach out to steady him, but it's too late. He topples into my arms. I see it coming, so I catch him around the waist and press into him for support. Reflexively, his arms wind around my neck, his face inches from mine. The current that flows between us jolts my body tense.

His glare softens as he stares into my eyes, gasping and scrambling to straighten. He must have felt it too because he swiftly puts more space between us, sinking down on the couch with another groan. The crutches clatter to the floor.

"I'm sorry," he says with a heavy sigh of surrender as he resettles on the cushions. With his eyes closed tight and his hand pinching the bridge of his nose, he asks, "Would you get me another pain pill?"

I leave his crutches on the floor, hoping the distance will dissuade him from trying to get up again. "All they gave you is a couple of prescription-strength anti-inflammatories." I dole out one pill from the container and disappear into the kitchen. "Let me get you some water," I call over my shoulder.

"Never mind that," he groans again, holding out his hand in a decisive manner. I detour back to him and drop the pill into his hand. He swallows it dry, lets his head fall back against a throw pillow, and closes his eyes. Opening one eyelid, he fixes me with a glare. "Wake me for dinner."

• • • •

I HATE MYSELF FOR THE way I'm treating Abigail. She doesn't deserve it. It isn't so much the pain. That's reasonably dimmed by the pills, finally. It's the thing of it. Being tied down, being unable to perform my duties as conductor and music director of the symphony. Malcolm and the board must be having a right good time of it, knowing I'm incapacitated. It gives them the taste of being without me. Having someone else in the director's position. It gives them ideas about not renewing my contract.

There hasn't been any communication about my contract renewal in weeks. Is that meant to tell me something? Perhaps it's time to move on. God knows I should have left after Cynthia's betrayal. However, I would have had to break my current contract, which would have had a detrimental effect on my reputation. People would want to know why I'd broken it early. I wasn't about to let her affair harm my career. Bad enough that it tainted my heart.

EVICTED

OVER THE NEXT FEW DAYS, Mr. Grant's knee settles into place, though his temper does not. He pushes his endurance to the limit before collapsing on his bed or the couch, refusing the anti-inflammatory drug, the ice packs, and prescribed physical therapy.

At his request, I set him up with his cellphone and laptop so he can conduct business, if not the orchestra. I suggest he retire to his bedroom instead of the couch, but he refuses. A weight lifts off my shoulders at this decision. I don't want to be in his bedroom more than necessary. It does strange things to my insides and always feels like an invasion of privacy.

I wait on his needs, having called out sick for the duration, so I can assist him and make sure he doesn't hail a cab to get to his office. He runs me ragged with his demands, interrupting every chore I try to do. Fortunately, he manages his own personal hygiene, so I don't have to assist him with showering or dressing, though he curses like a longshoreman whenever he does. It can't be easy balancing on one leg.

Helping him to the table for meals and then spotting him back to the couch afterwards is hard enough on my senses. Not to mention tucking the blanket around his pelvis, and propping his knee and lower leg on a pillow. A strange feeling circulates through me as he watches my hands touch his body. His breath stutters while I lean over him and try to make him more comfortable. Is it pain or the intimacy of the touch?

Sunday night, I receive a text message from Veronica.

The girls and I took a vote. We've decided to evict you. A more appropriate, younger woman wants your room. Since you haven't been here in weeks anyway, please remove your things and return the key before February 10thso Bethany can move in. V, M, J

My heartbeat falters as I read and re-read the message. What am I going to do now? My house is gone, and the thirty-day trial period here won't be finished for another week and a half. I'll be out on my ear, completely homeless, if Mr. Grant doesn't want me to stay on. A thousand worries ping-pong around my brain so rapidly that I can't think straight. I need to talk to Clare for advice. I hit speed dial.

"'Sup?" she answers.

I hear conversation in the background. "I need help."

"My couch again?" she teases. At my lack of a response, she replies, "Oh no. What happened?"

As succinctly as I can, I tell her about Veronica's text message. "What should I do?" I'm biting my fingernails like a seven-year-old, well aware of all the nasty germs lurking under and around them, but I can't help it.

"Did you tell them you were extending your room lease? Or has Maestro said if he's going to continue your position?"

"I never said I *wasn't* extending my room lease," I hedge. "My position here hasn't been...extended. Yet." I press my palm to my forehead and close my eyes. Why does everything have to happen at the same time?

"If I were you, I'd have a convo with the man. Ask if he's made a decision yet and if he hasn't, suggest you might have other opportunities." Clare offers, "If he intends to extend your employment, get your crap out of that filthy hellhole and count your blessings. Those dimwit party animals have done you a favor."

The metallic taste of blood stops my gnawing. "What if he hasn't decided?"

"Beg."

BEGGING

IN THE MORNING, I FIX Mr. Grant's coffee and bring it to him. He insisted at dinner last night that he'd get himself to the kitchen for meals starting today. I wait, my nerves tingling, my jaw tense for the coming discussion. At last he arrives, in a T-shirt and sweatpants, and using only one crutch. He sinks onto the chair and his crutch falls to the floor. I move to retrieve it, but he holds up his palm. "Later. I'm hungry."

"What would you like?" I ask, like I do every morning. You'd think he'd know by now to tell me in advance, or at the very least inform me without being asked. Fearful that I'll mess up my skirt and blouse, I tie an apron around my waist and slip the loop over my head, ready to make anything. Hoping to convince him I should stay, I've dressed and used a little makeup especially for him. He doesn't seem to notice.

"Whatever," he croaks as he unfolds the newspaper beside his placemat.

The temptation to slam a box of crackers and the jar of marmalade down on the table is intense. Instead, I play nice, needing his good graces today. I want him to make an early decision about my staying. Or going. Preferably staying.

He must sense my irritation because he blurts, "Omelet, sausage, toast," as he opens the newspaper wide and begins skimming pages two and three.

My fingers and shoulders tense, causing me to fumble as I get his breakfast together. How can I broach the subject without sounding obtuse? I set his plate down and he drops the paper. The pages slide, scattering on the floor at his feet.

He must see my dismay. "Sorry," he says. When I crouch to gather them, he barks, "Pick them up later."

This is it. My chance to ask the question is here, though his curt tone doesn't make it feel like the best time. "I am wondering how you think this trial period is going?"

He levels his gaze at me while he chews, making me wait. Is he doing it intentionally to fray my nerves? He swallows and says, "Fine so far."

"*Fine?* Mr. Grant, are you aware that I have called in sick this past week to look after you?" I'm skating on thin ice, but the words just keep coming. "I've helped you up and down the stairs, delivered meals so you wouldn't have to move, even plumped pillows to make you comfortable. And all you can say is fine?"

He takes another bite of omelet, his eyes still locked on me. My insides tremble at the uncomfortable silence. His face contorts as if he remembers something. "I should thank you for your help this last week."

Is that an apology? Did he mean to say that he really didn't want to thank me, but he *should*? Bile rises in my throat, and I grind my back molars, focusing on sliding the omelet pan into the dishwasher and dropping the eggshells into the trash. *What an ingrate.*

My silence must make him uncomfortable. "I mean, yes, I am grateful for your help."

Is he grateful enough to extend my term of employment? I confront him directly. "I've received notice that my lease is not being renewed after the end of this week." I clench my teeth, immediately sorry I gave more information than necessary. I go back to the kitchen sink and rinse out the sponge.

Steam rises inside at his continued silence. "Your highness, I really need to know now," I snap before I can hold my tongue. I lean against the counter to meet his eyes. "If there's even a remote possibility you won't want me beyond the trial period, I'd like to know now so I can begin searching for a room to let."

More silence fills the kitchen. He dabs his lips with his napkin then throws it down on the table. He stretches to pick up his crutch. "We'll discuss this later this evening."

And he hobbles back to the couch.

I fly up the stairs, the choking feeling in my throat that precipitates an ugly crying jag warning me to run. I press my weight against the door and let the tears flow. Losing Brannon, losing Kendall, my car, my home, everything that was normal and good and comfortable. The insecurity of my situation weighs heavily. It has been a nightmare from the get-go. The apartment was a rat hole, but at least it was a roof over my head. Noisy, dirty, and wrong for me in so many more ways than it was good.

Gone too are all my hopes that this maid position will pan out. Not after that snide comment I made. Then there's the promise my part-time job would become a full-time position. Well, at least that promise hasn't been completely broken.

A burning torch ignites in my core. I have to stop feeling the victim and start fighting—advocating for myself. I pull out my phone and text Veronica: *I will stop by this afternoon to remove my things and I expect my full security deposit returned in cash before I hand in the key.*

In minutes, Veronica responds: *3:00*

I set to work trying to confirm my suspicions. There's no time to lose.

All three of my flat mates are present when I arrive. They say nothing as they watch me wheel my suitcase past them. It takes less than thirty minutes to pack everything remaining into the suitcase and my overnight bag. I stuff the thrift store comforter and sheets into a plastic trash bag, determined to throw them in the dumpster on my way out. The twin-sized inflatable mattress, I leave behind. Bethany will need it since the room is too small to hold a bed frame.

With everything ready, I set the three items on the floor and beeline over to Veronica, who is in the kitchen watching me.

"There you go. It's all Bethany's." I try not to snarl. "She can use the air mattress. I don't need it."

"You are going to be missed." Veronica laments in a fake sing-song voice, opening her arms as if to hug me. I step back as she approaches. She frowns.

I hold out my open palm. "My security deposit." It's not a question, but a demand.

She looks at my palm and glares at me. She drops a sealed envelope in it. "It's all there."

Right. I tear it open, not caring about the shreds of paper that flutter to the floor. I take my time counting the bills. Meghan and Jenna sit on the futon watching, Jenna with a pillow pulled tight to her chest, Meghan pretending to check her nails while glancing at me every few seconds.

As I expect, it isn't all there.

I square my shoulders and thrust out my jaw. "Six hundred dollars is missing. I'm not leaving until my entire security deposit is in my hand."

"Well, there is the matter of the door damage...and the cleaning fee," Veronica trills and then laughs. She eyes our audience on the futon and tilts her head ever so slightly. Tweedle Dee and Tweedle Dum nervously start laughing.

I envisioned this scenario and did my homework prior to arriving. "Perhaps I should contact your parents in Millford, Illinois? Do you think they'll give me the missing six hundred dollars?"

Veronica's face drains of color. "Why would you call them? Th-they have nothing to do with this place." The tremor in her voice affirms that I have guessed correctly.

"Let's see, since *they* are paying your apartment rent, don't you think they'd be interested to know you're renting out rooms and pocketing the money? What a lucrative arrangement!"

Her face glows fire engine red. "You wouldn't." Her voice is husky and threatening.

I pull out my phone and hit speed dial, and then turn on the speaker. The phone rings a couple of times before a woman's voice comes on, "Hello?" Veronica lunges for my phone when her mother answers. I dodge her hand even though she grabs a handful of my hair and pulls...hard.

"Mrs. Parker, this is Veronica's roommate, Abigail. I'm having trouble getting my security deposit back. I'm hoping you can have a word with her. We signed a contract, and she's not returning all of my money." My voice drips with honey and concern.

The speaker is silent for a few heartbeats. Then Mrs. Parker croaks, "My daughter has been renting out a room in her apartment?"

"Yes, ma'am. Three actually. There are three of us renting rooms from her." I pull out my best acting skills. Inhaling deeply and noisily, I feign, "Oh! Oh my God, I thought you knew!"

Mrs. Parker curses, as if through clenched teeth. "Put her on."

Veronica dashes to her room as I hold out my phone. In seconds, she returns and holds out a small wad of bills. I count them slowly, enjoying watching her stew in her own deception. Satisfied the six hundred dollars is all there, I hold the phone to my ear again. "Mrs. Parker? Veronica has provided me with the remaining money. So *sorry* to bother you."

Mrs. Parker's voice booms over the speaker, "You tell her I will be discussing this issue with her father."

"Of course," I say, my voice saccharine sweet as I watch Veronica return to her room and slam the door. I disconnect the call and gather my belongings. Meghan and Jenna jump up from the couch.

Meghan asks, "What was that all about?" Her voice is edgy with concern.

I shrug. "Have you ever asked yourself why Veronica never wanted her parents to visit or to know she had roommates?"

The two girls give me blank stares before shaking their heads.

"Because her parents are paying for the apartment. By renting out the rooms, Veronica is pocketing our money as a side swindle." I wait a few heartbeats to see if they understand.

Jenna's eyes widen, and Meghan's a moment later. Bullseye! Time to go.

I pick up my suitcase and overnight bag. "Bye ladies. Good luck."

Meghan calls out as I reach the threshold, "Wait, you forgot this." She holds up the trash bag of sheets and comforter.

"You can keep it or chuck it in the dumpster. Thanks." I exit and tromp down those four flights of stairs for the last time.

Music wafting from the music room tells me Mr. Grant is home. The sounds are soft, almost mournful. I pause long enough to realize he's playing the piano. The last thing I want him to see is me arriving with my remaining belongings from that filthy apartment. Quietly, I take everything up to my room but don't have time to unpack. Dinner needs to be made. A meal that has me on edge. The stairs must creak as I descend. Mr. Grant sticks his head out the door.

"What time is dinner?" His tone is stern and tense, as is his jaw. His piercing look runs up and down my visage.

I halt a few feet from him. "Our usual time, six pm. If you would like it earlier than that, I will have to change the menu."

His jaw works like he's gnawing on the question. "No, that's fine," he grunts.

After a polite nod, I continue to the kitchen, feeling his eyes scorching my back the entire way. Inside the confines of the familiar space, I press my hands into the countertop and close my eyes. The short conversation rattles my confidence. We discussed this evening's menu last week, as a practice run for a future guest dinner. Mr. Grant intimated that Osso Bucco is his favorite meal. It's not a coincidence I'm serving it on a day I need to impress him with my cooking abilities. I've been making this dish for years. I know it will make a stunning impression.

But Veronica's antics have thrown my confidence awry. Even though I successfully won the standoff, it left me with a bad taste in my mouth and feeling off-kilter. It's like trying to walk while wearing two different-sized shoes. I have to get my mojo back before leaping into tonight's meal preparation.

Sitting on the kitchen floor in lotus position, the backs of my palms resting on my knees, I close my eyes, breathe deeply, and center my thoughts. After a few minutes of calm, I break off the exercise and get moving on dinner prep.

Forty-five minutes later, Mr. Grant limps into the kitchen and stops, sniffing the air. The rosemary and garlic focaccia, along with the simmering veal dish, fill the small kitchen with incredible scents. The table is set for our dinner. The everyday stoneware glows a brilliant midnight blue on the white tablecloth, the flatware and crystal gleaming in rays from the under-counter lights. A fresh garden salad sits beside each plate, and the basket of warm focaccia rests on the side of the table. I opened a bottle of fifty-dollar Barolo wine, lightly chilled, while I made dinner, allowing the slightly acidic, robust, and complex flavors to blossom as they aerate.

He sits down, picks up his napkin, and sets it on his lap. Grabbing the wine bottle, he pours us each a glass.

I plate two meals and set them on the placemats. A beautiful Osso Bucco shank rests atop a mound of risotto alla Milanese, accompanied by a side of roasted broccoli dusted with freshly grated Parmesan cheese.

His eyes bulge with surprise. "Wow, that looks good."

My jaw tightens. I worked my butt off planning, coordinating, and cooking this meal and that's all he can say? Steaming inside, I sit down.

There's little talk as we eat. He asks how my day went, to which I mutter, "fine." He gives me a troubled glance but says nothing.

I need his approval, and struggle to convert my peevish attitude into congeniality. It might help ease the tension already building about the coming conversation. "I heard the piano music when I came in. Is it for an upcoming concert?"

He nods. "The concert is at the end of the season, but I thought I'd get a start practicing it."

"Does it have a name? The piece?" I take too big a gulp of wine and choke. I snatch up the napkin and hold it over my mouth and nose, not knowing which might spew the expensive wine. My eyes water, and I swallow hard, deeply grateful that the danger of giving him a Barolo shower passes. My vision clears, and he is standing beside me, his hand resting on my upper back.

"Are you all right?" He stares at me, concern showing on his face.

"Yes," I croak out after a last cough. My back warms from the heat of his hand. The warmth of it spreads down to my belly and below until he removes it and returns to his seat.

"Uh, yes. It's called 'Consolation.'"

I dab my lips with my napkin and set it down. "Funny. It sounded rather melancholy. But it was beautiful."

He wipes his mouth, folds his napkin, and sets it down. His gaze hardens.

This is it. I steel myself for the imminent verdict.

"I've given your request some thought."

The curt formality of his statement is unnerving. My breath becomes shallow and erratic. I set down my fork and fold my hands in my lap, my back erect, my lips pressed tight.

"I've come up with a compromise." He pauses, takes a sip of wine, sets the glass down, and rests his elbows on the table, his hands clasped together. "Of course, you may finish out the remainder of the thirty-day trial."

I let out an audible breath. In response, he holds up one index finger, stalling. "If at that time, I agree to let you stay, then there isn't an issue. However, if I decide to forego an extended contract, I will provide you with notice and two additional paid weeks to find a new position and or a suitable place to live. Whichever comes first." He reaches for his glass but pauses before sipping. "The agency suggested not to let you stay beyond our arrangement, having concerns about theft or retaliatory actions. I told them I didn't think you were that type of person." He stares me down, a cold, hard glint in his eyes. "Are you that sort of person, Mrs. Davitt?"

My spine stiffens. "No, of course not, sir. Not at all." The heavy weight on my shoulders eases. It isn't a thumbs-up for beyond the trial, but it is a reasonable compromise. This news will keep me on my best game for another week and a half. I intend to do that anyway, but the stakes are high and I need to perform flawlessly. "Thank you, Mr. Grant. That is an acceptable plan."

He flashes a tight smile. "Good. Now, what's for dessert?"

I retrieve my homemade tiramisu, cut a piece the size of a deck of cards, and set it before him. The desire to up-end the plate on his head nearly wins. Instead, I'll let him taste it to further prove my worth. Tiramisu is my best-tasting and signature dessert, thanks to a former coworker's Italian family recipe.

Mr. Grant wastes no time digging in. "Outstanding." He doesn't stop shoveling it in until his plate is empty.

A little more weight slides off my shoulders. Now, I need to get through the next ten days to secure this position, the best thing that has happened to me in the last twelve months.

IN MY PRIVATE BATHROOM, I stare at my image in the mirror. I've behaved rather abominably, and my words were harsher than I intended. Being called "your highness" this morning took me aback. She's never snapped at me before. The look on her face shocked me, too. Her eyes were hard and wild with emotion. Like she could have strangled me for my uncouth words. A chuckle escapes me and I give in to a good belly laugh. She certainly gets furious when pushed. Her passion stirs something deep within me. Abigail Davitt is no pushover. The hint of a self-assertive feline replaces the Milquetoast I imagined her to be.

STOWAWAY

I USE SOME OF MY VACATION time to be available for the last few days of my trial period. I intend to give Mr. Grant my full attention and anticipate his every need and desire. I get his shoes shined after his comment about slush and mud-splattered shoes, and swipe his bathrobe for a wash. The grocery list gets longer as I order all the foods he likes to snack on while home. His shirt button comes unattached, and I hunt down my sewing kit and reattach it myself rather than send it out.

Anything I can think of to make his life easier, I do without sounding or looking like I'm sucking up. Because I'm not sucking up, not exactly. I'm used to the rhythm of the household and its owner, now I'm just hitting my stride. Yet, it doesn't feel like enough. I lie awake at night racking my brain, trying to think of something he won't expect. Something that might please him, or at the very least, make him consider me an irreplaceable asset he can't live without.

I peer out the window of my room that overlooks the backyard area. It's fenced in and overgrown with more signs of neglect than of care. Spring is creeping out early. The grass is starting to green in spots, and the day is warm. I open my window for some fresh air. A little breeze brings in the faint scent, promising more warm days to come. A few dry leaves rustle with each puff of wind, catching under shrubs and amid brown garden debris.

A peeping or chirping noise catches my ear. Something moves on the edge of a weed pile. It takes a long stare for me to recognize it is a kitten.

The tiny thing keeps returning to a pile of leaves. It must be stuck in the enclosed space, separated from its mother. At the very least, I can take it to the other side and shoo it away so they can be reunited.

I enter the area through a gate along the driveway, pushing through overgrown vegetation. The kitten mews beside the leaf pile, showing no fear at my approach. My nostrils flare at the stench of decomposition, and I halt. The tiny creature sits beside what must be its dead mother.

The urge to intervene is too strong to ignore. I pick up the scrawny brown striped tabby and cuddle it to my chest. It mews incessantly, struggling to get out of my arms and back to its mother. I place it in the grass and retrieve a shovel from the garage. Hopefully, the ground is no longer frozen so hard or deep I can't dig a hole to bury the dead cat.

After burying it in a rather shallow grave, I clutch the kitten to my chest again. It probably hasn't had any food since its mother died. There's some leftover meat in the fridge that I can puree for the tiny creature. Will Mr. Grant freak if I bring it inside to feed it? Should I call animal control or a local shelter? It mews and nuzzles my neck, and that decides it. I carry it into the kitchen, give it water and pureed cooked chicken, unsure if it can eat it. To my surprise, it laps up the puree and water without hesitation.

While it eats, I call any local shelters or animal control offices I can find online. None has room for this kitten. I stare down at the scraggly bit of fluff, brainstorming my options. Perhaps Clare can take it in? In the meantime, I'll set it up in my room to protect it and nurse it back to health. I hope it won't be the tipping point at the end of my trial period. If required to choose, I will choose the kitten over this job. Silently, I pray it won't come to that.

I tuck the furball under my chin and carry the water and food dishes upstairs to my room. If I hustle, I have just enough time to buy a litter box at the Sarte Street convenience store. Meanwhile, the cat settles in a box of towels I set out for a bed.

For the remainder of the day, I sit on the floor watching it sleep while calling more shelters, which proves useless. No one has room, not even for a kitten. Even Clare declines to take it, saying her husband may be allergic to cats. For the immediate future, it will have to stay hidden in my room. Mr. Grant never comes up the stairs as far as my door, so I'm not too worried about it being discovered.

Mrs. Farthing calls me in the early afternoon. "Mr. Grant needs something he left in the music room. Probably on the music stand or on top of the piano. Can you search for it?"

With the phone to my ear, I head to the music room. "Can you tell me what it looks like or says?"

"It's a score, the title is *La Mer*, by—"

"Debussy."

"What?"

"It's by Claude Debussy," I repeat without hesitation, searching for it. "Debussy is one of my favorite composers. I'm very familiar with his works." *La Mer*, or translated as "*The Sea*," is a favorite Debussy orchestral composition, after "Claire de Lune," my favorite piece, the third movement of his *Suite Bergamasque*.

"Yes, whatever. He needs it now. Right now. Can you find it?"

I find it on top of the piano. "Got it," I reply, waving it in the air like she can see it over the phone.

"Good. Grab a cab and deliver it with any additional paperwork attached to it."

"Me?" I'm reluctant to leave the kitten alone for even a short while. "Can't you send over a courier like you did when he was laid up with his knee?"

"No time. A courier will take too long. He needs it right away for rehearsal. The musicians are on break while we wait for it. I'll send a cab over now."

I resign myself to delivering the score in person. "Okay. I'll grab my purse and head over."

The ride to Symphony Hall is quick. I hold out the score and papers to Mrs. Farthing in her office.

"Take them to the room at the end of the hall." She points to the left.

I grunt as I turn on my heels and stride away. Frustration coalesces in the middle of my chest like a punch. This errand eats up more and more of my time. The left side door at the end of the hallway leads me through the wings backstage. Musicians mill about, murmuring and practicing various instruments while Maestro Grant confers with Haruka Satō at the podium.

I walk onto the stage, and light applause starts and spreads as I approach Mr. Grant. Musicians return to their seats, lifting instruments and settling back in for rehearsal. More than a few give me questioning stares. I surmise that they don't know the Maestro has a maid. Do they think I'm someone else in his life? I can't worry about it. Or about Haruka's evil eye when she loses his attention. My cheeks flush hot at all the inquisitive stares. It is not my place to explain.

He leaves Haruka, his long, lean legs eating up the distance in a few strides. He takes the materials from my hand. "Thank you. You've saved us precious time. Stay, if you'd like."

As much as I want to get back to the cat, I accept. He's never invited me to a rehearsal before. "I won't stay long," I say as he spreads the score on his podium. Forgetting me entirely, he picks up the baton and taps it against the metal stand to get everyone's attention.

I don't know where to go, and retreat to the wings. The rehearsal begins. The music fills me...my ears, my pores, and my heart. He frequently stops, providing directions to a section or particular musician. The stop-and-go of the rehearsal is familiar. The same I experienced during my high school concert band years.

I watch and listen, noting the musicians' respectful manner. Mr. Grant is also respectful toward them, treating them as professionals, and is polite and helpful in making them understand his expectations, while also being a firm and direct leader. They work well together.

This is a different scenario from what I'd read in the media. Is the arrogance he is accused of a misinterpretation of his actions? Yes, he brandishes the baton like a saber, sometimes pointing it at someone, sometimes jabbing or slicing it through the air with deliberate animation. While the musicians provide the sounds, he is the performer following a dancer's choreography. A sensual dance that ignites thoughts I shouldn't be having of my employer.

Rehearsal breaks off after an hour, though the piece isn't finished. I start to leave, and Mr. Grant calls out, "Mrs. Davitt."

I turn to meet him. "Yes?"

"I won't be home for dinner tonight or tomorrow. I expect to be late." I must be making a facial expression of some sort because he adds, "A few of the guys and I are going to a hockey game."

"Yes, sir. Thank you for the notice." I'm grateful to have the evening to myself. However, the discussion about my employment extension has been delayed. My spirits sink knowing my impatient wait for a resolution will last a little longer. Perhaps he means to make me wait until the thirtieth day. My teeth clench tightly at the possibility.

My cellphone rings as I enter the townhouse. Everything in my purse falls to the floor as I dig it out to answer the call. It's my lawyer.

"Mrs. Davitt, how are you today?" My lawyer asks, his words brisk and superficial.

Omitting the small talk, I reply, "What can I do for you?" I lean against the door and activate the alarm system. "Is my residual check coming soon?" Between the return of my security deposit and the few thousand dollars I expect to see from the house sale, I should have enough to get something, if necessary. If not within the city limits, then at least along the tram or bus line.

"There's a slight problem. Our accountant has completed the paperwork for your creditors." He pauses and his voice changes, becoming more solicitous. "There's a shortage of $2,752.00 for the hospital lien. The sale can't be cleared until we have those additional funds."

Stars swirl in my peripheral vision as I slump against the wall and slide down it, my rump hitting the floor with a thud. "I—will—" I'm unable to put my scrambled thoughts into a complete sentence.

"I know," he says, "it's a complete surprise to us as well." He pauses again. "I've asked the hospital to forgive the amount, but they declined. They have already reduced the amount owed by 30 percent. They won't budge. When can I expect to have the additional funds to complete this transaction?"

I close my eyes, the center of my chest hurting so much that I fear I'm having a heart attack. The security deposit money is gone. Along with a little bit of my paycheck. "I'll send it tomorrow, via express mail. Will that suffice?"

Clare calls me an hour later. "Hey, any chance I can take you out for a drink this evening?"

"Oh, you are a Godsend. Absolutely, I can go out. Dinner and a drink or just dinner?" I ask, my fingers crossed she's up for both.

"Sure! The Hayloft? About six pm?"

"I'll be there."

Clare finds me at the bar, halfway through my first drink. "Hey! I thought you were never going to get here. I've already shooed away several guys wanting to chat me up."

"They wanted to do more than chat, I bet." She settles on the bar stool. "I put our names in for a table. It should only be a few minutes." Clare orders a martini and nibbles on the crunchy snacks in the bowl the bartender gave me. "What's going on?"

I roll my eyes dramatically and grasp the edge of the bar as my head spins. The margarita is strong, but that's no excuse. I haven't had much alcohol lately, so it hits me like a brick. I better go easy on this stuff, or eat a lot of food. Screw going easy. I'll eat a lot to soak up the alcohol. "I told you about the eviction. But I haven't told you about the house sale."

"What about it? It should have been straightforward, yes?" She sips her martini and sighs with relief, rolling her eyes with pleasure.

"The attorney called. The sale proceeds ran short of the amount the hospital wanted. They refused to budge. So that returned security deposit will end up with the hospital."

Clare's eyes widen. "Holy crap! Those bastards, honestly. If people only knew what leeches they are..."

I hold up my palm. "Yes, well, it's done. I'm free."

Holding her martini glass toward me, she says, "Let's celebrate. You jumped the final hurdle, and freedom lies before you."

"Yeah, whoopee," I cringe, feeling emptiness instead of freedom. "There's nowhere but up from here."

MAESTRO'S DECISION

I SLEEP LITTLE THAT night, worrying about my future. Especially since all my savings are gone. The kitten sleeps most of the night in its box. At some point, I hear it bounding around the room and crying. Finally, it crawls up on me at five in the morning, kneading at the blanket over my chest. I should have brought the rest of the puree up to my room in case it got hungry during the night. Also, so Mr. Grant won't find it and ask questions. I might be out of a job if he finds out about the kitten.

I'm too late. He sits at the kitchen table with a mug of steaming coffee, the container of pureed meat sitting in the center of the table. A fist-sized knot twists in my core, my chest growing tight. This doesn't bode well. Deciding on pleasantry and surprise, I say, "Oh, Mr. Grant. I didn't expect you up so soon. Is there anything I can get you?"

He shakes his head. My insides tighten even more. I wait, not wanting to divulge or offer an explanation.

His eyes are narrow with suspicion. "I found this container of paste in the refrigerator. It smells like chicken. What is it for?" He cocks his head and waits.

My mind whirls. Can I get away without mentioning the ball of fur upstairs? "I saw a cat in the backyard yesterday morning. I brought it some food and water as it looked very hungry and sick."

He raises an eyebrow. "You kept the puree?"

I shrug, picking over possible answers. "I did. I didn't want it to go to waste. It's just plain cooked chicken."

Mr. Grant gives me what looks like a reluctant nod.

A thud sounds at the front door. Saved by the newspaper's arrival, I move to get it, but Mr. Grant raises his palm to stop me. "I'll get it."

He disappears from the kitchen, his limp much less noticeable today.

I stuff the puree into the freezer for the time being. I can retrieve it after he leaves for the office. "Breakfast?" I ask when he returns.

"One poached egg on a slice of toast, please," he replies from behind the newspaper, already open. "Smear the last of that puree under the egg. I'll finish it off."

My breath locks in my throat. "I —uh, just threw it in the freezer in case the cat shows up again," I stutter, trying to think of another excuse. "I don't think that's Kosher."

"What?" he erupts, his head popping up over the newspaper. "I don't care if it's Kosher or not." He cocks his head, his gaze holding me in place. "Never mind. Don't get into the habit of feeding every stray that shows up."

"Of course." At least his breakfast will be easy and quick. The faster he's gone, the sooner I can feed the furball upstairs.

He eats and leaves for the office within an hour, which seems very early after a late night out with the guys.

Free from his presence, I hurry to put the puree in my room, refilling the cat's dishes with it and water from the bathroom tap. It isn't the best water, but the tiny thing doesn't seem to care.

Entering Mr. Grant's bedroom, my insides twinge. The smell of his shampoo and soap lingers long after he leaves. The cedar and clove aroma is the same I've come to recognize as Mr. Grant's scent.

The fragrance fills the air as I wrestle with the king-sized bed sheets. My hand lingers over the smooth softness of the one thousand thread count, sea-island cotton fabric. My propensity to sleep nude died with Brannon. Yet the feel of Mr. Grant's sheets fosters a yearning to strip off my clothes and slip between them for a luxurious nap. Especially after my terrible night's sleep. I don't dare try it.

I continue to clean up, washing the breakfast dishes, checking the music room for order. I vacuum the floors despite having vacuumed them yesterday. But if today is my last official day, it eases my mind to know the place is in good condition. If nothing else, Mr. Grant should give me a good reference for the McAuliffe Agency. It will make a big difference in getting another maid's job.

In the afternoon, I play with the kitten and call a few more shelters looking for a spot for this spitfire of fur. A little part of me rejoices with every negative response. Yet, how will I keep it? What if he dismisses me? How will I ever find another job if I refuse to leave the kitten behind? How difficult will it be to find an apartment that allows cats?

Mr. Grant returns for dinner at six. The pork roast I cooked is succulent, the sauerkraut tamed with apples and sweet onions, and the salad crisp. We sit down immediately and eat in silence. When we are finished eating I clear the plates away.

He clears his throat. "Please sit, Mrs. Davitt. We have some things to discuss."

I take my seat across the table from him, my jaw aching from clenching. My insides taut as a trampoline. "Yes, Mr. Grant."

Putting his fisted hands on the table, he starts, "I've been thinking about our arrangement and have made a decision." He leans back and pauses, looking at me.

His stare isn't unpleasant. Yet the longer it lasts, the worse I feel. My blood cools as I wait, my eyes watering, blinking madly as I steel myself for a dismissal.

"I don't think the title maid suits you. I think we should reword our agreement with the title of housekeeper, with an upgrade in salary, of course." He doesn't smile or react to his own words.

My hand flies to cover my mouth. Long-held tension floods out with my tears, and I hunch over the table, my forehead resting on the surface as I sob.

His hand lands gently on my shoulder, sending sparks throughout my body. I can no longer deny that he sets me on fire with his touch. *This is not a good thing.*

"Are you all right?" he asks, squatting beside my chair. His free hand holds out a clean linen handkerchief. The one I embroidered with his initials in a spare hour. The one he never mentioned noticing.

I take it, wiping away my tears. "Oh, Mr. Grant. You have no idea..." Fresh tears prevent me from finishing.

"I'm sorry it was delayed, but I needed more information."

He gives my shoulder a light squeeze, and my insides squirm with pleasure.

"I do understand. I had a chat with Mrs. Wainwright at the agency. She provided me with answers to some of my questions. I've instructed her to draft a new contract with the updated position and salary. Double, I might add."

He returns to his chair. "I want you to know you've been doing a fine job. It's been like heaven to not have to worry about anything here. I appreciate that you're also a good cook, and I don't have to eat takeout all the time." He gives me a rare full smile. "I think I've actually lost some weight, though the guys are teasing me otherwise."

I half stammer, half chuckle, "Any self-respecting cook would see weight loss as a red flag."

"I don't. It's healthier food you're feeding me, and I appreciate your efforts to create nutritionally balanced meals."

"Thank you, Mr. Grant," I sniffle, wiping away stray tears still leaking down my face.

He stands to leave. "Now, you are welcome to call me Kent. No more *Mr. Grant*, please."

I nod, still wiping at my tears with his handkerchief as he strides to the door. "Oh, by the way...the kitten can roam the house at will." He disappears out the doorway.

My breath catches in my throat as my mind races, trying to figure out how he knew about the kitten. "How did you know?" I call out to him.

He pokes his head around the corner and smiles. "I heard something jumping around last night when I returned. I was concerned there might be a squirrel in the house. The noise was coming from your room. I heard meowing." He gives me a wink and leaves.

My laughter comes hard and I thank God for bringing Maestro Grant to me. For this man, whose deceptive bark covers a heart softer than my new kitten's fur.

THE INVITATION

TENSION DISAPPEARS overnight. Over the next month, Mr. Grant—Kent—is more at ease, more amicable, and forthcoming with conversation. More people, friends and colleagues come to visit. Some join us for informal dinners. Much of the time, the guests include Rick Weatherby and a few of the other male musicians or members of the crew. They all greet me merrily. At these events, I excuse myself from the table, leaving Kent and his guests to dine alone. My presence might hamper their conversations. I take my meals upstairs with my unnamed cat.

A frequent visitor during the day is Haruka Satō. The concertmaster comes on various missions, which sound more and more like pretenses. If it's really work-related, why doesn't she discuss the issues at his office? Why visit him at home? Of course, it's clear why. She is after him, flirting with him. Her clothing choices are on the skimpy side despite the chilly weather. Her lilting laughter punctuates their discussions in the music room, whose door Kent keeps open whenever she visits.

They're together in the music room this Thursday in late March. The discussion is brisk but friendly. I descend the stairs and turn to look down the hallway. Haruka stands at the door, her hand on the inside knob. She flashes me a mischievous smile and closes the door behind her.

Emotions tangle in my belly as I cross my arms over my chest with a huff. How dare she? He obviously isn't romantically interested in her. She's never been asked to lunch or dinner. As far as I know, she's never accompanied him anywhere.

I stuff the concern down. If this is something Kent wants, well, who am I to stop him? If it isn't wanted, he can deal with it himself. Back in the kitchen, I start peeling potatoes to make potato-leek soup, bending my ears for the slightest noise from the music room. I don't have to wait long.

A loud bang reverberates through the townhouse. I drop the peeler and the potato and run to the music room. Kent, dressed in more formal clothing than usual, holds the door open while a sobbing Haruka darts past him, her eyes lowered. She scurries past me in the hallway and out the front door.

Kent rolls his eyes and shuts the door as he disappears into the music room again.

Only then do I see the knob-shaped hole in the drywall and add calling a repairman to my to-do list.

It is nearly an hour before Kent joins me in the kitchen, looking for lunch. He finishes his silent meal of potato-leek soup, garden salad, and homemade biscuits and leans back in his chair. Rubbing his forehead, he asks, "Are you doing anything Saturday night?"

I pause in the middle of buttering a biscuit and stare at him, momentarily struck dumb. He's never asked me about my plans. "I don't have any plans that night." I don't even have to make him dinner that evening as he is going to some fancy soiree.

"How about being my plus-one at the fundraising event?" He scrutinizes me, but says nothing more.

A million thoughts race through my mind. Why is he asking now, two days before the event? What can I possibly wear? "I—I'm not sure I can pull it off."

He leans forward, conspiratorially, "Miss Satō was supposed to be my guest, but she has changed her mind."

It all makes sense. Haruka was probably going to be his date until Kent rejected her advances. "I'm not sure I can get something appropriate to wear in so short a time."

He folds his hands on the table. "What about that black sheath dress you wore to the Copland concert?"

I nearly choke on my inhaled breath. He remembers that concert, even the garment I wore. "I still have it. Will it be fancy enough?" For some reason, I envision needing a cocktail gown.

"It will work fine." He stands, resting his palms on the table and leaning over it. "Does this mean you'll go?"

My mouth opens and closes several times, but no sound comes out. Finally, I shrug one shoulder though my insides are sizzling at the idea. "I—I guess I can."

"Perfect. We'll leave about six-thirty. There's cocktails and small talk until eight when dinner is served. A presentation about the symphony orchestra fundraising follows. Music and dancing afterward." He walks to the doorway and turns back. "Do you know how to waltz?"

My throat goes dry at the thought of being held in his arms. Even for a short dance. Not trusting myself to say anything, I nod.

Still dizzy from his request, I go to tidy up the music room. There isn't much to do except collect a few coffee-stained mugs and a small plate with smears of peanut butter and jelly and breadcrumbs. On the way out, I inspect the hole in the drywall. I'm pulling out my phone to take a picture when it pings with a text from Clare.

Clare: *How are you? How's it going?*

Me: *Okay. Mr. Grant decided to permanently hire me as housekeeper at double the salary. And he asked me to be his plus-one at a symphony fundraiser Saturday evening.*

Clare: *Holy Moses! We need to stay in contact more often. BTW, Louis and I are going to that fundraiser. I'll see you there.*

Me: *What are you wearing? He told me the funeral dress will be fine. It doesn't seem correct attire for such an event.*

Clare: *Oh no! It's formal attire. You'll need a gown.*

Me: *Got an extra?* I have a formal gown, but it's buried somewhere in my rented storage units. And probably terribly wrinkled if not ravaged by mice by now.

Clare: *Sure. Can you meet me for lunch tomorrow at noon at Longueil food court? I'll bring the gown.*

Me: *Yes, see you there.*

LUNCH

THE LONGUEIL FOOD COURT is packed with customers. Located deep in the downtown business district, it's swarmed all day Monday through Friday, especially at lunchtime. Clad in a business suit, Clare waves me over when she sees me at the top of the escalator.

"Thanks for meeting me," I say, dropping into the chair opposite hers and pulling off my windbreaker.

"No problem. I can't stay long. I'm in a meeting at two, and want to go over my notes beforehand." She opens her takeout bag. "Want to get anything? Or watch me eat?"

"I'll watch. I don't have a deadline, and I'd rather talk to you."

She chomps into a tuna grinder, a trickle of mayo glistening on her upper lip as she chews. Is that an appropriate choice before a meeting? Tuna breath? "So, as I said, we're going to the fundraising event for the symphony. And you can't acknowledge knowing who I am...I'm under an NDA."

"Are you kidding?" she bursts out, her mouth full as she rolls her eyes and swallows. Bobbing her head to the chair beside her where a garment bag drapes over the seat back, she says, "The gown is there. It should fit. I threw in a few extra things like matching shoes and a purse."

"Thanks." Thank God, Clare and I are the same size for clothing and shoes. We often shared our closets during our college roommate days. As usual, I don't know how I would survive without her or her wardrobe. I blurt out, "I'm so nervous. How is he going to introduce me?" I hadn't realized how much this issue nagged at me. He won't admit I'm his housekeeper, will he? I believe he has more couth than that.

"I'll be there. Don't worry." She nods before taking a second bite. "Tell me about the extension." Setting down the sandwich, she opens a bag of potato chips. I snatch a few as I collect my thoughts.

"He's upgraded my position to housekeeper and doubled my salary. Which is good because I'm nervous about my hospital position. It was supposed to become full-time last fall, but that hasn't happened. I'm thinking it won't."

Clare slaps my hand playfully as I reach for more chips. "Do you think you can manage the housekeeping and a full-time job?"

"It's not too hard, but I had to take five days off while Kent was recovering."

"Oooh, on a first name basis now?" Clare chuckles.

Ignoring her comment, I continue, "The principal investigator, Dr. Tucker, wasn't happy about my sudden vacation. I've used up all of my vacation days until next month, though I do have two days of sick time left." I frown. "It doesn't feel right in the lab. Dr. Tucker told me he submitted that grant request to the hospital's Institutional Research Review Board nearly six months ago. It should have either been accepted or rejected by now."

"Well, wait it out. You never know. Maybe he had to revise his application." She pops the last bite of sandwich into her mouth and crumples up the wrapper.

"I know. I shouldn't complain. Truthfully, I'd rather not be working with him, but the health insurance is important."

Clare slides the potato chip bag over to me. "At least you have that."

I nod, remembering the hell Brannon and I went through with all his health issues. They started so quickly and ferociously; I immediately took Family and Medical Leave from my full-time hospital work. As his cancer lingered despite repeated treatments, the FMLA ran out, and I had to quit my job, just as Brannon's accounting business tanked. That left us with no health insurance and only our savings to live off. Not even enough to afford COBRA insurance. After Brannon's death, I tried returning to my old job, but I'd already been replaced. The only option was to take the part-time research job with Dr. Tucker and his promises of full-time employment. But at least it got me some health insurance.

The gray fog descends over my soul like a hood. Clare grasps my hand across the table, breaking the spell. "How are you really feeling?"

I know she's talking about my grief over losing Brannon. Just when he was feeling so much better, and we all thought he was going to make it, he had a fatal episode of difficult breathing. Six minutes. All it took was six minutes, and he was dead. Since he had previously signed a "do not resuscitate" order, the hospital staff let him go. Probably a blood clot in his lungs, the oncologist said.

The entire event, holding his hand as he took his last breath, has haunted me since that day. Daily, at first, but now only once in a while. "As appalled as I was to witness Brannon's end, I've come to realize he didn't suffer. Not for long. It started in his sleep, and he never regained consciousness. A blessing perhaps." I wipe the dampness from my eyes with a napkin that Clare hands me.

"It is a blessing, after all the chemo and radiation, and the surgeries. The bone marrow transplant alone...having to stay in a virtual bubble for months."

I nod as I crush the tear-stained napkin and shove it into the takeout bag of trash. "There." I brush a lock of hair from my eyes. "All better," I say, tamping down the grief that wallows beneath the surface of my composure like an ocean rip tide.

"What about Maestro Grant? He's handsome." She cups her chin in her palm, her elbow on the table. Her eyes glisten and twinkle with merriment.

"What? No...I mean, yes, he is very handsome. And much nicer now that the trial period is over." I can't admit more than this yet. "We actually have good conversations during our meals together."

"Together?" She raises an eyebrow in an inquisitive expression.

"Yeah. He doesn't like eating alone, so he eats informally in the kitchen with me."

A twinkle sparks in Clare's eyes. "Hmm, sounds interesting," she says saucily.

I hold up my palm. "Stop. Don't make it into something it's not."

"Do you have any romantic or lusty feelings for him?" She winks.

I stand up abruptly, nearly knocking my chair to the floor. "No!" My stomach gives a little flip at the suggestion. As usual, Clare has figured out the truth. I stammer, "I—it would be out of place. He's my employer. I've never had a workplace affair, and I'm not going to start now, no matter how great he looks." Peeved at Clare's insistent Cheshire cat grin, I add, "You better get back to work."

"This discussion isn't finished." She grins even wider. "See you on Saturday." She winks one last time and heads for the exit.

GARDEN PLANS

RETURNING TO THE TOWNHOUSE after an errand, I wander around looking for something to do. Kent is a fairly neat person, so there isn't much that needs my attention. The groceries were ordered and delivered earlier in the week, as was the routine laundry and the dry cleaning. His symphony concert and formal attire are handled by Mrs. Farthing at the symphony's expense. Other than cooking, I'm left with cleaning floors and dusting...neither of which takes a lot of my time. Even Glee, the female kitten (short for glissando, a musical term), naps away most of the afternoon in a sunbeam with nothing better to do.

Tonight's event has my stomach in knots. I need something to distract myself. The beautiful early spring sunshine beckons me into the backyard. I walk the entire perimeter, noting what plants are there. As the gardener at my former house, I'm familiar enough with the way plants look throughout the different seasons, provided some color, bark pattern, or budding leaves are present. I ponder different ways to make the space more pleasant and usable like an oasis amid the metropolitan setting, or a backyard barbeque party site.

I envision a meditation bench tucked under the small birch tree, a water or pond feature in one corner of the yard for habitat. And more flowering plants for bees and butterflies to enjoy and draw nectar from over the coming summer. Excited by all the thoughts racing through my head, I retrieve paper and pencil from the kitchen and sketch the current yard and its plant inhabitants. When done, I draft several plan options for development. I need a big project. Something big enough to keep me busy while the symphony is in residence at Sutton Lake for the concert series in June, and when they tour Western Europe in July.

I sketch and resketch, sitting on the ground, looking up plant species and their sunlight requirements on my phone. A voice behind asks, "What are you doing?"

Reflexively, I bolt away before realizing it's Kent. "Oh...you scared me." I clutch my chest to keep my thundering heart from bursting through. Strands of his hair lift with the breeze, softening his features. He's removed his suit jacket, and the baby blue button-down shirt stretches taut against his sculpted chest. My mouth waters at the sight.

Looking over my shoulder, he asks, "Plans?"

"I was daydreaming of making over this space." I wave my hand, encompassing the entire garden. "It could be a charming and peaceful oasis. A great place to hide and rejuvenate. A place for barbeques and lawn parties."

To my surprise, he sits down on the grass. "Explain what you envision."

Unnerved by his nearness, I chatter away, explaining what is already in place, then add my thoughts on features and beneficial plants, pointing out several of the different ideas I've drawn on the sheets of paper. Noting his interest, I say, "Most of these changes I can make myself. A pond or water feature would have to be professionally installed. The garden bench would need to be selected and delivered."

Kent takes the papers out of my hand and shuffles through them, giving each a hard look. Gruffly, he says, "This is very impressive. Where did you learn about this?"

"I love gardening. It was my happy place at our house." I wonder if the new owners will appreciate the lush beds I cared for so lovingly. Kent is watching me, and I give him a quick smile, shaking off my melancholy.

He says, "Let me think about it. I'll give them back tomorrow."

He tucks the papers under his arm. "Oh, I came out here to tell you that the plans for the end of season dinner are solidified. Give Evelyn a call at your convenience. She has all the details." Once more, he starts for the townhouse, turns, and frowns as he looks at his watch. "We're still on for tonight?"

I check the time on my phone. "The fundraiser event? Yes. I'm going to get ready soon."

"The car arrives at six-thirty. Three hours from now." He raises his eyebrows. "Don't women need hours to primp?"

"I don't." I chuckle. "I realize the time. Don't worry. I'll be ready." I shoo him away with both hands.

As I watch him disappear inside, a little niggle in my gut twitches, wondering if I'll ever see those plans again. He might actually give me the okay to make the changes too. Changes that would turn this secluded spot into a secret garden and give me something to do while he's away. I consider that outcome a long shot.

I meet him downstairs in the living room at twenty after six. When I step down the final riser, he turns to look at me. Inspect me, is more like it. His eyes literally roam up and down my body. My cheeks flush hot at the attention. The tuxedo he's wearing fits him like a glove, highlighting his finely toned body. Unlike his performance attire, his bow tie is white, and his cummerbund is a satiny-black.

"That's not the black dress you wore to the Copland concert," he says, gesturing up and down with one hand.

"No, it's not. I heard tonight is a very formal event, so a friend lent me a gown." I did a little twirl, letting the navy chiffon skirt and its underlying silk flutter out like a bell.

"You look lovely," he says, instantly turning to look out the front window for the luxury town car hired to drive us to the event.

The rather dismissive comment strikes my ego. I'm happy with the way I look and present myself tonight. My makeup is subtle and natural-looking, like I don't have any on at all except for lipstick. I've tamed my long tresses into a chignon with a thin braid of my auburn hair wrapped around the base.

I stare down at my hands. I've painted my nails a light, shell-pink color and moisturized them. My wedding ring gleams in the lamplight. That won't do. It will look unseemly if Kent's plus-one is a married woman. The gossip would be brutal. I slide the ring off and place it in the Colts stein on the fireplace mantel.

Kent surprises me by asking, "Do you have any jewelry you could wear?"

"I have these earrings," I motion toward the diamond studs in my earlobes. "My watch isn't fancy enough. It will look out of place with this outfit."

"A necklace?" He cocks his head quizzically, studying my neck again.

A necklace. I hadn't owned many expensive necklaces: a garnet drop, my birthstone, a few gold chains, and a diamond pendant. All were sold little by little to pay for Brannon's treatments, or our mortgage, or the utilities, or medicine, or food. My grandmother's pearls were the last to go. "No." My voice is harsh. Kent raises an eyebrow and opens his mouth to say something else when the doorbell rings. The car is here.

Tucked inside the car's back seat, I take charge of the conversation so it doesn't return to my lack of a necklace. "Tell me who's going to be there tonight."

Kent grimaces. "All the usual suspects. There are the members of the symphony's board of directors. All white men, all old, obnoxious, and controlling. Members of the staff will be there, of course. Including Evelyn, should you need anything."

The car makes a sharp maneuver to get around a bus, knocking me against Kent's arm and side. An electric zing courses through my body, forcing me to pull myself upright. Kent's gaze holds mine. "Are you all right? I can have the driver slow down."

I straighten my shawl and pat my chignon, embarrassed at the strong reaction to his rugged torso and his hand on my arm as he helps me regain my seat. "I—I'm fine. Thank you."

Can he tell I'm not fine? It has nothing at all to do with being knocked around the back of the car. I'm acutely aware of his presence, the heat that emanates from him, his usual cedar and clove aura mixing with a woodsy, sage and lemon grass cologne. The very manliness of him sitting beside me in that immaculate tuxedo causes me to quiver inside.

He clears his throat. "The, um, ah, various directors should be there also, of marketing, operations, community outreach, etc. Plus the executive director."

"Please tell me there won't be a name test at the end of the evening." I need to say something light to break the tension rapidly building between us after that touch.

"Definitely not. Several musicians will attend, especially our endowed chairs. You'll see Rick Weatherby too."

Remembering the incident with Kent's dislocated knee, I ask, "It wasn't Rick who stepped in for you when your knee went out."

"No, Rick's a rehearsal conductor. He and I go over the score after I've examined it and decide how I want it to sound. Rick works with the musicians to get them acclimated to my vision. Then he rehearses them a few times before I step in for the final ones, days before the concert."

The car stops in front of the Elliot Hotel's banquet entrance. I gather the bell of my dress and my clutch. Kent's hand on my forearm stops me from exiting the car. "Don't find yourself alone with Malcolm Trier, the president of the board. Not even for a dance. He's a groper. And while I'd love to get him dismissed from the board for doing it again, I don't want you to have to suffer the attack."

THE EX

A RED CARPET LEADS the way from the curb to the double doors manned by two footmen in scarlet uniforms reminiscent of British Beefeaters, minus the tall furry helmets.

Camera bulbs flash like sparklers as we mount the stairs lined with fans. Like a gauntlet, we pass hundreds of women shouting for Kent's attention. Reporters and photographers beg us to stop and pose for pictures at the door. Kent's hand rests on my back, drawing me closer to him. Its warmth seeps into me, providing assurance and support. "Smile," he whispers.

I smile amid the flashes before we disappear through the doors into the ballroom.

A large crowd mills about the dozens of elegantly staged tables. Several people, Mrs. Farthing among them, approach to shake Kent's hand and welcome him. Mrs. Farthing sidles up to me and whispers in an angry tone, "Don't look so shell-shocked. Paste a smile on your face if you have to. You need to look happy to be here with Maestro."

I immediately smile broadly and laugh like she said something funny. This event is far bigger than I had anticipated. Kent didn't mention that photographers, TV crews, and other media outlets would be jockeying for images. What do they consider me? His date? The plus-one? Will word get out that I'm his housekeeper? How pathetic that would sound for both of us.

Kent steers me with a hand lightly touching my back. A gentle jab of a finger turns me ninety degrees to an approaching elderly man.

"Malcom, let me introduce Abigail Davitt. Abigail, this is Malcom Trier. Malcom is president of the symphony's board of directors."

This old sock is the man I'm supposed to be wary of? He's balding yet stocky, and about seventy years old. Unsure what to do, I hold out my hand for a handshake.

"A pleasure to meet you, Miss Davitt," he says, taking my hand in his. "You look ravishing tonight." His leer scans my body from head to toe. Turning to Kent, he says in a lowered voice, "Lucky dog, you."

As much as I don't like being eye-candy for an elderly lech, I appreciate the compliment. Clare's dress fits tightly around the bodice, exposing more cleavage than I'm used to. Malcolm's eyes are glued to the plunging neckline.

I sense Kent go rigid beside me. His face is frozen in a Mona Lisa smile. Suddenly, he looks past Malcolm's shoulder and waves to someone. I crane my neck but can't see who it is. Kent excuses us and steers us away, leaving Malcolm behind. He weaves through the crowd until we are on the other side of the room. Only then does the tension in his shoulders ease. Unclenching his teeth and smiling at me, he apologizes, "Sorry about that. I was hoping to stay clear of Malcolm..." He pauses as others approach him with a greeting.

Over the next hour, I am introduced to dozens of people. Some of them are also on the board of directors, some musicians from the symphony, a bunch of prominent city politicians and leaders, including the mayor of Baymont, Michelle Rousso. Fortunately, Kent handles the conversations and steers away any questions about my presence.

I startle to hear someone whisper in my ear, "Hey, you." The tension in my chest eases, and I turn to hug Clare and Louis.

Clare smiles, a glint in her eyes. "You look gorgeous. How's it going?" she whispers in my ear.

"Good," I reply, my voice low so no one else can hear. "Thanks. It's going okay so far. I do feel like a fish out of water." Kent reaches out to me for yet another introduction. "Got to go..." I whisper, hoping Kent didn't notice my conversation with Clare and Louis.

As I turn my attention to the new couple standing beside Kent, he whispers, "Who was that?"

"My college friends and symphony subscribers, Clare and Louis," I mutter as I smile prettily and greet the couple, all the while hoping I won't have to recall their names later. I've already been introduced to over three dozen people. There is no way I can keep track of all their names and positions.

When I think this cocktail hour will never end, Mrs. Farthing shows us to our table near the front center of the room, before the raised dais holding a podium.

Our dinner table is comprised of Kent and me, Malcolm Trier and his wife, and three other directors and their wives. All the wives must know each other because they sit together and whisper, frequently glancing in my direction. Are they trying to guess who I am? Only Clare and Louis, Mrs. Farthing, Rick, and a few of the musicians know me. Or at least, that is what I hope. How many others know the truth?

Dinner is delicious, though I don't eat the scallop appetizer. Again, Kent comes to my rescue, telling the waiter I am allergic to shellfish and taking the plate himself. Malcolm takes the information bone and rattles on about such a terrible allergy to such delicious food. Only the next course's delivery breaks his babble. It is clear that Malcolm enjoys hearing himself talk, while the rest of the table, except for the wives, feigns attention.

After the main course—chicken with chasseur sauce over whipped turnips, and a dessert of cheesecake with blackberry compote—the ceremony begins. The master of ceremonies starts with the mayor, followed by Malcolm, who seems perfectly happy to drone on about the work he and the symphony's board have undertaken to mold and direct its past, present, and future. His wife wipes her forehead with a white napkin, possibly a signal, because Malcolm, on seeing it, abruptly ends his oratory mid-sentence.

Kent is the next speaker. His comments are short, as the audience is stirring after Malcolm's long-winded remarks. Kent thanks the donors sincerely for the help they provide to the mission of the symphony, the musicians, and himself. He mentions the Sutton Lake series and the summer tour to Europe, generously funded by donors. He concludes by mentioning the community work he is privileged to provide to the school system's children in musical education, also because of their unwavering financial aid. In conclusion, he thanks everyone for their support, in spirit, in donations, and in attendance, which together promise a bright future for Baymont's renowned symphony orchestra.

The applause is thunderous as he returns to his seat beside me. Clearly, he is appreciated, if not for his comments, then for acknowledging the donors' support rather than tooting his own horn as Malcolm had done.

His words warm me to the core. Succinctly, he shows how grateful he is to be doing the symphony's work, whether on the stage or in the community. The symphony benefactors love him for it.

The hotel staff clear the dance floor, and a live band commences playing, inviting everyone to dance.

I'm not sure if Kent intends to dance with me. I stay by his side while he is bombarded with well-wishers. He graciously greets each by name, sometimes introducing me, but mostly not. It's all fine with me. I'm not there to make an impression. Only be his "plus-one," as he stated earlier. Thankfully, Clare and Louis stay well away, although she winks at me as they walk past. No one seeks me out until Kent excuses himself and leaves my side for what I assume is a bathroom visit.

While he's gone, an elegantly couture-dressed, dark auburn-haired woman approaches, looking me up and down. She's not much older than I am, and I don't like the severe look in her hard, dark eyes or the tiny, controlled sneer on her face. "So, you're the flavor of the night," she says flatly.

I give her the same treatment, my eyes roaming over her gaunt figure. Does she ever eat anything? The clavicle bones framing her neck stand out prominently, as does her sternum. It's visible nearly to her navel behind a nude colored chiffon fabric in the low-cut bodice. She is so anorexic looking, I feel sure I can count every one of her ribs had they been exposed. When she holds up her martini glass, I can even distinguish the two separate, yet parallel bones of her forearm. My spine shivers at the creepy look of it.

When I don't reply to her comment, she adds, "Nothing to say?" Her sneer broadens. Beyond her, I catch sight of Malcom's wife elbowing her friend to draw her attention to me. Apparently, this interaction is going to be gossip fodder.

The heat of Kent's hand and presence at my back floods me with relief. Kent says, "Cynthia, go pester someone else." His hand grips my elbow, and he steers me away to the bar. Away from the menacing woman, the muscles in my shoulders and back ease my rigid stance, and I begin to tremble. Kent orders two vodka tonics for us.

My knees stop shaking after the fourth gulp. "W—Who was that?" I can see her staring at us, a smoldering look on her face.

Kent turns and slips between me and Cynthia's line of vision. He leans closer and whispers, "My ex-fiancée." He slugs back his drink. "Come on. Let's dance," he says, as the band starts playing a waltz.

Slipping his arm to my waist and grasping my other hand, he draws me into the dance. Not knowing where else to put it, my free hand settles on his upper arm. He pulls me close, far closer than some of the other couples. I step back, putting more inches between our torsos.

Why am I surprised that this man, a musical conductor, is a terrific dancer? After the first few seconds, my feet flawlessly follow his. He smoothly leads me around the dance floor in the steady, flowing rhythm. His hot breath grazes my neck, raising goosebumps on my arms.

"Comfortable?" He hesitates for half a second before twirling me under his arm into a side-by-side open position and pauses, swaying left and right as if marking time.

I am more than comfortable. I am completely turned on, heat blossoming in my lady parts. "You're an excellent dancer," I blurt, as we come back together in the normal stance.

He gives a brief chuckle. "I took lessons. Can you imagine how it would look if the conductor couldn't hold his own on the dance floor?"

"I see your point." I laugh so hard at his statement, I snort and stumble momentarily.

His eyes search mine, filled with concern. "Are you tired? I've made all my rounds and talked to everyone I need to. We can leave at any time," he says as the waltz ends.

He bows to me. My heart flutters, and I curtsy. "Yes. Let's leave before I embarrass myself somehow."

Approaching us as we leave the dance floor is Haruka Satō. Her face red with rage.

Rather than dodge her, Kent holds my hand tighter and leads me past her swiftly. "Okay, time to bail out of here before one of them makes a scene."

Now I'm really worried. Far more than I was about Clare perhaps spilling the beans. Haruka knows I'm Kent's housekeeper and cook. Will she retaliate against his rejection by disclosing my true connection to him? Or is she also under an NDA? I pray that is the case for his sake and mine.

Our ride back to the townhouse is quiet at first. I'm not sure if it's because he is exhausted or if he doesn't want to give the driver anything to spread as gossip. I remain silent, enjoying the city lights and the congenial comfort of the man beside me.

A warmth radiates to my hand as it rests on the seat. A quick glance, and that warmth runs up my arm and into my chest. Kent's hand is beside mine on the cushion. Will he take it? A lump in my chest grows with anticipation. Does he expect me to touch his hand instead? It would thrill me to no end to do so. Before I can gather the nerve to touch him, the cab comes to a halt outside the front door. I withdraw my hand and clutch it to my side.

Inside the townhouse's door, Kent stops my passage. "Thank you for being my date tonight. I know it was rather boring for you." He takes my hand. "I do hope it wasn't too tiresome."

Lightning sears up my arm at his touch, the electrons racing through my chest and down further. "I—I had a good time. Even the food was delicious." *As was being held in your arms while we danced,* my mind adds silently.

He pauses, looking at me with a strange, penetrating stare, his lips parting. Ever so slightly, his head inches toward mine. My breath catches, and my pulse pounds. It looks like he's going to kiss me.

Abruptly, he lets me go and straightens as he steps a pace backward. "Well then, good night." He brushes against my arm as he passes, heading directly for his bedroom.

Again, the electricity is palpable where he brushed against me, adding fuel to the smoldering in my core. Swiftly, before I do something most unsuitable, I retire to my room upstairs. My body still tingles with the almost kiss and his touch. My mind floats in a daydream as I remove my clothing. Would he like to do that for me? Unzip my gown, slip it down past my hips to pool on the floor? Would he like the matching black lace bra and panties I must admit I wore especially for him?

I squeeze my eyes shut and shake my head. He's my employer. I can't forget that, no matter how attracted I am to him. And I'm Brannon's widow. The two issues combined make it impossible for me to act on my strong feelings for Kent. No matter how much I might wish otherwise.

Sleep eludes me as my mind ruminates over Cynthia's words. To say she is obnoxious is an understatement. I hadn't realized Kent's ex-fiancée moved in the same circle he did. Perhaps she did it to stalk him, or simply to be a perpetual pain in his behind. Whatever the reason, it doesn't bode well for him, and I hope not to be the recipient of her stinging words again. That's unlikely to happen, as this was a one-time occurrence. I finally drift to sleep, remembering he'd called it a date. Not a plus-one arrangement. The tingling feels his words made in my core keep me company all night.

THE PHOTOS

THE BED SHEETS BEAR witness to my turbulent dreams. The sun has yet to rise. I slip on my robe and descend the stairs, lusting for a cup of coffee. I need it to release me from the dream's images. Images of Kent's arms around me, sashaying over the dance floor, then the bottom falling out beneath our feet. Cynthia's face ridiculing me, Kent chained to a cold stone wall. My husband, Brannon, coming to save me, pulling me away from Cynthia, her cackling laughter sounding like Veronica's as Kent hangs limply from the wrist manacles that bind him to her will.

With the steaming mug in hand, I return to my room and take my time getting ready for whatever this Sunday brings. The local church bell rings eight times as I take one last, examining look in the mirror. I have nothing on my calendar today, so I dress casually in jeans and a light cotton jersey long-sleeved shirt. If Kent doesn't have anything for me to do, I might head to the library or dally in the backyard garden. Kent said he'd give my drafted plans back to me today with a decision. Positive mantras circulate in my head, willing a best-case decision.

Downstairs, Kent is already at the breakfast table, skimming through the newspaper with his coffee mug in hand.

"Good morning," I chirp as merrily as I'm able. If my attitude is upbeat, it might entice him to decide in the affirmative.

"Good morning." He folds the open newspaper in quarters and holds it out for me. "Check out the photos from last night."

A jittering in my stomach sparks as I take the proffered newspaper. There are several photos highlighting the event, one of them showing Kent and me locked in our waltzing stance. I am looking straight at the camera, which I hadn't even noticed last night. Kent is looking at me with a tenderness I definitely didn't see.

The photo caption reads, "Baymont Symphony conductor Kendrick Grant dancing with his date, Abigail Davitt."

"How did they get my name?" I ask, returning the paper to him.

He sets the paper down on the chair to his left. "If I had to guess, either Evelyn or the symphony's PR staff gave them your name. I had to provide it to get you on the guest list." His gaze holds me still, his eyebrows drawn together. "I'm sorry, I should have asked your permission. Is this disclosure going to detrimentally affect you?"

What can I say? Who would care? Chances are that my former extended and alienated family will never see the photo. "No. That's fine. It just surprises me."

"Why's that?" He tucks the paper under his arm.

I raise a shoulder, "I guess because I was just a plus-one."

He cocks his head. "You could never only be someone's plus-one."

My breath stops and the tingling in my belly spreads to my skin. Goosebumps erupt on my forearms. What does he mean? Did he imply I'm special in some way? I breathe in and hold it, then slowly release to ease the thudding of my heart against my chest wall.

He no sooner finishes his statement than his phone rings. "Evelyn," he says, retreating from the kitchen with the newspaper.

In a few minutes, I hear him wrestling with his lightweight jacket, keys jingling, as he walks back into the kitchen. "There's a problem. I have to get to the office now." He's changed into his business attire. He walks toward the garage door, then turns back. "Oh, by the way. Go ahead with the backyard garden plans. Gather some pictures of benches, and we can select one at dinner tonight."

My heart nearly explodes with joy. He said yes to my proposal. *And* he said we would select the materials together. Not just him, but *we*. The giddiness in my belly spills through me. I make a list of things to do on my Sunday off, including finding garden benches and water features. Before I stuff my to-do list into my jeans pocket, I add one more item. Today's newspaper. I want a copy of that picture of Kent holding me in his arms.

As expected, Clare calls me after breakfast. "Did you get a look at the newspaper?" she asks.

"Kent showed the pictures to me this morning," I reply while getting my stuff together for the garden center trip.

"You two looked pretty cozy on the dance floor." Clare chuckles. "Did you have a good time?"

I know her well enough to visualize her waggling her eyebrows suggestively. "It was very interesting. So many people to meet. Including Maestro's ex-fiancée, Cynthia."

A sharp intake of breath sounds. "OMG, are you kidding. Did he introduce you to her?"

"Actually, no. She started taunting me. Kent came to my rescue."

"Holy crap! Is she frightful?"

I nod. "Yes. Overbearing, beautiful, immaculately clothed in haute couture. Perfect makeup and hair. Talk about making me feel like Cinderella before the ball."

"You looked beautiful in that gown." Clare asks, "Did he tell you anything about why they never married?"

"Not a word," I say, stuffing the garden plans into a tote bag. Better to have the plans than try to recall them from memory. "She looks and sounds like a piece of work."

"Do you think they'll get back together?"

"From what I see, I doubt it. But if they do, I'm outta here."

THE MUSIC ROOM

WHEN I RETURN FROM the garden center, Kent is already back. He rarely comes home for lunch, but today is Sunday, not a work day. I find him in the recliner in his music room listening to a CD. His eyes are closed, his expression serene as if he's asleep. I turn to leave.

"Do you need something?" He speaks softly under the stream of soothing music.

I jump, not realizing he'd known I was in the room. "I'm sorry if I woke you. Would you like me to fix you some lunch?"

"No thanks. I'm expecting Miss Satō any time now. Please show her in here and don't disturb us."

He's never asked me so formally before. What can he possibly want to see her about? She was his original plus-one for the fundraising event. Perhaps seeing us last night and the picture in today's paper stirred her jealousy? Were they going to make up their differences? Or would she rage at him again? Whatever happens today, my knees are already feeling squishy about it. I try to control the chip on my shoulder from turning me green with envy.

When the doorbell rings, I let her in and escort her to the music room. She's dressed up fancy, her makeup alluring with cat's-eye liner and bright red pouting lips. I've no doubt she'll use sex appeal to get on his best side again. Is she taking lessons from Cynthia? A hard knot grows in my gut, making me angry. I don't want them to get back together, if they ever had been. I want our relationship to continue as it has grown. My life revolves around his needs and filling them makes me happy. I sigh heavily remembering I'm just the housekeeper. Kent is simply my employer. I have no stake in the matter of his love life.

I retreat to the kitchen to eat a bowl of homemade kale soup. Minutes later, Miss Satō screams obscenities at Kent, interrupting my peaceful lunch. I can't hear whether he answers her or tries to calm her down. My fists clench tightly as I pace the kitchen. I don't know what to do. Kent gave no further instruction than not to interrupt. Should I ignore the obscene epithets or follow Kent's demand? There must be something I can do to be ready in case the scene escalates badly.

Positioning myself between the music room and the front door, I wait, alert and furtively watching. I'm worried the woman will cause a lot of trouble. Kent had told me earlier she is a firebrand, and I don't think he meant it in a good way. Her filthy language continues, her accusations impossible not to hear. She claims he led her on, believing they had a mutual understanding, a growing relationship. On and on she drones loud enough to send Glee scurrying up the stairs to higher ground and quiet safety.

The door flies open, the knob striking the repaired drywall and punching a new hole in it. Miss Satō storms out, takes one look at me, and glares maliciously. "Housekeeper, indeed!" She spits at me. Her spittle hits my T-shirt. Satisfied with her insult, she marches off, slamming the door open. The alarm sounds, blaring loudly as she flies down the stairs.

I rush to the alarm pad and enter the code. The siren still rings in my ears in the sudden silence. Kent is at my side.

"Are you all right?" He holds out a hand but doesn't touch me, his gaze searching my face before dropping to the wet spot on my shirt.

My trembling hand brushes through my hair. "I'm okay."

We stare at each other for several minutes before I stutter, "I—I'm going to go clean up."

Kent nods. "I'm sorry for that."

I blurt unexpectedly, "You do raise emotions in people."

He looks at me, a quizzical expression on his face. "I do?"

Rather than admit he raises them in me, I take the stairs to my room, two at a time.

137

By the time I return to the kitchen and my now cold soup, Kent is gone. A note beside my bowl says, *Meeting up with the guys. Dinner out.*

I bolt upright in bed when the house alarm blares at three-twenty in the morning. I hesitate until a thud downstairs has me surging out of bed to investigate. I find the front door open, the alarm still ringing, while Kent slumps against the wall, cursing. "I can't remember the code," he slurs, a strong smell of bourbon emanating from his breath. I look outside, catching the wave of the cabbie as he drives away.

I silence the alarm and grab Kent's arm as he slides sideways. "Let me help you to your room." One arm around his waist, my shoulder under his armpit supporting much of his weight, I nearly carry him to his room. We stumble upstairs to his bed, where I set him down. He immediately slumps over sideways.

I can't tell if his snoring started before or after he hit the mattress. Lifting his feet, I put them on the bed and pull off his boat shoes. I look at him. He's fully dressed. Should I remove or loosen his clothing? I reach out and begin opening his shirt buttons, but the sight of his muscular bare chest stops my fingers. It feels too intimate, an invasion. He'll have to sleep in his clothes. I position him on his stomach, hoping he doesn't vomit and choke. Lastly, I pull the blanket over him, the soft, tender gesture surprising me. With one last look, I return to my room. Twice during the night, I peek in at him. He's still in the position I placed him in, snoring. No signs of sickness. A maternal instinct warms me as I brush a lock of hair aside from his face. My fingertips brush his forehead in same spot I'd like to press my lips. Retracting my hand, I return to my own bed.

The next morning, I get ready for work and set up Kent's breakfast place. Except I don't hear any stirring in his room. It is after eight o'clock. He is usually up, dressed, and ready to eat breakfast by now.

I listen at his bedroom door for any noise. Nothing. My heart stutters thinking he might have died overnight after all, choking on vomit or dying of alcohol poisoning. I knock hard, then fling open the door. His breathing body lies exactly where I last saw him. "Kent? Are you all right?" I call out, hoping to wake him.

An indistinguishable mumble rises. I clench my hands, twisting them with indecision. I take a deep breath and exhale, approach the bed, and nudge his shoulder. "Kent?"

He sleepily replies, "What time is it?" With half his mouth pressed into the pillow, it comes out sounding like "Wot ime-zit?"

"It's after eight. Are you going to work today?" I ask, stepping back a pace. He reeks of alcohol and sweat, and his face is pale.

"Yez." The sheets rustle as he moves, turning onto his back. "I'll be down in ten minutes," he groans.

Satisfied with his response, I return to the kitchen and wait. It's so unlike him to over-indulge to the point of inebriation. Did the argument with Haruka cause this? Did she threaten to expose that he took his maid to the fundraiser? Or was it something else?

Thirty minutes later, Kent stumbles into the kitchen in a navy blue suit, his hair wet from his shower, his feet bare, a pair of socks in one hand and one shoe in the other. "I can't find the other shoe," he mutters, dropping onto his chair. The socks and shoe thump to the floor. He grasps the steaming mug I hand him and drinks deeply.

"Last I saw of them, they were both beside your bed," I reply, as I drop some eggs and sausage in the frying pan.

As the aroma of fried food fills the air, Kent groans and shoves the placemat away. "Ugh. No food. Not a good idea yet." He holds his head in his hands, elbows resting on the table.

The sight makes me smile. He is human after all. I shut off the gas and take the offending pan of food out to the back porch, leaving it there for whatever animal wants it.

"Hair of the dog?" I ask when I return. He does have a slight shade of lime green about his features.

"No. I did my liver enough damage last night," he mutters through his hands. "My shoe. I need it." He tries to stand, but slumps back onto his chair. Grasping the table, he asks, "Can you help me?" His voice is weak and pitiful.

I've never seen him look or act so...helpless. It makes my heart squeeze. "Stay here. I'll find your other shoe." I search his room and find the lost shoe tucked behind the bathroom door.

"Thanks." He leans over to put them on, only to sit up again, groaning. Taking the hint, I put his socks and shoes on and tie them. His palm softly cups the side of my face before I can stand up. "Thanks."

I look at him, an unsettling feeling in my chest. This is so far beyond how he usually treats me, I wonder if he is aware of what he's doing. "Are you sure you should go to the office like this? You don't look good at all." He looks horrible. It is so far from his usual well-kept, robust, and perfectly manicured visage that I don't think it prudent to let him go.

"I have a meeting with Rick Weatherby this morning. It can't wait."

"Can't he come here?"

"No. I need Evelyn too."

"Fine. At least let me call the livery to pick you up."

He capitulates to my suggestion. It arrives in five minutes, during which I collect his briefcase, wallet, and suit jacket from his bedroom.

Assisting him, we walk out the front door and down the stairs to the curb, him white knuckling the iron railing. After tucking him inside the backseat, I stand back and watch as the car drives away. I mount the front steps and grasp the doorknob. I'm locked out. Without the key or my cellphone. Again.

THE LAY OFF

AFTER THE FIRST LOCK-out episode, Kent hid an extra door key in a flowerpot of soil in the backyard. It takes walking down the street and around the backside of the row of townhouses to reach Kent's driveway. Reaching the garden, I fish the candy tin out of the pot's soil. Then I reverse my trek back to the front door.

I call ahead to notify Dr. Tucker that I am on my way, but I will be arriving late. He grumbles and hangs up. It figures I actually have a real experiment to do today.

I bustle into work thirty-seven minutes late and don't dally prepping for today's project. Usually, I get called into the diagnostic laboratory to assist with testing tissue samples. Today, no summons arrives. Instead, I have a few surveys to perform. It's tedious work, but it keeps me in a paycheck and health insurance.

Just after noon, I knock on Dr. Tucker's door to drop off the microscope slides from today's experiments. He calls out, "Enter," but doesn't look up from the oculars.

"Your slides," I say, placing the cardboard flats holding thirty-six slides on his desk. "Let me know what you think after looking at them, so I can update the records."

"Sit down, please," he barks, still not looking at me.

This request is unusual and does not bode well. The expectation of bad tidings makes my breath shallow and choppy. Can he really be so angry over my being late for work?

"Yes, sir." I sit in the chair opposite him at the two-headed microscope. Only then does he raise his head and look at me, his features hard and unyielding.

"My research application has been denied. Without funding, I must let you go." His focus goes directly back to the microscope.

Just like that, I'm dismissed.

I can't breathe. My pass, my pay, my health insurance gone? "Is there another opening somewhere else in the lab? The diagnostic lab, maybe?"

His voice goes cold and hard. "You'll have to discuss that with human resources."

He's done with me. No words of thanks, no apologies for getting my hopes up all these months. No sincerity and no help. He knows what I've been through with Brannon. He knew I had to give up everything in my life, my hobbies, my joys, my car, my house, and so much more to pay medical bills. Everything of any monetary value had to be sold or pawned. A numbness settles over me as I walk out of his office and pull the door shut with a final click. I lean against it, my chin trembling as I fight to hold back tears.

Back in the lab, I clean out my few personal items and walk over to HR. No human resource counselors are available, so I make an appointment for the next day.

As I leave the building, my throat is parched, and a thousand thoughts roil around like tangled noodles in a pot of boiling water. How can I survive? What will I do if I can't get another part-time position that syncs with my housekeeping job? There are other hospitals in Baymont. Surely, one of them will have a job for a certified laboratory technologist. I can type and understand medical terms, biosafety, and related concepts. There has to be something available somewhere.

The first thing I do when I get back to the townhouse is fire up my laptop and search for another lab tech job in Baymont. An hour later, I conclude there aren't any. Increasing the search to hospitals and laboratory companies outside the city's environs doesn't help. There isn't a single position available for a certified, registered, and experienced lab technologist. Frustrated, I shut the computer and escape downstairs to begin dinner preparations.

While prepping the meal, I mull over Kent's reaction to Haruka's outburst. It confuses me. She backed out of being his date for the fundraising soiree. He found a replacement, and she exploded over my presence at the event. Had he intended to make Haruka jealous? Did I serve a dual purpose in that matter? Yet, he didn't seem to have reconnected with her. He hasn't appeased her, kissed up, or made up with her, as far as I know. He let her spew vile words and stalk out. It doesn't make sense. And his night of binge drinking afterward makes it all the more puzzling.

"I'm back." Kent arrives home earlier than expected. He still isn't feeling well after his night of overindulgence. He disappears into his bedroom, no doubt to change into something more comfortable than his suit.

Over dinner, we are both extra quiet. There are no words from Kent beyond a simple thank you for a delicious homemade chicken pot pie. I can't muster a reply.

"Is something wrong?" he asks as he butters a homemade biscuit.

Where do I begin? Without any thought, I blurt out the truth, "I was laid off today."

The spreading motion of his knife stops. He looks up, his eyes fastening on mine. "Because you were late? What happened?"

I puff out my cheeks and let the air out slowly, thinking about how to explain. "No. I was hired for a specific research project. The doctor I worked for needed funding from the NIH to conduct the study. He told me today his funding application was denied. So he had to let me go." I drop my gaze to my half-eaten dinner. Wincing, I say, "I have an appointment tomorrow with human resources to see if there's another position in the hospital I am qualified for."

"How about at the other two hospitals in Baymont?" Concern etches his handsome face.

My shoulders slump forward a little more. "I looked online. There aren't any openings in my specialty anywhere in Baymont or the surrounding towns."

We are silent again, each stewing in our own thoughts. Kent takes a few more bites of dinner. I'm poking at the peas to pop them.

"Do you really need that work?" he asks, grasping my hand across the table.

I look at my hand in his. His feels warm, soft, and yet muscular. Secure. "It is nice having the extra money. Plus, the hospital gave me a discount transportation card. But mainly I was there for the health insurance." After what I'd gone through with Brannon, health insurance is more important than food in my estimation. I will pay whatever exorbitantly priced health care insurance I can get rather than go through that ordeal and lose everything all over again. Not that I have much to lose right now. It's all gone already.

He looks at me, our gazes locking across the small kitchen table like at a poker game, as if we are trying to read each other's minds. "The message I received yesterday from Evelyn might help with your dilemma."

I stare at him. A change of subject? Rather than wallow with me in my self-pity?

"You see, in eight weeks, I'll be leaving with the symphony to tour Europe for ten days. In addition to the musicians, there are a dozen or so other people who travel along as support staff. The person who keeps everything together, keeps everyone on schedule, told us she's pregnant. She's miscarried several times and, understandably, she's refusing to go with us. The stress—" As if reading my face, he adds, "You could do it."

"I—I wouldn't know the first thing about an orchestra tour," I stutter, surprised he'd really consider me for the position.

"Gabriella has all the information you would need, including checklists to rely on. Everything is pre-planned. It's only a matter of herding everyone to the next location, be it a restaurant for dinner, making sure everyone checks in for the concert, and making sure the crew gets the stage arranged as needed." Before I can speak again, he says, "I've seen you get everything here under control. Your organizational skills are exemplary. I believe you can do it." His eyes sparkle as he says, "The pay is good."

"That's not the point, Kent," I plead. "It's unseemly."

"To whom?"

"What will people think?" I hiss.

"Look, you won't be staying with me. We'll be at the same hotel, but if you want, it can be a different hotel. But I think that *would* look unseemly. If you and I are open about your presence there...and we don't have to hang out together. Just come, keep everyone on schedule, and enjoy the sights. It's only ten days."

I ache to say yes. Europe is one of my favorite places, especially Paris. "I'll think about it."

"Come on, Abigail. They need to know now. If you can't, or won't, they need to hire someone else." His eyes are round and sparkling, and he squeezes my hand. "Say yes."

My brain descending into chaos, I can't come up with the pros and cons of doing it. As I stare off, trying to harness my emotions, Glee pads into the room. I've forgotten to feed her in my distracted state. My eyes fly open. "What about Glee? We can't leave her here alone for ten days!"

Kent chuckles. "I'm sure we can find someone to take care of her while we're away. What say you?"

His pleading eyes melt my heart. He's coiled up like a spring waiting for an affirmative response. My answer sways back and forth. What do I have to lose? I'm no longer tied to anything but this job. Why not?

"Okay," I groan.

I don't know what possesses me to give in. Maybe it's to see the sudden brilliance in Kent's eyes. Maybe it's the enthusiasm in his voice and words. Or maybe it's just a need to get away, to escape my reality for a little while. I've only been to a few parts of Europe. This might be the excuse I need to see more.

• • • •

"EXCELLENT!" I SHOUT so loud that Glee runs for cover. "Awesome! Let me call Evelyn right now before you change your mind!" My insides sputter with excitement, and I fight down the urge to give Abigail a huge hug.

The elation I feel is beyond any excitement I've experienced before previous tours. There wasn't any comfort on those trips. I got through by wandering the city's tourist sites or just lazing about the hotel bar with a few of the guys after the concerts. Because of my position, I'm always the outsider, the tag-along.

Meals are a particular hardship. Everyone dines on their own. Unless the local symphony conductor invites me to dine with them, I eat room service in my room. These isolating dinners are the reason I like to hold pre-event dinner parties at my townhouse. Now, after dining with Abigail most evenings over the past months, I can't think of eating alone yet again. The thought of having her there to at least have dinner with every evening, maybe even breakfast, makes my spirits soar.

The outlook for this tour seems far better than I previously anticipated.

I tamp down my excitement.

"There's one other thing I need to discuss with you. That dinner party I'm hosting for the performers in our final show in May. It's two weeks away. We've discussed it briefly, but it's time to make some concrete plans. Did you get a chance to speak with Evelyn about it?" I ask.

"I'm sorry, I, ah, didn't yet."

"Contact her tomorrow. Okay?"

She looks up in surprise. "Okay. I don't have any plans tomorrow afternoon. I'll do it then."

• • • •

HUMAN RESOURCES DOESN'T have any part-time or full-time positions I'm qualified to fill. There are some per-diem positions, but I'm reluctant to take them. Working per diem doesn't make me eligible for any benefits. I told them I'd think about it, but truthfully, I've already decided to decline.

I also learned that I'm not eligible for unemployment benefits as a laid-off worker because I have another job — this housekeeper job. I can apply, but the result will likely be a denial.

With that great news, I call Mrs. Farthing about the dinner party. She emails me the specifics regarding the guests, including their food allergies and likes and dislikes. From what I hear, I'm to devise a six-course menu and review it with both her and Kent for approval. With nothing else to do, I begin planning several different menus for them to choose from.

My cellphone rings half an hour later. It's Clare. Perfect timing. "Hey."

"Hey, yourself. Meet me for dinner tonight?"

"Can't. I have to cook for Kent. Plus, we have some things to discuss."

"Huh? What's going on?"

Her question stumps me. Where do I start? "I've been laid off at the hospital. Dr. Tucker was unable to get funding for his project, so my position has been eliminated."

"That's insane! Don't they have anything else you can do? Did you check around?" Clare's voice is full of indignation, which matches what I'm feeling.

"I did check. There's nothing right now," I momentarily debate telling her about accepting the tour-herding job. "I have a temp job this summer. Maestro Grant asked me to fill in for someone on the ten-day European tour."

"Ten days? In Europe? On their payroll and all expenses on their dime?" Her voice crackles with excitement.

"Yup. In July."

"I could take a week's vacation and meet you there. We could explore all the tourist sights," she says, excitement bubbling in her voice.

I shake my head. "I don't think I'll have any time to do that." I sense her disappointment. "Maybe next time."

Not long after, Mrs. Wainwright calls me. "I want you to know, as of next week, Mr. Grant will provide you with a full range of benefits, including health insurance."

Relief erupts in my chest, and I blurt out, "Really?" Tears slide down my face as I cover my mouth to silence my sobbing. Mrs. Wainwright prattles on, but I don't catch what she says after that, because I'm falling to pieces with gratitude. Adding those features to my employment status will cost him another small fortune. My heart is near bursting to think he listened to my problem and thought enough of me to find and activate a solution.

The next week flies by as the plans for this dinner party undergo a dozen revisions. I get the impression that this dinner is special, and for some reason, neither Kent nor Mrs. Farthing is willing to divulge why. Kent wants me to cook and serve all the food. He'll select the wines and serve them during the dinner, a different wine for each course.

We decide to run a trial a few days before. He chose the best china and classic table settings, which signified to me how much he wants to impress his guests. I set out all the dishes, silverware, and glasses to see how much room the table will allow. Kent reviews the setup and the seating chart with me. Just one day before the guests arrive, he gives me the thumbs-up, and everything is a go.

THE MENTOR

THE GUESTS ARRIVE AS scheduled. Kent plays the suave, charming host as usual, greeting each of them at the door. It isn't a concert night, but he's in navy blue pants, a crisp white shirt, and a plaid bow tie.

I'm dressed in black pants and a white peplum blouse cinched with a thin black belt. Ballet flats finish my attire. I station myself behind him, ready to take coats and drink orders. I keep an eye on the charcuterie board on the coffee table in the living room. As we wait for one last guest, I check my detailed list, making sure everything is set and ready to go either on the table or into the oven when the proper time comes.

Previous weeks of planning and serving Kent's informal guests, family, and friends do little to stem my willies. Tonight's celebrity dinner guests are special, participants in the last symphony event of the spring season. I get the chills every time I look beyond the kitchen doorway. Of the celebrity guests, tonight's group includes Franco Cartoni, the seventy-year-old conductor of the Venetian Opera Symphony; Andrew Peal, the twenty-four-year-old violin virtuoso; and three members of Honeyed Meade, an a capella Irish ballad group from Dublin. One guest, the beautiful diva Antonia Resnic, a mezzo-soprano from Brazil, is yet to arrive.

For the first time since the first football party, butterflies bound around my stomach. I'm waiting for the signal from Kent to start.

By a quarter to eight, Miss Resnic still hasn't arrived. Kent pops his head into the kitchen, "Call the livery service. Make sure they went to pick her up."

I call the service and inquire. Upon questioning, the driver reports that he waited over an hour after ringing her room, but no one answered. Going further, I call the hotel manager. She informs me that Miss Resnic left the hotel in the company of a man hours ago, their destination unknown.

I signal Kent to the kitchen door and relay the information.

Kent nods and directs his guests to the dining table, where everyone takes their seats at their name cards. When all are seated, Kent gestures to the unoccupied extra place setting and announces, "It seems Miss Resnic will not be joining us this evening." In unison, everyone turns to the empty chair and then to me as I enter with the soup tureen.

"Well, we must not let this empty chair go to waste, perhaps this beautiful young lady will join us, especially since she'll be sitting beside me," says Franco Cartoni with a sparkling, mischievous smile.

Caitriona adds, "Aye, we shouldn't eat in an odd-numbered party. It's bad luck."

I stop ladling soup into bowls, staring at Kent, who is speechless for a few seconds, staring back at me, and then over at Franco. Franco's smile broadens as he watches the unspoken words pass between us.

Finally, Kent says, "Yes, Abigail, if you can join us, please do sit down and round out our dinner party to an even number."

"Certainly, Mr. Grant." After ladling myself a bowl, I sit in the empty chair between Franco Cartoni and Mauren Smyth from Honeyed Meade.

Everyone begins eating while I glance around the table, careful not to make eye contact with anyone. They are content for the moment between the soup and hot dinner rolls. My bowl remains untouched as I try to figure out how to serve and eat the entire meal. Everything else, including the salad, pasta, and Osso Buco, is prepared and ready to go.

I feel Kent's eyes upon me and look up to meet them down at the head of the table. He gives me a subtle wink and nod, then turns to Riley O'Sullivan on his right with a question. Franco Cartoni leans toward me and whispers, "My compliments to the chef, this kale soup is outstanding! Antonia will be sorry she missed out on this Portuguese favorite!"

With the warmth of a blush on my face, I smile. "Thank you, Maestro Cartoni. I am so pleased you are enjoying it." I reach for my wineglass, take a demure sip instead of the hearty swig I desire, and set it down. Kent's eyes meet mine across the length of the table again as the soup course continues in gentle, congenial conversation.

The remainder of the meal goes smoother than I could have predicted. Kent rises and assists me, joking with his guests as he smoothly removes bowls. The next course is a salad, followed by the pasta course. The unending supply of wine boosts the guests' spirits. Everyone eats with gusto and without complaints. With the most difficult part of the meal over, the tension in my body eases. The main course, Osso Bucco, is served with a side of steamed broccoli topped with shaved parmesan cheese and a splash of lemon juice. Laughter and animated discussions erupt around the table, and everyone is talking and acting like old high school friends.

After clearing away the entrée dishes, I pass around the cheese platter in the French fashion before serving the final course. Dessert is a simple caramelized Pear Tarte Tatin served as much for its lightness as for its rustic visual impact.

At last, I serve the tea and coffee, as Kent, to everyone's delight, passes around Italian liqueurs. Somehow, it ends up being a successful meal, despite my constant ups and downs at the table, serving and then sitting beside Franco Cartoni to partake of each course. He proves a delightful dinner companion, as does Mauren Smyth of Honeyed Meade on my other side. The two regale me with funny, off-kilter moments from their previous concerts.

The night has been a refreshing way to enjoy the food and conversation of the evening's dinner, rather than eavesdropping from the kitchen door.

I clear the last of the dishes away from the table as the guests move to the living room. Not long after, they move to the music room for some playful banter at the piano, started by a continually energetic Cartoni.

I hum along with the show tunes they sing while washing the pots and pans. With the dishes stowed away in the dishwasher, I try to slide out of sight up the stairs to my room, but I hear my name being called.

Franco Cartoni stops playing mid-song at his perch on the piano bench and calls out, "Miss Abigail! At last you grace us with your presence again! Now our celebration is complete! Come, come, here, sit beside me, tell me you know how to read music and turn pages."

All eyes land on me. I am caught, slightly disheveled and fatigued from the evening's wines, food, and entertainment. Not to mention the hours of preparation that went into it before the guests arrived.

I seek Kent's eyes. He waves me in, indicating his acceptance of his guest's requests.

"Thank you." I smile first at Kent and then more broadly at Mr. Cartoni and settle on the piano bench beside him. "Of course I can read music. It was a prerequisite of the job here with Maestro Grant!" Everyone laughs heartily at my quip, including Kent. I wonder if he remembers our little repartee about that subject during my interview.

We all sing and play for nearly an hour. When the clock chimes eleven, we break off the merriment for a good night's sleep. I call for the livery cars as they bid adieu to Kent.

The last to leave is Mr. Cartoni, who makes a special effort to thank me for a delicious and enchanting evening. While standing a half step behind Kent, Mr. Cartoni adds, "You've got a great girl here, Maestro, don't lose her."

A hot blush creeps over my face while Kent stammers, "I have no intentions of losing her." Maestro Cartoni gives me a kiss on each cheek before descending the steps to the waiting town car with Kent by his side. The two chat for a few more minutes before Kent retreats up the steps as the car pulls away.

After closing the door, Kent grasps my right forearm. "Wait," he says. I stop and turn back to him, finding myself inches from his chest. "Thank you for what you did tonight. It was above and beyond what we agreed upon. I want you to know how much I appreciate it."

I smile tiredly. "It was fun in a way to get to know them as normal people. Instead of their talented celebrity persona."

"Yes. They are all jolly good, normal people. Maestro Cartoni was my mentor when I started out. At the time, he was with the National Symphony. I love him dearly, so I am exceedingly pleased that you were so kind to him tonight. He is one of my dearest friends. And unfortunately, very sick."

I'm struck speechless momentarily, glaring at Kent's grime expression. "Very sick? Oh dear, will he be all right?"

"No, I'm afraid not, but at least he enjoyed the time he spent here tonight. That's all I can ask. Thank you for giving him and me, one last great memory." Kent slips his arm around my waist, pulling me gently to him. I let him pull me close, my pulse thundering against my chest. His gaze bores into mine in silence.

Is he going to kiss me? Butterflies swarm in my belly, though he doesn't move. Finally, he kisses my cheek before letting go and walking in the direction of the music room.

Stunned, I can't say anything. I walk back to the kitchen to start the dishwasher, still feeling the heat of Kent's arm around my waist, the warmth that burned between our chests, and the softness of his lips on my flushed cheek. I cup my cheek, hoping to keep that feeling there as I go off to my room.

THE WALK HOME

THE CONCERT FEATURING all of last night's dinner participants is this evening, and I attend, sitting in the balcony. Before the curtain goes up, an usher delivers a message from Kent.

I don't anticipate bringing anyone to the house after the show. I will be going out. Don't wait up. Whatever I might need I can get myself. Thanks. K

I release a sigh of relief despite the mild sense of disappointment at not seeing Maestro Cartoni again. Spending another few hours with Kent and Mr. Cartoni would have capped a pleasant evening. Perhaps they will spend a little more time together before Franco returns to Venice.

The program is sensational, certainly the best of the season, and definitely worthy of the season finale. No more dinners until the fall season, at least none directly related to the concert series. Kent is no social slouch and likes to entertain, often doing so casually with friends.

After the performance, I decide to stroll in the crisp evening air, enjoying the solitude. A measure of melancholy slowly envelopes me as I try to view the stars. It is impossible in such a large city with all its light pollution. I remember sitting in the perfectly dark yard in Crabtree while star gazing. With that memory, the loss of my home, and all the wonderous times there, floods me like a tsunami. In seconds, the memory of everything I lost presses down on me. Silent tears slide down my cheeks as the ache I have worked so hard to tamp down explodes from my chest. I stop walking when I can't see the sidewalk beneath my feet through the stream of tears blinding my vision.

"Are you all right?"

His words startle me. I wasn't aware he had followed me. A stupid mistake this late at night, even in this good section of the city.

But I know that voice, even if it holds a softness I haven't experienced before. It's Kent.

I stop and turn around. "I'll be fine, thanks. What are you doing here? I thought you were going out."

He rubs his hands together as if they are cold on this rather warm May evening. "I saw Franco off to his hotel. He wasn't feeling well, so I decided to walk home." He cocks his head questioningly. "Why are you crying?"

I sniffle again. "I was just thinking about some things that always make me sad." I try to put a brave smile on my face while wiping away my tears with the backs of my hands.

"Is there anything I can do?" Kent asks, offering the crook of his arm to continue the walk.

I slip my arm through his. "No. These are old tears revisiting from a past life, long gone."

"Ah, past lives...creeping up on you in the dark. They do that to me too." His smile falters.

"Yup, on a beautiful night no less. There should be a law..." I try to lighten the conversation with humor.

Kent stops, taking both my hands in his. "I know I'm a relative stranger despite the fact that we've been living under the same roof for nearly half a year now, but I want you to know I care. And you can tell me anything if you think it will help."

I look into blue-green eyes so full of concern. There's an overwhelming urge to tell him the truth, tell him the whole story. Fall into the warmth of his soft eyes and the embrace I know he can provide. I don't need to be strong around him. His very presence makes me feel...safe. Yet the private, solitary woman in me feels it's almost too personal to share, especially with someone who, no matter how concerned, is my employer. I stare at my feet, gently pulling my hands out from his, and continue to walk on. Kent matches my stride in silence. Maybe it will be easier to explain if I don't see his response.

"Some of this you know. Before I moved here to Baymont, I lived in Crabtree. My husband and I spent five years there...the happiest of my life. We had four acres of quiet, undisturbed land with all kinds of wildlife. Kendall, my dog, was like my child." I stop, glancing over to look Kent in the eye. "And then my husband's cancer was found."

Kent blinks rapidly several times but remains silent.

"We both lost our jobs during his treatments, which were astronomically expensive without health insurance. My husband died one year ago in February. It was expected after his long battle with acute myeloid leukemia." Tears spill down my face again.

"You sold the house recently. Why was that?"

"Brannon was a self-employed accountant. He didn't earn enough money to afford great health insurance. We never dreamed he'd end up with the most fatal type of leukemia. Between the chemo and stem-cell transplant, we were wiped out financially. He couldn't work, so the business folded. I took care of him. Without an income, everything of value had to be sold to pay for his treatments. In the end, it wasn't enough. A medical lien was placed on the house before his death." I shrug, closing my eyes to the bitter memories of our struggle. "I was trying to pay it off by renting it out, at first. But it wasn't fast enough for the hospital. I had to sell it."

"How did you end up in Baymont? Was it work?"

"I came to Baymont looking for work after Brannon died. Work that would give me health insurance and a change of scenery. A chance to get beyond the grief. Sometimes now, I actually forget for a whole day that I had that other life, and all those good but painful memories it brings."

I try to turn away as my emotional restraint slips further. I openly sob with the heartache of my lost loves and the years we would never have together. Kent catches my arm and gently wraps his arms around me and holds me. I relinquish my control and sink against him, letting the firm strength of his arms hold me upright. It's sweet security in his arms, and I mold myself against his broad chest.

Minutes later, when my tears have subsided, I'm pressed tightly against his muscular body, held protectively. My head on his chest, my sobs lessen. Quiet enough to hear his heart beating beneath my ear. As more of my senses leave the black pit of despair, I notice his hand gently stroking my hair, slowing and then stopping as my weeping ends. Both his arms are around my waist, holding me secure to his torso.

I revel in the sturdiness. Behind his intense exterior lies a tenderness so deep and comforting that I don't want to move. This man, who says little, who is maligned by some for his portrayed arrogance, is the kindest, most generous person I have ever known.

"I'm so sorry you had to go through all that," Kent whispers.

"Me too," I whisper, pulling away a fraction of an inch and meeting his eyes, feeling myself lost in the depths of those blue-green orbs. The memory of his soft lips on my cheek after the dinner has me yearning for another. Danger sirens blare in my head. It is time to put some distance between us.

I pull out of his arms, resuming our walk home. Turning onto Newfane from Ackerman Avenue, we walk on without speaking, side by side, the rest of the way to Kent's townhouse. Once inside the door, we drift to our respective rooms in silent contemplation.

THE FUNERAL

A WEEK LATER, KENT comes down to breakfast on Monday morning, his shoulders tense, his face set in a sort of sad scowl. This unusual demeanor rattles my senses alert. Not knowing what else to do, I wish him a good morning and set his coffee mug on the table beside the newspaper.

"No, it's not," he curtly replies, his voice hard as flint.

It isn't like him to reply so harshly. Not anymore. Whatever affects him must be serious. "I'm sorry. Is there anything I can do to change that?" I spoon the flaxseed and fresh blueberry fortified oatmeal into his bowl.

He reaches for the pitcher of maple syrup, pouring a generous amount of the dark amber liquid atop his hot cereal. "No."

I sit down across from him, my own oatmeal before me. I wait to see if he decides to tell me whatever has upset him.

His shoulders sag. "I received some bad news this morning."

I stare at him, wondering if he is going to share the information with me or not. He hasn't picked up the newspaper to browse the contents as he does every morning. Something is seriously wrong. The creases in his forehead deepen, and the sudden glint of tears in his eyes accelerates my rising anxiety.

"What's happened?" My stomach churns that it has something to do with his mother and her breast cancer.

"Maestro Franco Cartoni died in his sleep last night." He scoops up a spoonful of oatmeal and brings it halfway to his lips. The spoon falls back into his bowl with a clatter. "Sorry, I don't have much of an appetite this morning."

"Maestro Cartoni?" No wonder he is distraught. Franco Cartoni has been a special part of his career, his life. Heck, in the short time I got to know him during the dinner party, he wiggled his way into my heart too. "I'm so sorry," I whisper and reflexively place my hand over his.

His fingers intertwine with mine and hold on tight. He clears his throat. "Well, we knew it was coming." He throws his napkin down beside his cooling oatmeal. "I just—I—" He swallows hard, his Adam's apple bobbing several times before he steels his composure. "I didn't think it would happen so fast."

"I didn't either." I blink rapidly, trying like mad to keep my tears at bay. "Will you go to the services? In Italy, I suppose?"

"I hope to. It depends on what events are happening here. We're getting ready for the Sutton Lake concert series. I'll ask Evelyn to see what arrangements we can make."

I nod, watching him stir the congealed oatmeal around his bowl. "Would you like me to warm it up in the microwave?" As much as I'd like to, there isn't much more I can do for him.

"No thanks. I'm done." He leaves the room.

Mrs. Farthing calls hours later. "I'm wondering if you're going with Kent to Venice. He said you might want to go with him to Maestro Cartoni's funeral. He leaves Friday evening, returning late Sunday night."

Her question surprises me. Is this Kent's way of asking if I would go with him for emotional support? Or is he being kind, knowing I became fond of the man? Kent's thoughtfulness warms my heart. "Do you have to know this minute?"

She sighs. "Yes," she says, drawing out the S like a hissing snake. "I'm in the midst of making hotel and flight reservations. Maestro Grant told me to charge your room and airfare to his personal credit card if you want to go."

Her words make me pause longer. He recognizes the cost will be prohibitive for me at this stage of my financial recovery. Venice in late May can't be cheap. Taking Kent up on his offer causes a shift in my mentality, like the shift of tectonic plates during an earthquake.

The part lifting higher than the other says, don't go, no matter how much you'd like to see Venice. How could I ever pay him back for such an expense? Do I want to feel beholden to him for however long it would take to pay off yet another debt? "No, I won't be going to Venice with him."

I know my words are rather curt. I certainly don't intend them to be rude. Already, I hope Mrs. Farthing doesn't repeat my words to him. I don't want him to get the wrong impression. Because I would love to go with him. Aside from the cost issue, it just doesn't seem appropriate on an employer-to-employee basis, especially if it involves a financial debt between us.

"Okay," Mrs. Farthing says and disconnects the call, leaving me mulling over my response in dead air.

That evening, Kent seeks me out in my room. He's beside the open door and knocks on the doorframe. "May I have a word?"

I lower the book I'm reading in the overstuffed chintz-covered armchair beside the living room window, Glee snoozing, curled up in my lap. "Sure, what's up?" My spine tightens. I'm not sure what he's going to say. I can only guess this has something to do with declining the trip to the funeral.

He approaches but stops an arm's distance away.

The tension I can see in his shoulders and the tightness of his jaw warn me he is uncomfortable or angry about something.

"I'm disappointed to hear you don't want to join me at Franco's funeral," he says while stuffing both hands in his pants pockets. He rocks up on the balls of his feet and then down again. "Did the offer make you uncomfortable?"

"It did. It's only for a few days." I avoid saying the word *nights*, which would make it sound almost salacious. "That's a lot of traveling. I don't think I'm up to it." I position a bookmark in the book and place it on the side table. I gesture toward my lap. "Besides, someone should stay here with Glee."

He nods, scratching the back of his head uncharacteristically. "As long as it wasn't, or doesn't seem—" He stops trying to explain and simply frowns, his brows knit together.

I understand what he's trying to suggest. "No," I interject. "Perhaps next time, if the trip is longer."

He's visibly relieved. Rubbing his palms together, he says, "Well, okay then." He doesn't move. He's watching me. For what I don't know. "What are you reading?"

My brain freezes. I don't want to name the book or tell him it's a steamy romance. "A historical romance set in Regency era London."

He raises his eyebrows. "Huh. I didn't know you read those types of books."

"I read pretty much everything except horror novels. But literary fiction and historical romance are my favorites."

He presses his lips together and nods. "Good to know."

Over the next four days, I work with Kent to get him packed for the trip. Luckily, Maestro Cartoni's family realized how much the music community revered him and delayed his funeral so that anyone could make plans to attend. On Friday evening, the livery service takes Kent to the airport, leaving me in a silent house until his return.

I keep busy working in the garden over the weekend, following the plans Kent approved. With it being the first days of June, things begin to really come to life in the garden. Now, it's easier to recognize plants that were too withered to identify during the winter months. Allium, irises, and peonies spring up, surprising me with their variety of colors. I update my original garden map and inventory and check the new garden plan to see what changes might need to be made. My bones and muscles ache from the gardening workout, ensuring I pass out with exhaustion each night and sleep deeply.

The workmen come to install the water feature in the back corner of the fencing. The solar-powered spout gives off a soft, soothing gurgle. It doesn't take long for the birds to find it. Kent has yet to decide whether he wants it uninhabited or if he wants koi.

The garden bench is delivered and placed under the birch tree. After the delivery men leave, I decide to take a break.

Retrieving my book from my room, I sit in the dappled shade of the birch, the leaves creating a swishing sound overhead as the soft, fragrant breeze sweeps over the stockade fencing.

A notification comes to my phone that the front doorbell is ringing. Opening the app as I go to answer the door, I stop. The camera shows Cynthia at the door. Kent's ex-fiancée. Should I open the door to find out what she wants? Or just ignore the summons like I never heard the doorbell ring? I decide to talk to her through the cellphone speaker app to see what she wants. "Hello. How may I help you?"

"Well, someone *is* home after all," she slurs. "Who are you? I want to speak to Kent."

I don't want to identify myself as the housekeeper, especially to someone who might run off to the newspapers with the information. Ignoring her first question, I reply, "Mr. Grant is not home right now. Please contact his office at Symphony Hall to make an appointment. Have a good day," I say and click off the microphone. I watch her through the doorbell camera as she scowls and stamps her foot. I can hear her cursing and yelling, "You don't get to dismiss me, I insist on speaking with him."

Biting my lip, I hold to my plan. I don't answer her and watch for several minutes. She rages, then stomps back to the waiting cab and leaves. Only then do I breathe easier. The last thing I want is to be truthful with anyone who might use the information maliciously. Someone who might have an axe to grind on Kent's reputation.

I try to return to my book, but my mind keeps replaying the encounter. Thank God Kent had the doorbell camera and speaker installed and connected to the app. Opening the door to Cynthia might have created a huge problem. I can easily imagine her brushing past me into the house and refusing to leave until she saw Kent. Despite the fact that he is airborne between Rome and Venice by this time.

The incident is unsettling. A thousand questions arise about Kent's relationship with such a curse of a woman. How did it happen, and what did he ever see in her? And why is it I've spilled my past into Kent's lap, but he hasn't reciprocated? I set aside my book and start yanking up weeds in a portion of the garden. Pulling them up with such a ferocity that more soil than roots come flying out.

Later, Kent calls while I wait for my frozen dinner entrée to reheat in the microwave. "Hey, I made it." His voice sounds weak or tired. Is it the transatlantic connection, or has the travel worn him out? Perhaps it's both.

"Good. No problems with luggage and such?"

"No, surprisingly enough. I expected lost luggage after two plane changes, but everything arrived with me."

I consider whether to tell him about Cynthia's attempted visit or wait until he returns to the States. I opt for giving him advanced notice. "Your ex-fiancée, Cynthia, came by to speak with you. I didn't open the door but told her, via the speaker, to make an appointment through your office."

I can hear him sigh over the clicks and pops of the connection. "Yes, I heard. Mrs. Farthing emailed me, asking if I wanted to see her."

He says nothing more. No mention of whether he would see her or not. *Fine by me. Not my problem.* Even so, my skin tone must be a little green.

"I wish you had come with me," he murmurs.

My inhalation catches in my throat, and I start coughing. He'd wanted me to join him? Does he not like being alone? "Surely, there are other people you know who are also there for the funeral."

"Yes, I saw a bunch of them bellying up at the lobby bar. Perhaps I'll go down and join them for a bite to eat." He sighs. "Or maybe I'll order room service. I haven't decided yet."

The timer for the microwave oven beeps.

"What are you heating up?" he asks, his words soft, almost wistful.

"Fettuccini Alfredo with broccoli and chicken. It's a frozen entrée." I struggle to remove the container from the oven with the cellphone slipping between my ear and shoulder.

"I'm sure it's not nearly as good as your homemade."

Again, there is that tone that makes me think he's feeling homesick. "Well, I'm not up to doing dishes tonight. I worked hard in the garden all day."

His chuckle buoys my spirit. "You should be having a mini vacation while I'm gone."

My laughter joins his. "I should! As for cooking and such, yes, I am. But I'm steeling myself for the suitcase full of dirty laundry you'll bring me as a souvenir from Venice."

His laughter ebbs. "Is there something you'd like as a souvenir?"

There's no way I mentioned souvenirs to suggest I want or expect one. "Heavens, no. You won't have time, and I don't have any idea what I'd want." Before I can stop them, more words tumble out, "Just come home safely."

"Sounds like you care about me." His voice is soft again and a little like he's pleased or surprised.

"Of course I care about you." I bite back the rest of my statement. *That's part of my job as housekeeper...taking care of you.* I don't say the rest because I know my words are not entirely truthful. I do care for him. Far more than I should. The lines between us are blurring. It's getting confusing and scary, like walking blindfolded through a minefield. I don't want to step into something that can foul our relationship. The memory of it would stay between us long after, causing problems we never intended.

Kent returns on Sunday night after eight o'clock, the look on his handsome face showing a deep-seated weariness and a grief I'm familiar with. Losing someone who means a lot to you can break your heart.

"Welcome home," I greet him as he walks in the door. It's evident by his rumpled clothing that it's been a long flight and a similarly long extended weekend.

"Thanks. Good to be back." He leans over unexpectedly and kisses my cheek. It's an unconscious action that, frankly, feels so natural and normal, I barely register the impropriety.

I must have uttered something because he promptly realizes his error. We both freeze, and he sharply pulls away. "I...I'm sorry. That was uncalled for," he says, his voice shaking.

My hand covers the spot he kissed. "It's Okay." What else can I say? Should I do something? Call him out for crossing the line? And how can I do that when my first reactive thought was to take him in my arms, and turn my head until our lips met?

Fortunately for both of us, the livery driver lumbers up the steps with Kent's suitcase in hand. He glances between us as he sets it down and hands Kent his laptop case. Taking the case, Kent heads straight for his bedroom.

The driver looks at me and rolls his eyes. "Sorry about the bad timing."

I shut the door and re-arm the alarm system behind him as he leaves. He clearly realized something was happening between Kent and me. My hand cups my cheek again. I can still feel the softness of his lips on it, the sincere, if unconscious, emotion behind it. I dash away thoughts of what might have happened had the driver not interrupted us.

Kent returns as I head for the kitchen. "Are you hungry? Would you like something to eat?" I ask, not knowing what else I can offer.

He scrubs his palm over his face. "No. I think I'll wait until morning." He stares around the room, realizing Glee is weaving around his feet. Picking up the cat, he buries his nose into her soft fur and hugs her. She squirms, and he lets her down. "I'm going to bed."

Kent never leaves his room the rest of the night. Was he deliberately trying to put time and space between the incident? It doesn't matter. It's all I think about in the early morning hours when I should be sleeping.

THE SOUVENIR

I TREAT THE NEXT MORNING as any other. It being Monday, I assume Kent will be going to his office. A pot of coffee is ready and waiting for him. Everything is prepared for his breakfast request. Usually, it's oatmeal with all the fixings on Monday. All the newspapers since he's been away wait in a stack beside his placemat, should he wish to catch up on news he missed.

"Good morning," Kent says, entering the kitchen with a medium-sized bag in hand. He sits down as I place his mug of coffee on the table. The bag is set in the middle of his placemat. "Sit, please." He gestures with his index finger to reinforce his wishes.

The unexpected directive surprises me. He's never done so before, and I have no clue what's coming...not after last night's faux pas. I sit across from him and fold my hands around my coffee mug. He pulls a sturdy box out of the bag and holds it out to me. "For you. Careful, it's fragile." He grins, his eyes sparkling like a toddler's on Christmas morning.

"Oh!" I can't help but feel surprised and excited that he brought me a souvenir after all. Another thought flits through my mind. Embarrassment at the intimacy it alludes to. Heat rises up my neck, to my cheeks and ears. He's watching me intently, wiggling in his chair ever so slightly as if anxious or impatient for the unwrapping.

I open the eight-inch-long, five-inch-tall box. Inside, swaddled in bubble wrap, is a glass morning glory blossom. The robin's egg blue of the trumpet-shaped blossom and the green of the stem and vine it's attached to are a bright Kelly green, the colors matching a true living blossom. I hold it up. "My God, Kent. It's gorgeous! How did you know it's one of my favorite flowers?"

His smile is ear to ear. "You gave yourself away on the garden plan. You wrote 'morning glories along the fencing' on it and underlined the words 'morning glories' about five times. How could I not assume it's a favorite?"

I hold the blossom up to the light, admiring the beautiful, authentic-looking glass object. "I can't thank you enough. It's so lovely. I'm going to put it on my desk upstairs."

"Hurry back," he says. "I'm hungry."

I get up to do just that, but as I pass Kent, he reaches for my free hand. "It reminds me of you...beautiful, simple, and natural." He lets go of my hand and glances away as if he senses my embarrassment. Or did he see the flushing heat scorching my face again?

I don't know what to say, and prefer to run up the stairs to my room, where I can set down the glass sculpture and splash myself with cold water to ease my blushes. Did we cross a line during our time apart? Based on the three out-of-the-ordinary actions, the kiss and the present, and the statement he made, it feels like we're in unsettled and uncharted territory.

At dinner that night, Kent launches into a discussion about another fundraiser. He digs into the coq au vin I cooked in a crockpot all afternoon. Between forkfuls, he explains the situation, "Over the next two weeks, I have several evening symphony events at locations not far from Baymont. The livery will pick me up in the late afternoon and bring me home after the concert, much like it does now. It could be midnight or one a.m. before I'm home. I'll have Evelyn email you a list."

He continues eating, as I ask, "Do you want me to pack something? A change of clothes, maybe, so you can return in comfort? Or snacks or a meal you can eat when you arrive?"

"I'll change back into my street clothes. Evelyn is setting up restaurant reservations for the early staff. The musicians will have time to eat before being bused to the location." He sets down the fork dangling from his fingers. "There's also another fundraising event. At the Clairview Hotel, coming up on Sunday. I know it's technically your day off, but you really don't seem to leave." He cocks his head. "If you aren't busy, would you be so kind as to accompany me?"

There it is. Another event on Kent's arm. He's not calling it a date or a plus-one. He's tiptoeing around calling it anything but an accompaniment. The memory of being on his arm through the last event stirs the butterflies in my stomach. Their wings flap quickly, then slow into a guarded posture with one question. "Will your ex-fiancée be there?"

Kent's eyes narrow. "She could be. I'll ask Evelyn to check the guest list. Is that an issue? Will you still go if she attends?"

I want to say no, but I nod instead. However, her attendance will dictate what I wear. Cynthia's expensive couture means I need to find the most stunning evening gown I can afford and have my hair professionally done this time. Maybe even a stunning mani-pedi? Can I afford all that? "It might alter my attire. I'm assuming it's another formal wear event?" My voice hitches up and cracks.

Kent nods, smiling. Too broadly. He must be thinking it's a vanity thing.

I shake my head. "It's not vanity. I just want to look good enough to be on your arm."

"Hmm," he mutters, apparently not believing me. His smile erupts even wider. "If you need an outfit, let me know. I'm sure I can come up with money to cover the expenses."

"No, it's not that," I say, even though it is, kinda true. "It's..."

His voice turned husky and sexy, and he whispers conspiratorially, "Are you jealous of Cynthia? Because if that's the case, please know I don't think she can hold a candle to you."

Whoa. My lady parts zing into quivering awareness. The butterflies take flight like a swarm of bees on the queen. I swallow when I catch my breath and say, "If you're sure, I'll do it."

He gives me a wink. "One hundred percent sure."

A wink. His words, his actions, his demeanor are rather loose. I don't know what to make of them. This is not something I expect from someone who just came back from the funeral of a close mentor and friend. Between my wobbling knees, the butterflies, and this shift of status in our employer/employee relationship, I'm speechless. So, I do what I usually do when confronted with unexpected changes. I bury my head in the sand and ignore the blaring alarms.

For the rest of our meal, electricity sparks between us like a balloon on a sweater. Kent finishes eating, gives me a nod, his eyes sparkling in the kitchen light, and leaves the room.

I slump in my chair, fanning my face and various overheated body parts with my napkin. When every part of me has cooled down a little, I pick up my phone and call Clare. "I need your help. Again."

This fundraiser will be held in the Clairview Hotel's ballroom. Fortunately, Clare had been there on one occasion and knew its size, elegance, and beauty were beyond the Elliott Hotel's. Armed with that information, we go shopping, browsing all the haute couture shops but finding nothing I consider wearing. Time after time, Clare holds something up for my inspection.

"What about this gown?" she asks. For the hundredth time, she's showing me a gown that reveals far too much.

"No," I say firmly.

Clare takes a deep breath and releases it, letting her shoulders slump and the bottom of the gown drape on the floor. "Why not?"

"I have limits. No excessive displays of female parts I don't want to show off." What I don't tell her is that Brannon had very strict rules about what I could wear. Rules that still warp my choices.

"But you'll look stunning." She pouts, putting the hanger back on the rack.

"It's Kent's night to wow the crowd. I don't want to steal his limelight. I'm only his plus-one, not his date."

Clare rolls her eyes. "Sure. Tell yourself that." She adjusts her purse on her shoulder. "Let's try another tactic."

We poke around vintage stores. In a little shop that doesn't look very promising, we find my gown. It's exquisite, with an intricate, geometric, flowing beaded design that shimmers with every move. A sensual, asymmetrical neckline accentuates the décolletage, offering sophistication and allure without exposing too much cleavage. Cap sleeves cover my shoulders, overly tanned as they are from gardening. The full-length black skirt features similar beading and a knee-height side leg slit. I consider my legs my best feature, so the glimpse of leg boosts my confidence. The crystal beaded design runs from my left shoulder to my right foot, curving dramatically at my waist, giving a slimming effect. The gown fits me like a leotard.

I put the outfit on at Clare's house, and examine myself in a full-length mirror. I look stunning, even to my critical eye. This outfit gives me far more confidence than I had at the last fundraiser event. Clare loans me a pair of black satin gloves that reach above the elbow. With her black, sequined strapless heels, Art Deco-styled dangling crystal earrings, and her black, sequined handbag, I am prepared.

"Well, what do you think?" I only hope I haven't overshot the event's fanciness. It feels uncomfortable, like I still have too much skin showing. Brannon would never have let me out of the house in a clingy dress like this. A thrill runs through me as I look at myself in the mirror. I do look phenomenal. It's not too revealing for *my* taste.

"I think the gloves add that extra 'je ne sais quoi.' You look ravishing," Clare gushes.

Ravishing. The same word Malcolm Trier used to describe my appearance. Would he be at the party? Would I have to spend my night like a bobble-head doll, looking this way and that to avoid him *and* Cynthia?

After fully dressing on the night of the event, I grab my left ring finger to remove my wedding band before putting on the gloves. My eyes narrow when I realize it's not on my finger. Thinking back, I don't remember retrieving it from the stein on the mantel after the last fundraising event weeks ago. I'll have a look for it tomorrow. For now, I slip on the gloves, grab my purse, and head downstairs.

When I glide down the stairs to meet Kent in the living room, he stares at me, his mouth hanging open.

I cringe, instantly regretting the gown choice. "Too much?" I ask, my confidence wavering at his look.

He shakes his head vehemently. "Oh, no. You look absolutely divine. Don't change a thing. Except...hmm." He presses his lips together as if displeased about something.

My heart starts to plummet. "What is it?"

"It's the necklace thing again." He approaches me.

"The straight line of the gauzy fabric covering my collarbone doesn't really allow a necklace," I say. "It's better without something around my neck."

He raises his eyebrows in surprise and scrutinizes me. "I guess you're right. Let's go. The car is here."

CLAIRVIEW HOTEL

ON THE WAY TO THE HOTEL on Bond Street, Kent says, "I want you to be forewarned. Cynthia will be there as someone else's guest. She's a nasty piece of work, as I almost found out too late. Steer clear of her as best you can."

The trembling of my knees reverberates up through the rest of my body. Unlike last time, I know what she looks like. "I'll keep watch and walk away if she tries to lure me into conversation."

One corner of his lips lifting, Kent makes a hissing sound on an inhale. "It infuriates her to be ignored. I don't recommend that approach."

I never get a chance to ask what will work, other than staying home. Whatever bravado I experienced earlier rapidly evaporates.

"Ah, here we are." Kent scooches out of the back seat and holds out his hand to assist me. "Ready?" he whispers, as the cameras flash and Maestro Grant's female fans scream and call his name.

I don't feel ready. I attempt to twist my thinking, picturing my gown as a suit of armor. I'll have to stay on my toes and keep my radar locked on Cynthia's every movement. This time, she will not be allowed to invade my physical or emotional space.

The event's schedule is much like the last one: cocktails, dinner, speakers, then dancing. Kent introduces me to some of the same people as last time, and many new faces. Again, I try to ingrain the names and faces. One face I know by heart, and I cringe when he heads in our direction. Malcolm Trier saunters over, without his wife this time. Kent notices his approach as well. I can tell by his body stiffening even more than mine.

"Aah, Maestro, how are you this evening?" Without waiting for an answer, Malcolm leers at me, his eyes roaming my body. "Beautiful, dear. You are stunning this evening."

Clenching his teeth, Kent replies in a low, hard voice, "I'm fine."

Malcolm's gaze stays on the leg slit and the hint of exposed calf. "Good, good. It's an important night. A new batch of millionaires to seduce into writing large checks to the symphony." His fake smile breaks, and his face hardens as he shifts his glare to Kent. "Make it happen." He grasps my hand and kisses the back of it, leaving a slick spot where his tongue touched my glove. Gross. He gives me a wink before striding off to speak with someone else.

I glance at Kent. His face is full of thunder, his eyes piercing Malcolm's back like a dagger. "Bastard."

The word shocks me. I've never heard Kent swear. Certainly never to someone involved in the orchestra. Spotting an elderly woman approaching us, I say, "Let it go. Here comes another fan."

The lady introduces herself as Mrs. Matthews and begins picking Kent's brain about the next season. I know its planning is well underway, maybe even finished by now. Clueless, her talk turns into a lecture about what *she* wants to hear in the fall season. Kent stands still, focusing his eyes, if not his attention, on her, as if he's taking in all her suggestions. Her monologue ends with a not so subtle warning that the size of her donation check will be commensurate with the number of her suggestions in the fall season's lineup.

"I'm sorry to hear that, Mrs. Matthews. I wish you had addressed your suggestions much earlier, like last fall. The next season's lineup has been finalized, and all the contracts have been signed already." He nods at her. "But I will make sure your suggestions are discussed for the following spring. Will that do?" He gives her a courteous smile as he presses his hand into my back to steer me toward Mrs. Farthing.

"Insufferable." His thunderous expression returns, but only momentarily, as a man approaches. "Ah, Gabriel, thanks for coming," he says, holding out his hand.

The man shakes Kent's hand and turns to me. "Good evening." His eyes sparkle, and a loose curl of hair falls over his forehead, giving him a rakish look.

"Abigail Davitt, this is the new concertmaster, Gabriel Carvello."

My gaze shifts to Kent, my eyebrows shooting higher. He never mentioned that Haruka Satō was no longer concertmaster. Did she leave voluntarily, or was she pushed? Not that it matters. It's better for Kent to have a new concertmaster after the hard feelings Miss Satō harbored against him. "A pleasure to meet you," I respond with a friendly smile.

The emcee at the microphone interrupts the cocktail hour and asks everyone to be seated.

Mrs. Farthing guides us to our table, where name cards indicate that Kent is seated across from me. Dread rips through my gut when I see Malcolm will be sitting to my left. Instinct tells me to switch Malcolm's name card with Kent's. Starting to reach for it, I hear Malcolm's voice over my shoulder. "Are you going to deny me the pleasure of getting to know you better? I was so looking forward to having a nice conversation with you."

I turn and study his face. It looks pleasant, but the undercurrent of his words suggests his designs are likely something sinister. "I thought you'd rather sit beside Maestro Grant. I'm sure there are many things you two can discuss. He's the man of the hour, after all, isn't he?" I raise my brows as I watch Malcolm's countenance switch to anger.

"He and I have had our discussions. We understand each other perfectly." He pulls out his chair, slides it a couple of inches closer to mine, and sits down, angling his body toward me. I follow his glance to Kent across the table. Kent's face is full of fury. His body tenser than I've ever seen it. Something is going on here that goes far beyond the seating arrangement.

A waiter arrives and begins distributing plates of salad. I push the endive leaves, grapes, feta, and red onion slivers around my plate, every so often glancing at Kent to see if his mood is better. He politely chats with another elderly woman, who captures his right arm as she blabbers away. Kent's tension escalates again. It's his conducting arm. The one Mrs. Farthing said is insured for a couple of million dollars.

As the salad plates are exchanged for dinner plates with filet mignon and steamed green beans, Kent removes the woman's hand from his arm and cups it between his hands. The gesture silences her, and a coy smile grows on her face. I can't hear what he says to her, but she happily focuses on her plate. Kent glances at me, an expression of relief on his face.

It is then that I feel Malcolm's knee rest against mine. My face must have telegraphed that something is wrong, because Kent's eyes narrow and his jaw tightens.

I move my leg away from Malcolm's. He presses again. My fist clutches my steak knife as I cut into the medium rare beef. I cut a small piece and set it in my mouth, my eyes never leaving Kent's dangerous expression. As I chew, Malcolm makes another move I anticipated.

"Miss," the waiter says, "Is that filet too rare for you?"

I look at the meat and the pool of bright red juices around it. It's definitely rarer than medium. "It's fine, thank you for asking." I give the waiter a smile and a nod, and he walks away.

Malcolm's right hand alights on my left thigh. I blink rapidly, trying to signal to Kent that something is terribly wrong. His scowling attention diverts to Malcolm's face.

If Kent does something to Malcolm, the president of the symphony's board of directors, it could cost him his job. *I* must stop the unwanted physical contact myself.

I turn toward Malcolm, my steak knife pointed forward, the blade bloodied from my rare steak. I push it forward ever so slightly as I pull my leg away, but his grip becomes harder. "I must have gotten the sharpest knife in the drawer. Why, I think it could even cut a bone in two with one swipe," I say to Malcolm, as softly as I can so no one else can hear.

He meets my stare. His leering smile melts away, and the color washes out of Malcolm's face as he notices the closeness of my knife. His hand instantly leaves my thigh. Bringing his napkin to his lips, he holds it there, his eyes wildly racing around the room.

I give Kent a smile filled with relief. He lets out an audible breath and nods.

Malcolm stands up abruptly. "I believe I left my speech notes in my coat pocket." It's a lie, of course. The temperature outside is over seventy degrees. He wouldn't have worn a coat tonight. He leaves, heading for the men's room and never returns to finish his meal.

When dinner service ends, Kent takes Malcolm's seat. He draws close to my ear, his jaw tight. "Did he grab you under the table?" he whispers.

"He put his hand on my upper thigh. I showed him my steak knife and told him it was sharp enough to cut a bone in two."

Kent's eyes widen before he throws back his head and roars with laughter, drawing the attention of everyone within twenty feet of us...including Malcolm. Kent's outburst sparks a warm glow in me. He wants to protect me. While I am grateful for any help, should it be needed again, a burst of pride in handling it all by myself has me sitting taller.

When he collects himself, his face darkens. Kent whispers, "I'll get that bastard. How dare he?" The menace in his eyes sends a shiver down my spine. If Kent is as angry as I think, Malcolm had better watch his step.

The emcee begins the presentations after dessert is served. Same as last time, Malcolm is first. His hands tremble as he holds his notes, the top edge of the paper jerking. His words are jumbled and unintelligible, and his voice cracks often. Whispers start around the room. Sitting beside me, Kent's tension eases. "He really took your threat to heart," he mumbles. "Good."

As everyone watches, the emcee cuts off Malcolm's presentation and escorts him from the stage.

"I guess so." I didn't think he'd been that shaken by my words, though he certainly took them for gospel. One weight pressing on my shoulders lifts. Chances are good he'll never touch me again. Such a pervert, and to behave like that in a room full of three hundred and fifty people. It's unfathomable how some men feel able to get away with that kind of behavior. I hope he remembers how that bloody steak knife looked for the rest of his life.

The audience's applause draws me back to the moment. It's Kent's turn at the microphone. He barrels up to the stage and pulls an index card from his inside jacket pocket. He thanks everyone for being here and launches into a description of how their donations help the symphony bring beautiful music to the city and beyond. Briefly, he discusses the upcoming European tour to five cities and how the reputation and presence of the Baymont Symphony bring pride to them all. When he finishes, the audience's strong and lengthy applause reverberates through the ballroom.

The CFO accepts the microphone from Kent as he leaves the stage and returns to sit beside me.

"Great speech," I whisper in his ear.

He shivers, gazing at me for a few seconds, then focuses his attention on the stage.

When the presentations are over, the band strikes up "Come Dance With Me," and couples crowd the dance floor. The jaunty tune makes my toes tap along to the beat. Despite what happened earlier with Malcolm, I'm not going to let it ruin this night.

Kent tenses beside me. His eyes roam the dance floor as though he is looking for someone. Cynthia? Or is something else wrong? I touch his shoulder, drawing his attention and hoping to break what appears to be a slow, angry simmer. Gathering some courage, I ask, "Dance?"

"I hope you don't mind, but I think we'd better leave." He stands up suddenly, grasps my hand, and pulls me along toward the trickle of people leaving.

"Maestro."

I hear the sultry tone of voice and know who it is without looking. Cynthia tracked us down and is making her move. No wonder Kent's body went rigid, and he wants to leave immediately.

Kent freezes mid-stride. "Cynthia. We're leaving. Save your barbs for next time." He glares at her as she juts out her leg from the hip-high slit in her Dior gown that shows off a considerable amount of skin.

"Never put off for another day what you can do today, my mother always said." She winks at him and juts her hip out saucily. "No time like the present."

"You and I are finished. You got what you deserved."

"That pre-nup didn't provide me with enough money after you broke our engagement. I'm almost destitute," she whines. It's ludicrous that someone who claims to be destitute is wearing such an expensive evening gown.

"That's too bad, Cyn. Maybe you should have waited until after the 'I dos' to have an affair with Malcolm."

She shrugs. "Who knew you were bright enough to notice before the wedding?"

My sharp intake of breath is audible. Her betrayal was the cause of their breakup.

Kent's hand slips to my lower back, and he presses into it hard. We stride toward the exit. Her shrieking laughter echoes behind us over the music.

Our ride back to the townhouse is in silence. It all makes sense to me now. Malcolm had an affair with Cynthia before she married

Kent. Now, Malcolm is attempting to get at me. No wonder Kent can barely contain his fury when Malcolm is around. Especially after his behavior tonight. How does Kent manage to work under the man?

Once inside, Kent goes straight to the bourbon decanter in the living room, unstoppers the bottle, and pours himself a hefty dose. "Would you like one?"

I nod and settle on the couch, peeling off the satin gloves. Kent hands me the glass and sits beside me.

"So, now you know that backstory." He takes a long sip of the amber liquid. "At first, I was so angry with the man. Of course, it wasn't entirely his fault. Cynthia accepted his advances." He rests his head on the back of the couch. "It's taken me a while to see he did me a favor by exposing her true nature. He freed me from a terrible marriage before I recognized it as such."

My heart aches for him. Clearly, he has not come to peaceful terms with his breakup any more than I have come to terms with my loss.

His hand rests on the cushion between us. I put mine over his and say, "I know, sometimes a painful turn of events changes your thinking. Wakes you up to the reality you couldn't see beforehand."

That's when it hit me square between my ears. I nearly reel from the revelation. My hand shakes as I take a good, long sip from my glass. My face must have paled because Kent grasps my hand firmly.

"Are you okay?" He raises my hand and kisses the back of it.

The feel of his lips on my skin sends sparks igniting in the periphery of my vision. A queasiness makes me choke back a reply.

Whispering, Kent asks, "Did that happen to you too?"

"Sort of." I don't meet his eyes, watching him intertwine his fingers through mine. "I—I thought Brannon was my world. He was for a long time. I was happy. Then...so incrementally, I didn't even notice, his behavior changed. I had been working out, trying to get fitter through yoga and walking. I lost twenty pounds. I felt better, moved more easily, and my mood improved. Next thing I know, he was driving me everywhere as my chauffeur. It didn't matter where I was going, he'd drive me. He even started dropping me off and picking me up from work. I couldn't go anywhere without him. When I tried to meet friends for dinner or a movie, he accused me of cheating on him. He thought I was having an affair. It took a long time to recognize all the changes...recognize that he was controlling me. When he got sick, I felt guilty for thinking that, and he became my entire focus.

I close my eyes, the images of the past flipping through my mind like a slide show. "I confronted him about his accusations. He promised he'd change. Be better, build the business back. Get back everything we'd lost." I cradle my head in my hands, my fingers sinking into my hair. I inhale slowly and exhale. "I promised to stay with him. Help him get well again. He—he didn't make it."

I stare at Kent before turning away. "I truly was grieving. The loss of all our hopes and dreams, and our second chance. Over time, I realized I was set free by his death, and then I felt guilty for even thinking that. Losing everything gave me a second chance. It still feels traitorous to be free."

When I look back at Kent, I find him staring at me. "I'm not saying I'm happy he died. I'm saying I regret the time we didn't get. But I'm thankful for another chance at life." *And maybe love,* I finish in the silence of my heart.

I down the remaining bourbon, and stand up. "Goodnight."

• • • •

I WATCH ABIGAIL CLIMB the stairs to her room, my thoughts and feelings jumbled. She truly is a good person, and I understand her guilt. I've dealt with guilt as well. Cynthia blamed me for her infidelity, saying I was distant, always thinking of my career or the symphony. I admit it did consume me and still does. Cynthia also increased her own efforts to ingratiate herself with the local in-crowd. She loved the attention, the more the better. When money wasn't enough, she aligned herself with powerful people. Especially Malcolm, who had both power and a great deal of money. She knew he controlled my purse strings. Were her actions designed to get him to give me a larger salary? I'll never know.

Was she really going to marry me? I don't think so, unless she intended to divorce me later after a respectable amount of time, and collect a sizable alimony. But Malcolm foiled her plans, making odd comments about her. Making it clear, when all of the comments were put together, that something intimate was going on between them. When I caught them, literally walked in on them having sex in our bedroom, well, there was no explaining that away.

I gulp the last of my bourbon and contemplate having another. But my stomach is already churning, whether from the alcohol or the memories, I can't say. I double-check the alarm, shut off the lights, and tread the steps to my bedroom. But sleep doesn't come while recognition dawns that Abigail and I are emotionally free of our pasts. I'm not sure she realized it during her explanation, but her right hand kept going to her left ring finger. The one no longer sporting a wedding band.

Perhaps the attraction I feel for her is worth exploring.

SUTTON LAKE

SUMMERTIME IS EASIER for me, but it involves a more challenging schedule for Kent. The Summer Breezes Series of concerts takes place at an equally punishing clip for a smaller subgroup of the orchestra. The series is set in an outdoor amphitheater, located two and a half hours outside the city limits, in the resort town of Sutton Lake. Kent says he owns a lakeside condo and stays there when back-to-back concerts are scheduled.

His absence from the townhouse pitches me into a melancholy mood. Glee and I spend a lot of time together, reading books I've checked out of the library and keeping up with the gardening in between the few household chores.

Over the next week, Kent pops in and out unannounced to pick up bundles of clean clothes, CDs, musical scores, and sporting equipment when he's in the office. Planning sessions for future seasons are always on the agenda. Some days, the disappearance of the pile of materials I collect for him and leave on the dining room table is the only way I know that he's stopped by.

It's a good time for cleaning too. With Kent out of the house, I can be more thorough and not worry about disturbing him as I work. While dusting a few days after the Clairview event, I retrieve my wedding band from the Colts stein on the mantel. Not wanting to remove my rubber gloves, I slip the ring into my jeans pocket before continuing my chore.

This is also the time to fine-tune the backyard garden. Much of the area is shaded more than I anticipated, so some plants need to be replaced with others that can tolerate less sun. In addition to consulting with the garden supplier, I spend my time researching various plants. Over the course of two weeks, I manage to create a comfortable, green, grassy woodland garden of native plants around the bench and pond for solitude and relaxation. It reminds me of the Connecticut woodlands surrounding my childhood home. The stream provides water sounds and attracts birds, wildlife, and a surprising number of dragonflies and amphibians. While it irks me that Kent hasn't noticed the transformation, I secretly enjoy the notion of having it all to myself. I flee to the shady oasis in late afternoons, after a day of cleaning or running errands. A glass of wine and the comfortable bench give me the respite and chance for reflection I desperately need after the chaos of the last few years.

My wedding band still resides in my jeans pocket. It digs into my flesh through the denim, not allowing me to forget its presence. Alone on the bench, I pull it out and roll it over in my hand. I start to put it on, but stop, remembering something. Putting it back on reminds me of the manacles in that dream I had weeks ago. It was Kent wearing them, but they were keeping me from him, and him from me. Just as this little circle of fourteen-carat gold is keeping me from him. It is the revelation I had during our conversation after the Clairview Hotel event. Putting it back on may cost me a future chance at love. I exhale sharply through my nose and slip it back into my pocket.

Kent finds me out there one late afternoon, asleep on a blanket as the day cooled and the light faded. His dark silhouette stands between me and the house door.

"Abigail? Are you all right?"

The sound of his voice instantly awakens me. I bolt up from the blanket. "Oh, thank God it's only you! Yes!" I brush nonexistent bits of grass from my shorts, trying to calm my racing heart. "You frightened me. I had no idea you were coming home today!"

Kent steps close enough to meet my eyes. His intense gaze silent and searching.

I stare back, my chest tightening. There is something unnerving in the power of his regard. "Do you need something?" I gather my feet beneath me to stand.

"Let me help you," Kent murmurs, grasping my elbow to pull me up. His touch is warm and pleasant. Flashing memories of the feel of his hand slipping around my waist catch me off guard. I stumble momentarily, but Kent steadies me. He guides me toward the back door and into the kitchen.

"Are you staying here tonight?" I ask. I've made no preparations for dinner since I wasn't expecting him.

"Yes, until tomorrow morning. I have a meeting with the board of directors at seven tonight," Kent says. "In the morning, I'll return to Sutton Lake for the evening's performance."

The meeting time is unusual. On the few occasions I've known about his meetings with the board, they've been during his workday. Something must have come up that requires their immediate attention.

I open the refrigerator, unable to think of what we could have for dinner together. My focus on food, I don't understand Kent's question. "What, I'm sorry, I didn't hear that."

Kent leans his shoulder against the kitchen doorframe, his hands in his pockets. "I asked if you wanted to come to Sutton Lake tomorrow for the performance. It's Debussy and Chopin. I thought you might like it. You could stay at the condo tomorrow night and return the following morning."

A strange warmth creeps from between my breasts and up my neck, exciting and yet foreboding. I have nothing official planned for the next forty-eight hours. Tomorrow is Friday and the start of a listless weekend of lackadaisical chores designed solely to keep me occupied. A day in the country, on the lake, would be a treat. An outdoor performance of Debussy and Chopin sounds like heaven.

Then I think about the condo. Kent described it as small, with only one bedroom and one bathroom. My knees get rubbery, and I sit down at the table. What exactly is he suggesting?

As if reading my mind, Kent says, "There's a sleeper sofa in the living room. I'll sleep there." His words come out soft and intimate, almost like a caress. "I'll bring you back the next morning. I have to be in the office the next day."

I look at Kent across the kitchen, calculating his casual manner and directness. The bobbing of his Adam's apple and the tick in his cheek suggest anxiety on his part. Does he have something up his sleeve? The thought that this is an attempt to romance me sends a tremor down my spine. My abdomen tightens.

If that is his intent, am I ready for an intimate relationship with him? Would it even be right? What if it doesn't work out? He's my boss, and this townhouse is my workplace as well as my home. Even if I am ready to enter another relationship, it's not the smart thing to do. Losing the security I've managed to find over the last six months as his housekeeper might break me. But the idea of a day away from the city heat with delightful music under the stars sounds too good to pass up.

Kent raises one eyebrow at me, his head tilting to the side, questioning.

"Yes. I'll go to the lake. I could use some Debussy."

"Good. Get your things together tonight. We'll leave first thing in the morning."

He starts from the room but glances back. "No need for you to cook tonight. We can get takeout. Your pick and my treat."

LAKESIDE DINNER

WE ARRIVE BY EARLY afternoon. Whatever transpired at Kent's meeting with the board last night left him in a smoldering mood. He is silent much of the trip, his thoughts clearly elsewhere as he drives. The tick in his cheek is back, alternating with a clenching of his teeth. Once at the condo, I get ready for tonight's concert. My dress's Kelly green print goes well with the reddish highlights in my hair. Finished inspecting myself in the mirror, I return to the living room to view the lake.

He calls it a condo, but it's actually a small cabin. The front door opens into the living room, while the galley kitchen is off to the left. Going farther into the back portion, there's the full bathroom and the bedroom. The right side of the living room features French doors that lead onto a spacious deck, complete with a small table, two chairs, and a lounge chair. Trees surrounding the cabin filter much of the sunlight into dappled shade.

Kent suggests I walk down to the lake by a short trail. He wants time to unload the bags of groceries he had specially delivered to the townhouse this morning. I'm unsure what all those groceries are for, since he told me he would be doing the cooking.

The mile-long lake's surface is placid, reflecting the freshly leafed-out trees and the rich blue, cloudless sky above. Only a few people have homes on the lakefront, and by agreement, they adhere to a no-motor policy. One boat carrying two figures with fishing poles bobs on the water at the far end of the lake.

The serenity eases the misgivings dancing in my gut. Even the lapping of the waves and the birdsong in the trees envelope me in peace and calm. Calm. I need to settle my nerves over being here alone with Kent for the next twenty hours. I close my eyes, breathe deeply, and silently chant my calming mantra. When my heart rate slows and my nerves relax, I head back to the condo.

The smells wafting from the kitchen dance all the way out to the deck that overlooks the lake. Kent hands me a glass of white wine, which I sniff appreciatively and sip.

"You should have let me cook," I say, not knowing what other topic would be more benign.

"Nonsense. I can cook. This is practically a one-pan meal." Clearly, it's Italian, from the smells of chicken, garlic, and pesto. I step out onto the deck. A subtle breeze kicked up while I was inside. It flutters the leaves, matching the fluttering in my stomach.

I break into a smile as I catch the sound of Kent humming while he bustles around the galley kitchen. Chopin's Nocturne opus 9, number 2, which I can only guess is on tonight's program.

He appears at the open doors, holding a tray with flatware and a baguette of French bread in hand. He sets the napkins, flatware, and cutting board holding the bread on the small patio table.

"Table for two, Mademoiselle?" he inquires playfully in a poor rendition of a French accent.

"Oui, Monsieur!" I reply, keeping the lighthearted play going. Gosh, he's in rare form tonight. *What's up?*

He pulls out the chair that gives me the best view of the lake. "Have a seat at the table, Mademoiselle, dinner will be served momentarily."

I pretend to hold aside a voluminous skirt so I can sit down. Kent tucks the edge of the chair underneath me and bows before sauntering back into the condo. The lighthearted humor of our banter and actions amuses me, easing the tension between us.

Kent re-emerges with two steaming plates and a bottle of wine tucked under his arm. As I watch, the bottle begins to slide out of the crook of his elbow. I jump up and snatch the bottle as it falls, preventing it from shattering on the deck.

"Merci, Mademoiselle," he exclaims, setting the plates on the table.

We both settle in. Kent tops off the wine and raises his glass in a toast, "To you!"

How could I hide my shock as my mouth drops open? Gathering my wits, I exclaim, "Me? Whatever for?"

He sets his glass on the table. "Yes, it's been nearly six months since you came into my life, and for that I am truly grateful," Kent replies, serious and intimate in a way I had never heard him. "I can't imagine what I did before you arrived. You are more than a housekeeper, a maid, a cook, or a party planner. You have become a cherished friend." Kent's voice is deeper than usual, filled with a tiny quiver of emotion. "Someone I can trust."

"I'm—so pleased." It's all I can stammer out before lapsing into silence. This is so out of the ordinary that it leaves me unsettled, almost wary. First, that he'd even remember the day I walked into his office for an interview. It wasn't the kind of thing an employer might celebrate. Men don't usually remember those kinds of things, do they?

Yet, *he* has remembered. What or how can I begin to tell Kent about my happiness at being with him as his housekeeper? It feels more like a partnership between an unmarried couple. At times, it's more emotionally intimate. Other times, the space between us vibrates with anticipation. Here on this deck, a late afternoon aura surrounding us, the air is heavy with unspoken feelings.

The corners of his smile fall ever so slightly as I agonize over what to say.

In desperation, and to prevent him from getting the wrong idea, I let loose a torrent. "I'm sorry, I'm speechless that you remembered! I really like working for you. Ah, I mean, um, this situation has worked out better than I had hoped for, and I'm so glad you and I are such good friends too." I blunder on, "I can't think where I'd be without you."

My eyes drop to the cooling and congealing chicken scampi with pasta. When I look up at Kent, he's holding his glass up as if waiting for me to clink the rim of mine with his. I raise my wineglass and meet Kent's halfway. "Thank you. Cheers."

He lets out a stuttered sigh as he replaces the glass in his hand with a fork.

"Time to eat up. I have an orchestra to conduct," Kent says quietly into the charged air between us. He's not meeting my eyes, and that's so unlike him.

Have I offended him? My heart sinks with the guilt of not expressing myself better. Of not sounding as grateful as I really am. *Of not telling him how I really feel about him.* There, I thought it. He is very special to me. Perhaps too special, and I don't dare express it.

Ignoring my internal wavering, Kent discusses the difficulties of tonight's performance, going through the pieces as if he is reviewing the score. I focus on his words, listening intently, amazed at the details in the music. It is fascinating to hear his precise inner thoughts on the piece. No doubt that is why he is such a great Maestro.

I say very little, not knowing what more to say, so I nod my understanding, even with descriptions that evade my comprehension.

When we are finished eating, he reaches for our plates and flatware to take to the kitchen.

"Please, leave it. I'll get this cleaned up. You go get ready."

He downs the last of his wine. "Okay, but don't overtax yourself tonight."

I clear the table as Kent puts on his tuxedo in the bedroom. The kitchen is in good order, as if Kent cleaned as he cooked. A good habit, I think, with a smile on my face.

I hear him clearing his throat behind me and spin around. Kent enters the kitchen fiddling with his bow tie. He looks amazing in his concert attire, even without his jacket. Since he usually gets ready for performances in his dressing room an hour before a concert, I rarely see him decked out in his finery up close. The cut of his tux is immaculately tailored for him. One of the many tuxedos he told me is available, some of varying fabric weights to match the seasonal temperatures for the Sutton Lake concert series.

"Do you have any experience with these? It doesn't seem to want to cooperate tonight," he murmurs, trying to look down at the fabric below his chin.

"Sure." I wipe my hands on a dish towel. We stand chin to forehead as I wrangle the cloth into position around Kent's neck. The scent of his aftershave fills the air between us. Citrusy, spicy, and so alluring, my focus moves from the bow tie to his lips. Then lower, to the tiny space, mere inches, between our chests. My knees go wobbly and heat flames at the apex of my thighs. Frustrated in more ways than one, I wrestle with the noncompliant fabric.

"Easy woman, don't strangle me!" Kent's voice cracks.

"Sorry," I mutter, unaware I've been so rough with the tie and my own unruly thoughts.

With a final smoothing of the ends, I step back. "There. All set," I throw over my shoulder as I put my back and more distance between us. Kent goes to check his reflection in the full-length bathroom mirror while I head to the bedroom for my shawl. As we emerge simultaneously into the hallway, the doorbell rings. The livery car is here.

"Are you ready?" Kent asks, grabbing the garment bag that holds his tuxedo jacket.

"Ready." I nod, snatching up my purse from the sofa table. As I stand, Kent's free hand touches the small of my back. Shivers and sparks fly up my spine where his firm hand contacts my body. Damn it! I chide myself. The man makes me dinner, thanks me for being his housekeeper, and everything about him arouses me.

It's a good thing Kent is getting into his pre-performance focus, as it leaves me to gather my wits and settle my senses while the car speeds to the performance location.

• • • •

I NOTICE ABIGAIL'S hesitation when I compliment her on her work, and thank her for being a friend. My mind revisits all the times we spent together, over breakfasts, over dinners, and dealing with issues. I thought she would be more receptive because her wedding ring is still missing. Isn't that a sign she's ready to move on? If that's the case, why does she ignore my fumbled advances? This overnight event may not work out as well as I hoped. Not that I expected her to jump into bed with me. But I thought...hoped, maybe, she would affirm that she felt the same depth of feelings for me as I feel for her.

Having her so close as she tied my bow tie was frustratingly erotic. How her lips were a tiny movement away. How much I wanted to invade that space to capture them.

Being her employer complicates things, and I'm sure she feels that complication too. Maybe that's what holds her back. Because if we tried to have a real relationship, and things don't work out, she'd have to leave. Find another position. Another employer. That's the last thing I want her to do.

SUTTON LAKE CONCERT

SIXTY-SIX MUSICIANS wearily plod around backstage, packing up their instruments and returning sheet music to the ensemble's music librarian. Others continue to practice difficult passages for the next concert date. I wait on a folding chair outside the door of the dressing room marked Maestro Grant. Violin music, short musical phrases, are repeated over and over again inside. To an untrained ear, they would sound exactly the same. After half a year with Kent, I can hear the different intonation in each repetition of notes.

The voices of Kent and an unrecognizable male become louder as they approach the door. I stand, hoping Kent and I can finally leave for the night. Between the ride and the tension at our dinner, I'm ready for sleep. The door opens, and the new concertmaster, Gabriel Carvello, emerges laughing, with Kent following in similar good spirits.

"Abigail! I apologize for keeping you waiting. Gabe and I were going over a part that keeps giving everyone grief."

"No problem."

"What did you think?" Gabriel asks, his gray-blue eyes sparkling.

"The performance?" I ask, tapping my index finger on my chin as if being critical. "It was, um, it was. Oh, what can I say? It was great!" I smile mischievously.

Gabriel bursts out laughing as Kent erupts, "Ah, your common ear! You never hear the mistakes! Half the flutes were out of tune, the brass couldn't keep to tempo, and the violins always got the phrasing wrong! I need some wine. Let's get out of here." He grabs his jacket and shuts the door.

The ride back to the condo is filled with Kent's prattle about the performance, the good and the bad. Half listening, I muse that no one in the audience ever heard half the errors Kent noted. Despite the difficulties, he is pleased with the performance in general, and his good mood surrounds him like the moonlight bathing him through the car window.

The aura of congeniality continues in the condo, where Kent shucks the uncooperative bow tie, shoes, and socks. In bare feet, a white button-down shirt and red suspenders, instead of his usual cummerbund, I'm reminded of an illustration of Frodo I'd seen once in a *Lord of the Rings* book. How boyish he looks tonight! Aglow with the excitement that a performance always brings him.

It's like Christmas morning for him after a performance. The joy and energy still course through him even though the instruments are packed away and the music hall is silent. It will take a few hours to subside. I know this from experience, having heard and secretly watched him after a few concerts, walking about the townhouse humming, trying to dispel the kinetic energy he absorbs from the musicians and the audience. While it lasts, he is wonderful to behold. A victor of the battle to eke out the best music from the musicians.

I try to keep up with his soliloquy, but he is exceptionally talkative tonight. After another half hour and a glass of wine, he starts to wind down and becomes more contemplative. He steps out onto the deck on this cool night, leaving the French doors fully open. Open in an invitation? I decide to join him.

Wineglasses in hand, we gaze up at the stars from the deck railing. It is a beautiful, clear night. The sliver of moon hangs like an apostrophe over the lake.

"I've always wanted to bring a telescope up here for such nights. But I never think about it until it's too late," he muses.

"I'll add it to my shopping list, if you'd like," I offer, watching him turning 360 degrees to see all the stars.

"Remind me. I don't know anything about telescopes, or the stars for that matter, so I'll have to find someone who can help me select a good one."

"I can't help you with the telescope selection, but I know some of the stars and constellations," I reply, my gaze directly above us.

He steps closer. "Teach me."

Why not? "Okay, so can you find the Little Dipper?"

Kent spins slowly around again, eyes to the heavens, holding his wineglass tucked securely against his chest.

"There," he finally says, pointing overhead.

"The brightest star in the handle is called the North Star or Polaris."

"Polaris," Kent repeats, still staring upward.

"Now, look off to the next two stars lined up. They are part of the Big Dipper where the handle attaches. The Big Dipper is part of Ursa Major." I point in the direction Kent should look.

Kent sets his wineglass on the table, freeing his hands to hang onto the railing while looking up. "Where....oh, I see it."

"Next, from the end of the handle of the Big Dipper, following the curvature of the handle, you will find a very bright star a little ways away. That's Arcturus, meaning bear-watcher."

"Really? Arcturus?"

I turn sideways, my arm outstretched and pointing. "The brightest star above the top of that tall pine tree is Saturn."

"We can see Saturn?" Kent asks, his eyes wide as he looks at me, questioning.

"Yup, if we had that telescope, or even binoculars, we could see the rings." I smile at his obvious delight.

"I am definitely getting that damn telescope when we get back to Baymont," Kent confirms, his eyes still roaming the heavens.

"Over here." I point in another direction. "There are two bright stars way up there, that appear side by side, they are—"

"I can't see where," Kent mutters, confusion lacing his words.

"At about two o'clock in the sky, if the moon is at noon." I try to point more precisely.

"Hmm," Kent says, as he leans up close behind me and brings his head down to my shoulder to sight up my arm. He steadies himself with his hands on the railing in front of me. His forearms graze my waist as I stand trapped between them.

I can't think about the sky anymore as my pulse bounds and races, and my knees wobble. The stars whirl before my eyes, and the electrical surge ignites a fire I haven't felt in so long that I have almost forgotten it. His arms touch my waist. My skin tingles with awareness of the warmth and light pressure of his body against my back. The scent of his cologne and sweat from the concert makes a heady mixture as his breath tickles my right ear. Distracted, I drop my arm and twist to face him. Kent doesn't move an inch. Our gazes lock, our noses mere centimeters apart.

In a meteor's flash, his soft lips brush mine, and I abandon all pretense. His strong, muscular arms pull me closer. My nipples rise to hard peaks and press against his rock hard chest. Our breathing accelerates, and I can't help but moan as his tongue delves into my mouth, searching for my tongue. Flames flicker through my core, igniting my center as my tongue finds his. I want—I need to get closer as the scent of our passion erupts.

His marvelous lips continue to ply mine as he palms my breast.

A memory flashes of my first night with Brannon. Doing all the same things. Feeling all the same feelings. My entire body goes rigid.

What am I doing? My brain screams as images fill me of Brannon's last breath, the feel of his hand going cold in mine, the casket's wooden shine marred by the handful of dirt I'd numbly thrown down on it. His memory still holds me tight. Even after everything, and having the freedom to live life again, he doesn't release his grip on me.

Then there's the issue with Kent, my employer. He's been wonderful, helping me gain the stability I so need and crave. If I give in to these feelings for him and something goes wrong, both Glee and I will have the proverbial rug pulled out from under us. Again. And I don't feel ready to risk that for either of us.

My body screams back. *This is what you want, what you need. It's been so long. Take it. You are free.*

"No!" I choke out an anguished cry as I forcefully push against Kent's chest, breaking our intimate connection. He's my employer. This can't happen.

Kent releases me immediately and steps back two paces. He stares, his eyes wild with passion and confusion.

"I can't. Please —I—." I burst into gut-wrenching sobs and flee into the bedroom, slamming the door behind me.

• • • •

WHAT THE HELL HAPPENED? My thoughts scramble, jumbling up and twisting so fast and hard I can't get a grip on any one idea. My insides are equally wrecked. I sink onto the lounge chair and cover my face. My hands come away damp with tears I didn't know were sliding down my face. A part of me wants to comfort her, but I don't want to intrude on whatever it is she is experiencing. If it's some kind of guilt, as I suspect, she needs to figure it out for herself.

I need to figure out what to do now. For tonight, for tomorrow, and for the days to follow. For more reasons than one, I don't want to lose Abigail. Not as a housekeeper, a confidant, or a friend. I need her in my life, everything about her, from her dirt-stained fingernails to her cooing over the cat.

I thought she was ready for this after our conversation days ago. Maybe she voiced more bravado than she has. Or maybe she's rejecting me. Technically, I am her boss, and what I've done amounts to sexual harassment.

I scrub my face with my palms, trying to pull away from all the questions. The night's spell is broken beyond repair. I curl up on the couch, pulling the Sherpa throw over myself. Sleep takes its time settling into me.

• • • •

IN THE MIDDLE OF THE night, I tiptoe out of the bedroom to get a glass of water. Between the wine and the flood of tears, I'm dehydrated. Light snoring coming from the sofa tells me where Kent has retreated. Like a cat to catnip, I'm drawn to the sofa. Even asleep, his face shows the anguished and confused expression I last saw on his face. Only this time, his face is tear-streaked and his eyes swollen.

"I'm so sorry," I whisper. "I can't be in love with you."

My belly in knots, I stare at the gorgeous man before me. So many women would kill to have been in my shoes on that deck. He is so good, so kind, and so incredible in so many ways. The arrogance and conceit I'd initially found have melted away. Over the last six months, I've seen the true man behind the baton and I've gained a far better perspective on his demeanor..

No matter how my soul is drawn to him, I cannot have him. He is my boss. He's become a friend, yes. I know as much as I will regret it someday, I cannot have him now. Not only because he's my employer, but also as the successor to my love for Brannon.

Brannon—just when I think I'm over you, you remind me of the good times...the in-love times. Even if that's not how we ended. Perhaps it's my guilt. I'd been contemplating a divorce before he got sick. He must have sensed it. Because the first thing he asked me to do after his diagnosis was to stay with him. I relented. Is this survivor's guilt? I'm too tired to explore such a question tonight.

I pick up the throw from the floor and drape it over his body, then return to the bedroom. Facing each other in the morning will be painful. Like waking up on closing day, not ready to let go. Not wanting to move on. It will have to be faced, but it will be extremely difficult. I hope Kent won't ask why I changed my mind so abruptly. Perhaps he's figured it out.

Despite all the things I told him after the last fundraiser event, I have no answer for him other than a dead man's name. The one I had hoped I'd left behind. Whose memory has risen like Lazarus to become alive again and stymy my future.

For all my worrying the remainder of the night, he is gone when I awake the next morning. There's a note left on the kitchen counter near the coffee maker.

> *Thought I would let you sleep in.*
> *I've taken a cab back to town for my 9 a.m. meeting.*
> *You'll have to drive yourself back. Here are the car keys.*
> *See you tomorrow. K*

The reckoning is put off, and the chill begins.

THE AFTERMATH

WE DON'T SPEAK BEYOND what's necessary for me to do my job. "Mr. Grant," as I have reverted to calling him, is brisk and reserved. Rarely does he spend more time than necessary under his own roof.

For four nights he doesn't come home. No notice or explanation, though he's probably staying at Sutton Lake. Instead, he has Mrs. Farthing call over for a change of clothes or other items which a courier picks up.

The walls of my comfortable room are pressing in and mocking me, yet there isn't anything to do downstairs. The house is clean and stays clean in his absence. The laundry and dry cleaning arrive and are put away. Since "Mr. Grant" has been eating meals out, there isn't anything to buy from the grocery store either.

Without someone to cook for, I don't bother to cook for myself. It doesn't feel right to cook his food without him eating it too. I nibble only when I feel hungry, which isn't often.

When he finally comes back, he's preoccupied with his work or schedule. Most of the time, he retreats to the music room or to his bedroom and shuts the door. In the mornings, he leaves for work without having coffee or breakfast. How long will this cold shoulder last?

Insomnia strangles me as I contemplate that question. It makes my nights endless bouts of worry, regret, and above all, despair. If this is the end of this job, do I have enough in me to start all over again for the third time? Lying in bed, I search my soul for answers. Answers I cannot find before dawn arrives and yet another day of solitude begins.

It's over a week after the downfall when the doorbell rings one morning. No one is expected, and without the need to make breakfast for Kent, I hadn't bothered to get up though it is past ten o'clock. I search for my cell phone to use the speaker, but its battery is dead. I jump out of bed, don my robe, and run down the stairs. Quickly, I shut off the alarm and fling open the door.

Immediately, I realize my mistake.

Cynthia hurtles past me into the townhouse. "My. While the cat's away, the housekeeper stays in bed?" Cynthia, with her perfect makeup and expensive clothes, sashays into the living room. She drops her handbag on the couch. With an elegant shrug of her shoulders, her lightweight jacket slides off with a swish. Dangling it from her index finger, she holds it out for me to take.

"What do you want? Maestro Grant isn't here." I don't move to help the woman, nor close the front door. I want to make it clear she's to leave immediately.

She lets the coat drop to the floor as she smirks at me, as if tempting me to pick it up.

My teeth grind audibly. "You're Kent's ex-fiancée."

"Nonetheless. Here I am." She smiles again like a Cheshire cat with a mouse.

"I'm not sure Mr. Grant would like you to be here. You need to leave," I assert, my knees knocking in my pajamas.

"Call him and see what he says." Cynthia saunters around the living room, checking out objects on the side tables, then going to the bookcases. Her manicured finger slides along the book bindings. Pretending to read the titles? She picks one off the shelf and settles into a chair.

I need to call Kent. He needs to know she is here. Clearly, she won't leave until she sees him. Will Kent answer if I call him directly? I opt to call Mrs. Farthing.

In seconds, I have her on the phone. "Cynthia has entrenched herself in Kent's living room," I say, hoping Mrs. Farthing knows who I'm talking about.

"Cripe sakes, this day just keeps getting better and better. Hold on."

When Kent comes on the line, I tell him Cynthia is here.

"What the hell?" His voice is curt and hard. "Give her the phone," he demands, the exasperation in his voice unmistakable.

I hold it out for Cynthia, who doesn't move a muscle to get up. Out of spite, I want to make her come get it. But Kent is waiting. And the quicker he can get her out of this house, the better. I bring it over to her, my eyes sending her as much anger as I can muster into a glare.

Cynthia takes the phone and, with a flick of her fingers, shoos me away for a private conversation. I retreat to the dining area, not taking my eyes off the woman. It isn't her manner that infuriates me so much. It's the fact that she probably slept with Kent while having her affair with Malcolm and then blamed Kent when he ended the engagement.

If there was a pre-nup, she probably got a chunk of money, and kept the ring and all her expensive designer clothes. Not rack or ready-to-wear either. I might not be able to afford so much as a shoelace in any of those stores, but I know their logos, and Cynthia is wearing many. From the interconnecting Cs on her Chanel sunglass frames to the upside-down triangle on her Prada shoes and the mirror image Gs of her Gucci handbag. The almost Mrs. Grant is a walking advertisement for haute couture.

"Here," Cynthia's voice drips sweetly as she holds out the phone from across the room. I take it from her and hold it to my ear.

"Mr. Grant?" I ask into the phone.

"I'm on my way. She can stay until I get there. Do not let her wander the house." And he hangs up.

Nineteen minutes later, his Carrera screeches into the driveway. I hear his footsteps bounding in the door as he goes straight to the living room. Should I stay by the kitchen door and perhaps overhear things Kent doesn't want me to hear, or disappear upstairs to my room and hope he yells for me if I'm needed? I head for the kitchen.

Raised voices shout back and forth while I make myself a cup of tea. I can make out a few words, so I hum to myself to disengage my ears from their heated conversation, if you could call it that. The words I heard won't leave my mind, pre-nup, settlement, engagement, Malcolm, affair.

Quicker than I expect, the front door slams so hard the floors shake and the windowpanes rattle.

Seconds later, Kent stumbles into the kitchen and slumps into the chair. "Don't ever let her in again. Don't even open the door."

"I'm sorry, I wasn't thinking. She burst past me—" I try to apologize.

Kent holds up his palm. "Stop. I understand." He scrubs his hand over his face. "Don't let it happen again." He heads for the garage door, throwing a comment over his shoulder as he leaves, "I'll be back for dinner."

Before I can ask what he wants to eat, he's gone.

The entire episode unsettles me. If he's going to be out until dinner, I have time to meet Clare for lunch.

Clare and I meet at the Hayloft restaurant and are seated immediately. After our drinks arrive and our order is taken, she sits back in her chair and looks at me. "You look terrible. What's going on?"

"I haven't had a chance to talk with you about what happened at the lake." I keep my voice low so no one can hear.

"What lake?" Clare asks, cocking her head to one side while sipping on the hollow swizzle stick in her negroni.

I never told her about Sutton Lake. Until our lunch arrives, I give her a rundown of our trip to his condo. When I get to the part about after the concert, her mouth hangs open in what can only be disbelief. "And we've been pretty much non-communicative since," I say. Though I'd sorely like to talk with her about it, I don't mention Cynthia's visit. Even if Kent hadn't revealed her reason for barging in, and what was said.

"So you're telling me he came on to you and you stopped it because of Brannon?" She looks at me like I've told her a UFO brought me to Pluto and back. "Are you crazy?"

I recoil. Clare has never talked to me in that manner. "I—I couldn't help it." Why is she getting angry at me for remembering my husband?

"Look, I know you loved Brannon and he loved you too. But I think you need to remember what he was doing to you. Yes, he stopped. But he stopped because he was sick, and you promised him you'd stay." She takes a long sip of her drink. "I want you to ask yourself," and she holds up her hand, "you don't have to tell me what conclusion you come to...just ask yourself, if you would still be married if he hadn't been sick. Would you have stayed with him and his manipulative and controlling ways?"

It's my moment to be stunned. I'd never considered what might have happened with our marriage if he hadn't been sick. Or hadn't died. Would he have resumed his ways? Made me account for every minute I was out of his sight and every dollar I spent?

We remain quiet as the waitress delivers our food. We silently stare at our plates. I'm considering her question. I can't fathom what she's waiting for.

Clare picks up her turkey club. "I have to eat and get back to work," she says, not meeting my eyes.

My appetite disappears. On my plate is a pulled pork sandwich with seasoned curly fries. It was one of Brannon's favorite meals. Who did I order it for?

THE EUROPEAN TOUR

OVER THE NEXT WEEK, no further words are spoken about either incident. Kent seems to go out of his way to keep our one-on-one conversations on a strictly professional level. At the end of June, the last concert of the Sutton Lake Series is over, but the musical events don't end entirely. The musicians, Kent, and essential staff, including me, are to board a plane for Barcelona to start a five city European tour lasting ten days. Months ago, I'd agreed to become part of the staff. Gabriella provided me with the training to fill in for her duties. The day before our flights, disaster strikes at the townhouse. Literally.

Construction workers strike an underground electrical transformer in front of the house. The resulting fire doesn't just take out the electricity for the adjacent two blocks of commercial and residential community, the power surge damages electrical panels in several townhouses on the street.

I have to stay behind to deal with the electrical contractors. Kent, who is finally speaking with me, is distraught. He doesn't want to leave me behind to handle the issues. "It can wait until we get back," he mutters over and over, trying to convince me to board the plane with everyone else.

"No, it can't wait. The security system isn't working." I hear him grumble. "Glee will be here all alone until Mrs. Farthing gets here tomorrow. The workers have promised they will fix your townhouse first. They said it should only take a day. I'll catch a flight to Barcelona tomorrow evening."

I try to make it sound like everything is completely under control. It is better this way, because when they arrive in Barcelona, buses will take them to the hotel to rest. After a quick rehearsal mid-afternoon, they will all dine at the hotel buffet prior to getting into their concert attire. By the time they wake the next morning, I'll be there to help shepherd them onto buses to the train station. The high-speed rail will get us to Lyon, France, in less than six hours.

He capitulates with a heavy sigh. "Abigail, I'm sorry I can't be there to help you with this nightmare."

"Mr. Grant—"

"Kent," He interjects forcefully, his face tense. "Stop calling me Mr. Grant." His exasperation is palpable. He kicks his suitcase like a petulant child who can't have his way. The suitcase falls over.

"Stop worrying about me and worry about the tour. This is why you hired me...to take care of problems that crop up when you're busy working." I right his suitcase. "Waste your anxiety on getting the tribe to rehearsal, dinner, and the concert hall without having a breakdown, okay?" I plead. "Think positive."

"I'm fine. We've done these pieces hundreds of times," Kent says.

"Well then, just enjoy the city and Palau de la Musica. Suck up the moments!" I enthuse. "Check out the food and beer. I want a full report when I get there."

He groans, "Don't worry, I'm going to get some beer. I try to stay with the guys to keep them from getting too sloshed in the local bars after the performance. Getting them up to make the bus on time the next morning is always a problem."

I can't help but laugh, a vision of hungover musicians stumbling aboard a coach bus flashing in my head.

"Don't laugh!" Kent says, trying to stifle a chuckle. "They act like high school band musicians trying to sneak beer onto the bus or train for the long ride to the next city!" He laughs outright. "Honestly, it's like they're all having a mid-life crisis at the same time."

"It could be worse. They could be picking up more than beer. It would get pretty ugly if their wives or girlfriends found out," I warn, half serious.

"I've already had that problem once, only it was with a couple of the women. Seems the Italian men were irresistible during last summer's tour." Kent slaps his fist against his forehead. "I've suddenly become a parent of sixty-six musicians and twenty crew and staff!"

The doorbell rings. Our gazes meet. Our words dry up. The livery car is here to take Kent to the airport. While the driver takes his bags, Kent places his hand on my shoulder. "Be careful. Meet me in Spain as soon as you can."

The next day, two teams of electricians arrive en masse. Because of Maestro's celebrity, they set his house as the first to be repaired. Each team replaces one of the two electrical panels. Meanwhile, I check in for my flight.

The work is completed by mid-afternoon and I give Glee a kiss and a handful of treats before leaving in the cab. By five o'clock, my bags and I arrive at the gate, ready to catch the evening flight out of Baymont's airport.

Since the concert is currently in session at their location, I leave a message for Kent at the hotel. I'll see him tomorrow before we leave for Lyon.

With a direct flight and no delays, I arrive at the hotel as the buses to the train station are loading. I spot Kent pacing the hotel sidewalk, trying to move people along. Every few seconds, he scans the area. When he looks my way, I wave.

He smiles wearily, visibly relaxing as he jogs over to me.

"Oh, dear God, thank you," he says. "I was starting to get worried you'd miss the bus and train as well."

"Here I am. Don't worry. I'm on duty now." I set my luggage on the sidewalk and pull a notebook out of my oversized handbag. Kent deposits my luggage in the mass of cases one footman is trying to squeeze into the bus's hold.

We travel by bus, then by high-speed train to Lyon, arriving shortly after one o'clock. The afternoon speeds by as I make sure the musicians get into their hotel rooms, and then on to the auditorium, for rehearsal at four. Kent and I don't have a chance to meet up until afterward, for a quick dinner in the hotel restaurant.

"I can't believe you've had so little time to decompress since yesterday," I say as I pick at my salade Lyonnaise.

"Today's schedule is the worst. In the rest of the cities, we'll have more time to catch our breath." Kent is obviously enjoying his dinner, chicken with a mushroom and cream sauce. "Everything is going smoothly. So far."

"What should I do during the concert? Gabriella never mentioned that," I say, yawning.

Kent sets his fork down. "You can wait backstage, or we can find you a seat in the audience." Seeing my second yawn, he adds, "Or you could go back to the hotel for an early turn-in."

As great as that sounds, we're only here in Lyon for the next twelve or so hours, and since I've never been before, I want to explore. "Maybe I'll play tourist. It looks like a safe enough city."

Kent narrows his eyes at me. "Be careful. Meet me at the hotel bar about eleven o'clock." His gaze softens. "I want to know you're okay before we go to bed tonight."

I can't help the blush that blossoms on my face.

He quickly corrects, "That is...before we go to sleep, in our separate rooms."

Kent buys me a drink at the bar after the concert. One Kir Royale wipes me out. I nearly fall asleep halfway through my cocktail. It is a little awkward as he helps me to my room. I can't stop giggling for some reason. *Is it nerves?* Nothing has ever been said about the night at Sutton Lake. He leaves me at my hotel door, then moves on to his own room one floor up.

I fall into bed exhausted, with two cellphone alarms and the hotel wake-up service set to make sure I get up early.

Then, it starts all over again.

Our travel from Lyon to Geneva is a quick three hours by train. This gives everyone some downtime to sightsee and relax prior to rehearsals in Victoria Hall. Kent and I have a lovely dinner on the lake before the concert. We sit on the waterside patio, making small talk. A companionable silence builds between us.

Kent clears his throat. "I'm sorry for what happened at Sutton." He looks out over Lake Geneva, not meeting my eyes.

My face goes hot. "It's okay. We don't need to talk about it." I don't want to ruin such a beautiful place with memories of a night elsewhere that I sometimes relish and other times regret.

"I think we do." He reaches across the table to touch my hand. "I'm sorry."

I sigh. "Apology accepted." It's my luck that our dinners are delivered that very instant.

He doesn't try again. The acceptance of his apology seems to mollify his feelings. But *I* haven't apologized yet. At some point during this tour, I hope to muster the courage to do it. Now is not the right time.

The rest of the evening goes as planned. I stroll the safe streets, doing a little shopping and testing my high school French, which I find to be abysmal. Luckily, a majority of the people also speak English.

Kent and I don't meet after the concert. We have an early wake-up call to catch the next series of trains to our destination.

The next morning, we move on to Cologne, Germany. Such a lovely city, the cathedral is mostly repaired after Allied bombing in the Second World War, though pockmarks of bullets remain on parts of the cathedral's stone façade.

While on one train, I tell Kent to try to get to the Heidelberg Castle someday. This leads to discussions about my travels in Europe. Kent is surprised to hear I traveled in Germany and France years ago.

"I really enjoyed Germany, especially along the Rhine and the Mosel rivers. Although my attempts with the language were terrible. But my favorite places are in France. Here, we have to go to the square in front of the Cologne Cathedral and the Früh Em Veedel restaurant across from it. You have to try its peculiar fresh beer."

"The Frühe Restaurant, huh?" Kent replies. "Sounds like a tourist trap."

"So what? You're a tourist, aren't you? Give it a try. Cologne is famous for this type of beer. You can't call yourself a beer connoisseur and not have tried it," I urge.

Kent is quiet for a few moments. "We'll eat there for dinner, how's that?"

"Great."

And it was. We both enjoyed the beer and ate a hearty meal before Kent had to leave for the concert at the Kölner Philharmonie.

I hang out in the tourist area during the concert, then go off to bed.

Unbeknownst to me until the next day, after the concert, Kent returned to Frühe with some of the guys. The next morning, I'm banging on a bunch of doors trying to get the over-indulgers ready for a three and a half hour train ride to Paris.

Paris. The anticipation of being back in Paris has my stomach in a knot. I haven't been to Europe in years. Brannon and I used to go every year until his cancer treatments interrupted our lives. We'd honeymooned in France, driven from the English Channel to the Saintes-Maries-de-la-Mer on the Mediterranean Sea. Could I face being there without him? Could I consider the possibility of seeing my favorite city with another man by my side?

"Another man in my heart." The words slip out, surprising me. I don't know where that thought came from, but I recognize the truth. I have fallen in love with Kent. I bury my face in my hands, torn. Torn between the memory of my deceased husband and this vibrant, handsome, living man. It dawns on me like a slap that they are very much alike—strong, energetic, charming, and intellectual. They have dynamic careers and lives, are socially adept, quasi-introverted but extroverted when necessary. More importantly, they are honest, caring, and trustworthy. Well, Kent is.

An urgent need to call Clare has me bolting up from my seat beside him on the TGV. Kent glances up, gives me a gentle smile, but says nothing as I head to the bathroom compartment.

Locked inside, I call Clare, the gently swaying compartment soothing my panic.

With her groggy croak, I realize it's only four in the morning in Baymont. "Clare, I'm sorry. Should I call back later?" I cross my fingers, hoping she doesn't say yes. Heaven only knows when I might have time to call back once we hit Gare du Nord train station in Paris.

"What's going on?" The sound of rustling sheets tells me she is getting out of bed, probably to not wake Louis.

"I have something to tell you and I need your help on how to deal with it," I blurt, sitting on the toilet lid. "I've fallen in love with Kent."

"Oh no," she mutters. I can picture her scrubbing her forehead with her free hand. A common gesture for her. "What's happened? Did you kiss Kent? Or more?" she asks.

"No, it's—we've been here together, nearly 24/7. Well, not together together, but working together. Not sleeping together either." I slap my palm to my face. Why can't I explain it better? "We're working toward the same goals. It's been interesting. Lovely, really."

Clare yawns into the phone. "So what...what major crisis happened?"

I groan, trying to put the tornado of feelings inside my chest into words. "I'm contemplating being in Paris, the city Brannon and

I loved visiting so much. Wondering how I can go there and be without him. Be with another man instead of him. It struck me that I want to be there with Kent. That I love him." I growl. "Arghhh, what am I going to do?"

"Kiss him, have sex, get it out of your system. Take a chance he feels the same." Her voice is sleepy, and I wonder how much longer she'll stay awake.

I close my eyes and sigh. "But he's my employer. What if I come on to him and find out he's not interested in that way, and then he fires me?"

"Hmm, point taken." She pauses, probably pondering the complex situation. I hear her yawn. "After your description of his kiss on the deck, I'd guess he'd be all for it." Murmured conversation tells me she is talking to Louis. "Look, I'm glad you're finally getting beyond your grief and feeling strong enough to move forward into a new relationship. It's a big step for you."

"But what should I do?"

"Do you really have to do anything? Especially when you're in Europe on the symphony's dime? I suggest you hold off until you get back to the US. There's only a couple more days left to the tour, right?"

"Yes." I chew on my lip. Then nod in agreement. "I see your point. Okay. I'll play it cool until we're back in Baymont." The tension in my chest eases with the truce. I'll focus on the job I'm supposed to be doing and ignore the roaring feelings for Kent.

"Unless, of course, he kisses you again."

"You are no help, girlfriend."

PARIS

OUR ARRIVAL IN PARIS unfolds surprisingly well. The bus takes us from the train station to our hotel, which is literally around the corner from the concert hall. In the same general area are other lesser known attractions, like the science museum, a movie theatre in a geodesic dome, a decommissioned submarine museum, and the Canal de L'Ourcq where pleasure boats venture. I can hear a bunch of the musicians talking excitedly about where they'll spend their free time.

Keycards in hand, everyone disperses to settle into their rooms. They have free time to explore until their afternoon rehearsal.

In my room, I drop my suitcase and flop on the bed. Travel has worn me out. A nap feels overdue. As I'm drifting off, someone knocks on my door. I groan my discontent at having to get up. It's Kent.

"What do you say we go for a walk along the canal?" His hands are stuffed into his pants pockets, and he rocks on the balls of his feet.

I'd like nothing better than to object and resume my nap. But perhaps stretching my legs and getting some fresh air will be better. "I must confess, I am secretly yearning for a nap. But I've been sitting far too long today already."

We walk through the Parc de la Villette to the edge of the canal and stroll north. The bright sunshine warms our backs as we stroll along the wide concrete sidewalks, watching boats float by. Joggers and power walkers lap us, and mothers push baby strollers with older children trailing behind.

As with every other time I've been to Paris, I marvel at the cleanliness, the beauty, and the roominess of the sprawling city. Everywhere I turn there are vistas: the Eiffel Tower, Sacré Coeur, and the new roof and spire of Notre Dame. I hope to see these beautiful monuments up close again. Most of all, Notre Dame. I cried watching the sacred cathedral engulfed in flames six years ago. It was so heavily damaged, I feared it was beyond repair. Yet, it has been reborn in a faithful renovation. I long to see its beauty again.

"Do you have dinner plans tonight?" Kent asks as I stop to scan the skyline for more Parisian treasures.

"No plans except to get some exquisite French food. What about you? Are you and the guys going out to the local brasserie?"

"Yes, some of the other musicians and staff are joining us. The concierge made the arrangements for after the concert. Want to join us?" His eyes beg me to say yes.

"Sure. But I want to be back here by eleven. Six a.m. comes too early."

On our way back to the hotel, we stop to check out the decommissioned French submarine near the Parc. From there, Kent scoots off to rehearsal. I retreat to my hotel room for a thirty-minute nap. A cup of coffee and a pastry from the lobby cafe helps me muster enough energy to stay awake through the concert.

Hovering in the wings as the performance begins, I watch Maestro Grant. He is in exquisite form during tonight's concert. The entire orchestra is too. The Philharmonie de Paris' audience gives them rounds of applause. Kent returns to the stage for five standing ovations. Only later do I learn that ovations are rarely given in France, and standing ovations are nearly extinct. It is a coup for the Baymont Symphony and Maestro Grant.

Afterwards, we walk down the street to Les Bancs Publics, where the service and rustic food are outstanding and far cheaper than we anticipated. I sit with members of the stage crew at a table far from Kent. Only once does he come over to chat with me. With all the ears around, he keeps it professional, asking about breakfast service in the morning...something we had already discussed on our canal walk. The symphony crew gets rowdy as the night slips by with round after round of libations.

Before I know it, it's one a.m., and while the crew is still going strong, I'm fading fast. I pay my bill and start walking back to the hotel. Hearing heavy footsteps running behind me, I strike a defensive stance, fearing I'm going to be assaulted, but see Kent coming to join me.

"I asked room service to put something in your room for tomorrow night. I hope you don't mind, but I made reservations for our last dinner in Paris."

"Oh? Where are we going?" I quickly add, "Please don't tell me it's the restaurant in the Eiffel Tower."

"No. Something better, if the prix fixe is any indication. Oh, and it's on me." He winks as he opens the hotel lobby door.

"Fine. Sounds like it's something I can't afford." I give him a questioning glance.

Together, we ride up to my floor, the fifth. Kent walks me to my hotel room. "Until tomorrow." He gives me a curt nod after I open the door and walks back to the elevator for his trip to the penthouse suite.

A sturdy, black garment bag is hanging on the closet rod. While I'm curious of its contents, I'm too tired to check it out before I settle into bed.

After our buffet breakfast, Kent disappears for hours. He doesn't mention the reason. I head off, starting my long list of "must see again" places. I start with my favorite spot, the Luxembourg Gardens in the Latin Quarter. From there, I re-visit Notre Dame, Sainte-Chappelle, and then walk by the Louvre into the Tuileries Gardens. Like me, the musicians and crew are on their own until this evening, when we will congregate at the concert hall. At that time, I am back on duty, making sure everyone is in position and ready for the eight p.m. concert start.

Kent sidles up beside me as I help a musician untangle her dangling earring from the lace of her collar. "Well, ready for tonight?"

I know he is speaking about our dinner date after the concert. "Yes," I say, first freeing the earring from her ear lobe and then working it free from the lace. I hand it back to her. She thanks me and walks away, her flute in one hand, earring in the other.

Now that we are alone, I ask, "Where are you taking me that requires a haute couture garment?" I opened the garment bag before I left on my tourist trek across the city. The dress is exquisite and, without a doubt, costs more than I earn in a month of wages. I'd demand he return it, but I fell in love with it immediately. The sleeveless, light peach-colored dress features a deep, scoop neckline made of silk. The lightweight, sheer silk chiffon of the skirt softly drapes with an airy feel. I feel like a princess in it, and Kent's admiring look makes me stand taller.

"Only the best restaurant in Paris," Kent smiles mischievously, a twinkle in his eyes.

"This isn't necessary," I insist. "It sounds far too expensive—"

He cuts me off, "I think it's deserving. For both of us."

The ding of a bell indicates everyone should be on stage. "See you later. Merde," I say to Kent.

"What does that mean?" he inquires, stepping into the wing he will emerge from onto the stage.

"It's American equivalent is 'break a leg,' but a direct French translation means 'shit.'"

He raises his eyebrows in surprise as his name is called. He bounds out onto the stage to exuberant applause.

As happened last night, the orchestra plays flawlessly, Maestro Grant conducts incredibly, and the audience roars and claps ovation after ovation. Half an hour later, Kent exchanges his tux for a beautifully fitted suit.

Behind the hall, a Mercedes cab is waiting to whisk us away on our night of gastronomic delights. The Mercedes breezes along Rue De Rivoli with its sparkling, fairy-lit trees lining either side of the avenue. In the back seat, we are quiet, each of us buried in our own thoughts.

Kent breaks the silence. "It's our last night in Paris, in Europe really. Let's enjoy this meal tonight. Besides, I know how much you like duck, and these guys handle it expertly. Or so I'm told," he teases.

"Duck, yum. Okay. If it's that good, you are forgiven. If not...you're in trouble," I tease back.

La Tour d'Argent proves to be all Kent has been told. How he procured a table is unknown, but it must have required lots of palm grease for the hotel concierge to pull such strings. The chandeliers are perfectly dimmed, and the white linen tablecloths glow in the soft light. The tables are set with real silverware, elegant French china, and crystal.

I feast on the best duck I've ever tasted in the dining room's divine opulence. The view alone is worth a couple of million euros. Notre Dame glistens in the bright lights surrounding it. I've never been so pampered by restaurant staff before in my life. It truly makes me feel like royalty.

"I can't begin to tell you how happy I am that you decided to join me on tour. I hope you don't have any regrets," Kent says, sipping his after-dinner drink.

"I did at first. It was rather awkward trying to explain why I was here to some of the musicians who know who I really am. Melanie understood and must have smoothed it over with anyone who asked," I explain, referring to the first flutist.

"I really enjoyed your little impromptu tour in Cologne. I don't think I would ever have gone to the Frühe on my own."

"I'm sorry you were so busy today. Too busy to come sightseeing with me."

An odd look comes over his face. "Couldn't be helped. Perhaps we'll visit Paris again in the future. Tell me where you went."

I flash him a gleeful smile. Comparing his expression now to what I experienced in Cologne is like comparing a rock to the sky. I'm glad he can relax now that everything expected of him is over. It's too bad we leave in the morning.

"My favorite spot in Paris was first. The Medici fountain in Luxembourg Gardens. It's a peaceful, relaxing, and secluded spot. Then I watched children sailing boats in the fountain basin in front of the palace."

"Sounds lovely. I wish we had time to go before our flight," Kent says, dawdling with a silver spoon on the white linen tablecloth.

"Everyone swarms to Tuileries Gardens, but I think Luxembourg is more beautiful." I sigh, remembering all the hours I have spent there over my life just soaking in the mystery and seclusion of the water feature and its majestic, sculptured fountain.

A wave of melancholy floods over me, dimming my vision with tiny unshed tears. I stare at my own silver spoon, still unused, on the table.

"What's wrong?" Kent inquires softly.

"I'm so grateful I'm here," I whisper.

"And..." Kent coaxes, as if sensing there is more to this feeling I'm not sharing.

"And we leave tomorrow," I whisper. "But," I clear my throat and sit up straighter, "I will return."

"Anytime you want. Let me know. You can take off any time. As long..." Kent trails off as if not wanting to say more.

"As long...what?" I ask. He clearly has something more to say. I breathe in shallow pants, waiting for his answer.

He leans closer to me conspiratorially. "As long as you bring me with you."

It is exactly what I hoped he would say. My pulse skitters crazily as my heart feels ready to burst. That's when I think of something and place my hand over Kent's.

"If you are ready to go, I have another favorite spot I want to show you. My favorite night spot," I say as I gather my purse and shawl. "I can't not go there tonight. It's said to have some famous musical significance, so I think you will like it."

"I'm game. Let's go."

It's just fifteen minutes from the restaurant, so Kent and I walk along the quay. We don't speak as we admire the Seine flowing beside us.

At an intersection with a bridge, we take a right and walk to the center, where I stop. Kent halts beside me.

"This is it. Do you know where you are?" I ask.

"Uh, on a bridge?"

"Correct! There are thirty-seven bridges over the Seine. Do you know *which* bridge we're on?" I inquire playfully.

"Not a clue," he says, looking all around for a sign or label.

"You, Maestro Grant, are on the Pont Neuf bridge. The oldest bridge in Paris." I throw my arms wide to indicate the length of the bridge.

Kent crosses his arms over his chest. "What, Mademoiselle, does that have to do with music?" He asks, his curiosity piqued.

"Well, one of many rumors says that a very famous piece of music was composed by a famous man after he stood on this very bridge. Others say it is music for a scene in a poem where two masked figures dance under the moonlight. Would you like to guess what composition it is, or do you want to listen to the music for a clue?" I dig into my purse for my phone.

Kent furrows his eyebrows and looks stumped. "I have no idea." With that, I cue up the music on my cellphone.

The first chord is nearly inaudible amid the traffic noise on the bridge. I increase the volume until the music and its sweet chords become recognizable.

"Clair de Lune! Debussy!" Kent says with a sense of awe. "You would know something like that." He smiles and puts his right arm around my waist, drawing me closer to his side. It is a friendly, amused gesture, but I can't help the shiver of excitement that runs through me at the contact. Together, we gaze out over the turbulent water of the Seine, listening to the music rise and ebb with beauty and sadness until the final note.

Kent turns me to him. His face reveals the same look I saw in Sutton Lake. He leans over and kisses my right cheek and then my left cheek as I stand very still. His thumbs brush each cheek, his eyes sparkling in the ambient streetlamps. Only then do I realize I am crying. He brushes away the silent tears on my cheeks.

"It's so beautiful, watching the water and hearing the music simultaneously," Kent whispers. "Especially with you by my side."

A tremor seizes my body. His eyes hold tightly to mine, keeping me breathless. I can only nod in agreement.

"Thank you for giving us this special moment," Kent whispers. "I'll never, ever hear or conduct that piece again without thinking of this bridge, and these few moments here with you."

There is something in his voice, his meaning, that makes me shiver. It sounds so loving and special, yet it sounds final. Like it is meant to foreshadow something ending. What, I can't imagine.

I nod again, my eyes cast down to the dark, flowing water. It matches the swirling sensation in my gut. A chaos of emotions rises and falls like the waves stirred by the bateaux-mouches. I have been here to hear that music with another man. The path of tears continues as the memories flow out of me. The warmth of Kent's arm around my waist steadies me as I clutch the rail, white-knuckled.

Another time, long ago, I'd stood here with my eyes closed as now, but in anger. The moonlight glistening off *his* golden curls, sky-blue eyes darkened to navy. A taller but thinner man who didn't understand the sentimentality of the music and the beauty of the moment, and laughed at my tears.

The same melody now wafts across the water with the smell of strawberry crepes from a nearby street vendor. Kent pulls me to lean against his sculpted chest, lending a warmth to more areas of my body than contact points.

Forevermore, I would have two memories to choose from when thinking of this bridge: hearing the music with an unimpressed Brannon, or hearing it with Kent. Of the two, I must admit, hearing it with Kent has been far more moving. Kent understood the music and the moment. Brannon never did.

"Shall we go?" It has to be after two.

Kent steps back and thrusts his right hand into his suit's inside breast pocket.

My heart stops. My breathing stops. My mind screeches to a halt. If he goes down on his knee...

He doesn't.

Instead of a small square velvet box, he holds out a long, narrow one. "For you."

I still can't breathe. My breath refuses to return as if I've been punched in the diaphragm. Seconds later, I'm able to inhale. The gulp of air sets my normal breathing back, faster and shallower.

Kent hovers over me, his face crinkled with concern. "Are you okay? Do you need an ambulance?" He holds me upright, his head swiveling manically, looking for help. "Oh, God, is the emergency number 9-1-1 here?"

I place my hand over his as I croak out, "I'm okay. It's okay." The box is still in his hand. "W-what's this for?"

"A little souvenir. I should have given it to you in the livery car. It would have looked sensational with your dress. But I forgot." He gives me a sheepish look of apology.

I remove the bow and open the box. Inside, on a velvet base embossed with the word Cartier, is a string of pearls. "Oh!" I exclaim. "They're beautiful! You shouldn't have..."

"Perhaps, but I did. It's a thank you gift for everything you do for me," Kent's voice is low and gentle. "Want help putting it on?"

"Yes, please," I say as I turn around and lift my hair out of his way.

Kent drapes the pearls around the front of my neck. I can feel his fingers at the nape, his skin brushing against mine in feather light touches. Each delicate brush sends shivers down my spine, and my pulse races. He struggles with the fishhook clasp in the dim light of the streetlamps. I turn slightly so he can see better in the lamplight. The fine hairs at the base of my head stand erect as his hands withdraw.

Light breath swirls against my neck as he draws closer. I'm expecting him to whisper in my ear. Lightning flashes through me when I feel his lips dropping soft kisses along my exposed neck. My breath holds, as his arms encircle my waist and turn me around.

His Adam's apple bobs and his head inches down until his lips find mine. And oh, sweet God, it feels so incredible that my toes curl and my knees weaken. I clutch the lapels of his jacket and lean in, giving him no doubt that I desire him. I press forward seeking more. He moans at the contact of my breasts against his chest, and he lessens the kiss before letting space between us.

He gazes into my eyes and says, "Let's go back. We both need as much sleep as we can get before tomorrow's flight."

"Sleep?"

"Yes. I can't—we can't—not here."

I know what he is saying. We can't risk getting caught. I nod my understanding.

He hails a cab and gives the driver the hotel's address card. The man glances at it and hands it back. In half an hour, Kent is walking me to my hotel room door.

I unlock it and start to say goodnight. Kent stops me and hands me the empty necklace box. "Whatever happens from here on out, please know there's a reason."

His piercing gaze reminds me of the first night we saw each other. The night I fell asleep during Copland's Third Symphony. I get an odd sensation in my chest at his words. Something does not feel right. "What do you mean?"

"Just as I said." Without another word, he retreats to the elevator for the ride to his suite.

I stumble to bed, shucking my Chanel evening gown and everything else until I am naked. The last thing I take off is the necklace. I return it to its box and place it in my regular handbag. My morning alarm is set before I crawl under the covers for a few hours' sleep.

Just before dawn I wake up in a panic, panting and my heart thundering. I dreamed of pearls in a sink full of water. The water begins to spin and curl, flowing down the drain, taking the necklace with it.

THE BOMB

IT TAKES FIVE DAYS for my body to adjust back to Eastern US time. I've spent the time doing laundry and making Glee feel special. We'd been separated for ten days, and despite the sitter, she's been skittish since we got back.

Kent hasn't been around much. Which is probably a good thing. I might have expected us to resume the affection we started in Paris. But that hasn't happened. Kent remains distant, preoccupied about something. The lack of communication baffles me. Is it because, now that I'm back as his employee, he chooses to keep me at arm's length?

He is out the door before seven without breakfast or even coffee. Off to work, so he says. It's rather odd, considering all that transpired on our last night in Paris. When he gets home from work, he changes into casual clothes as he usually does, but then holes himself up in the music room.

It's only from Mrs. Farthing that I hear about the fallout. The usual post-tour briefing was held to discuss any triumphs and any problems encountered. The board members in attendance expressed dismay at the cost. The Baymont Orchestra's share of the revenue from the different concert halls is months away from being known. Malcom Trier, in particular, emphasized his feeling that touring was unnecessary and too expensive to ever do again. She also reported that Maestro Grant was silent throughout the entire meeting, a murderous look on his face.

On the sixth day back, I'm in the backyard garden catching up on the weeding when I receive a call from the McAuliffe Agency.

"Hello, Mrs. Wainwright."

"Hello, Mrs. Davitt. I hope you are well after your whirlwind European tour."

"Yes. I'm finally back on American time. It's an improvement being back home. I'm finishing up a catch-up chore. Somehow the gardens became overgrown with weeds in only ten days." My tone, like my mood, is light and airy, however, I'm perplexed. I can't imagine why Mrs. Wainwright is calling. My next performance evaluation is six months away. Unless there is a problem I'm not aware of. I pull my garden gloves off and sit on the bench as my shaking knees feel too weak to hold me up.

"I have some good news for you. I've found you a new post with the head of the surgery department at Baymont Hospital," she says with a chipper tone. "He's willing to offer you five thousand dollars a month to work for him."

For the second time in less than two weeks, my breath halts, and my pulse races erratically.

"Mrs. Davitt?" Mrs. Wainwright asks. Seconds later, she sighs. "Oh, my dear. I'm so very sorry. He hasn't told you yet."

Finding my voice, I croak, "T-told me what?"

"Mr. Grant is letting you go."

My back stiffens. It doesn't seem plausible. The kiss, the trip, the dress, the pearls, all made it seem like he is happy to have me working for him. Happy with my services. Perhaps even in love with me. Fire me? Now? After all that? It doesn't make sense, and my head spins.

I want to call Kent for an explanation. But I don't. He's orchestrated this announcement in a cowardly manner, letting the agency break the news. Instead, as I usually do, the first person I call is Clare. At her greeting, my control dissolves. Wailing so hard I can't believe she can understand my words, I cry, "He's fired me!"

"What? You didn't know it was coming? Was a reason given?"

Clare is as surprised as I am. How many times did we talk on the phone about doing the housework, fixing up the backyard, the cat, whom I've already decided will go with me, and the two fundraisers? "N-not a c-clue," I stutter as I sob. "I—I can't believe it."

Clare's voice is calm. "You start packing, I'll bring over more boxes and borrow my neighbor's cat carrier. You're staying here until you can get this straightened out."

"What about Louis? His cat allergy?"

Her voice hardens. "He'll have to suck it up and take allergy pills until we can get to the bottom of this mess."

I wash up and spend the rest of the afternoon packing up my things. Clare brings over the extra boxes and the carrier. I clean out the mini fridge, strip the bed, and put the sheets in the washing machine. Time feels of the essence but I won't leave a mess behind. I don't want to see Kent again. Not ever.

Within the hour, everything I own is tucked into Clare's Volvo wagon. I put the sheets in the dryer and leave the key on the kitchen table. Beside it, I place the Cartier box holding the string of pearls. I don't leave a note.

• • • •

I RETURN TO MY OFFICE after the meeting with Malcolm and the rest of the symphony's board. The meeting, which was meant to sign my contract, didn't go as planned. Not for them, anyway. Except for Malcolm. Despite his obvious pleasure at seeing me squirm, I can't help but feel better. For the first time in a very long time, I feel...free.

My cellphone beeps to notify me there's a voice message. I left it on my desk so I wouldn't be interrupted during the contract negotiation meeting. The message is from Mrs. Wainwright at the McAuliffe Agency, asking me to call her as soon as possible.

"You were trying to reach me?" I ask when she answers the call.

"Oh, Mr. Grant. I am so sorry to disturb you, but I'm afraid I have created an incident," she says, her voice filled with distress. "I didn't realize you hadn't told Mrs. Davitt about letting her go." She sniffles. "I'm so sorry to have spilled the beans before you told her."

My heart stops as I realize what she's saying. I can barely breathe. "Abigail knows? You told her? How long ago?"

"I'm afraid so."

"How long ago?" I nearly shout, my insides trembling with electricity. I need to get to Abigail so I can explain.

"About four hours ago. I am so very sorry, Mr. Grant," She wails.

I remind myself it's an honest mistake. Mrs. Wainwright didn't know I haven't spoken to Abigail yet. It was my intention to do it after my meeting with the board. But the meeting was long and contentious. "I have to go," I say, disconnecting the call.

Driving like a madman, I think of how bad this is for Abigail. She trusted Brannon, and he failed her, leaving her insecure. She trusted that doctor to give her a full-time job, and he let her down. And now it looks as though I've let her down too. Uprooting her yet again, leaving her insecure, unstable, and homeless again. I slam my fist against the steering wheel, my molars aching from clenching them so hard. I have to tell her the truth. Get it all out into the open. Only then can she believe in me, trust in me, come back to me. I have to tell her I love her. No more hesitation and no more fumbling with the words.

When I arrive home, the townhouse is silent. I immediately see the key and the Cartier box containing the pearls on the kitchen table. Taking the stairs two at a time, I sprint up to her suite. The door is open and the room swept of her belongings. The bed stripped down to the mattress, the door of the fridge left ajar.

As if it is reverent ground, I walk in to look out the back window. The garden is lush with colorful blooms and greenery. The little pond with its waterfall still gurgling away. The garden bench, where I often found Abigail reading, devoid of her presence. I have to find out where she went. Probably at her college friend, Clare's house, but since I don't know Clare's last name, I can't look it up on the internet. But Clare and her husband are symphony season subscribers.

I call Evelyn, my jaw set tight. "Find the address of a Clare and Louis, who have a season subscription."

HOMELESS AGAIN

GLEE AND I SETTLE AS best we can into Clare and Louis's home. Thank God they have a nearly empty basement where I temporarily store my boxes. Glee timidly explores the new environment. The bedroom door is kept closed to prevent Glee's cat dander and fur from activating Louis's allergy where he sleeps.

Clare makes dinner for the three of us, but I decline. I'm too shaken to eat anything.

The cat cuddles on my chest as I lie on the couch, awake much of the night.

I feel like I did when Brannon died, except without the sense of relief that his suffering was over. Depression engulfs me like a heavy wool blanket, pressing down and making it difficult to breathe. Inside, my thoughts roar.

How could he do this? Leave someone else to inform me instead of telling me himself? Why? What did I do or did not do that caused this? My breath quickens at one thought. Was it because I didn't go to bed with him? If that is the case, I'm happy to be rid of him. My mind comes up with dozens of other scenarios. Still, I can't believe it's vindictive. There has to be something else. Something I don't know about.

In the morning, as Clare and Louis start to stir, I feign sleep with the blanket pulled up over my head so as not to disturb their privacy. Glee remains tucked against my side. Louis leaves first, giving me a chance to talk to Clare alone. I yawn and fling back the blanket. Glee gets up, gives her adorable kitty yawn, and stretches.

Clare joins me in the living room. "Please, make yourself at home. You don't have to go anywhere just yet, do you?"

I shake my head. "I have to call the agency. See if there's anyone looking for a housekeeper."

She smiles too wide. "Well, that's great. So you won't have—"

"—to be here very long." I finish her sentence. At that moment, I understand she's pretty sick of dealing with my repeated failures. Frankly, I am too, so I can't blame her reaction.

Her glare darkens, and her fisted hands settle on her hips. "That's not what I was going to say!"

"Doesn't matter. It's the truth," I murmur. Glee hops up on my lap.

A look of exasperation fills Clare's features. "I'll be at work. Call me if you need anything."

My composure crumples, and I start to cry. "You know what makes this so hard?"

Clare sits on the armrest and holds my hand. "Tell me."

Tears stream down my face, my heart aching, ripping to shreds. "This is worse than when Brannon died. He didn't have a choice. If given one, he'd have recovered and stayed. Kent made the choice to throw me out. Fire me. His abrupt rejection and departure hurts twice as bad as Brannon's loss."

Clare kneels beside the couch and holds me as I wail so loud that Glee gets scared and hides. After a few minutes, I settle down again. "You better get to work," I sniffle, my voice cracking. The last thing I need is to screw up Clare's life any more than I already have.

She stands to leave. "Call me if you need me. I can be back in twenty-two minutes tops."

Nodding, I take the box of tissues she hands me.

When she's gone, I pick up my phone to call the agency. My phone is dead and I'm not sure where I've packed the charger.

The box of my essentials is beside the recliner, and I search through it. Finding the cord, I plug it into the outlet and into my phone. Within seconds, notifications are ringing like a church bell, one after another.

Knowing Kent might have left one, I begin listening to my voice messages. Thirty-seven messages are from Kent. As soon as I hear his voice, I delete it. I don't want to hear what he has to say. It doesn't matter now. Three messages are from the agency. The doctor wants to interview me today. *Not today.* I delete the message. A second and third message from Mrs. Wainwright, asking me to call her. At least she sounds sympathetic to my position.

Shuffling to the bathroom with my overnight bag, I spend the next half hour showering and getting presentable. As I dress in my favorite pair of jeans and a button-down shirt, I mull over the situation. I need to move on, no matter how painful it is. Clare and Louis need their privacy back. A kernel of hope warms in my gut that I could be out of their hair in a few days.

Finished dressing, I fold the blanket and spread it over the back of the couch. Glee finds the recliner more comfortable this morning. Curled up on the fabric, she purrs away when I brush my hand over her back. "Hang in there, buddy. We'll find a new home soon."

Feeling refreshed physically, if not mentally, I call Mrs. Wainwright.

"My dear, I've been trying to reach you. The head of surgery wanted to see you in his office at seven this morning." She sounds perturbed that I missed the interview.

"My apology. I've been under the weather and my cellphone died."

Her tone changes. "I know, this is a shock to you. If it makes you feel any better, he's always sung your praises...said you were doing splendid work. I never expected this."

"That makes two of us." I stare at Glee, who is lapping at her paws. "One thing, Mrs. Wainwright. I have a cat. Mr. Grant allowed me to get her, and she's part of the package deal. I won't give her up. So, whoever is considering me as their housekeeper should know the cat is coming with me."

"Oh," Mrs. Wainwright says. "Hmm, let me get back to you. I had three inquiries for you, but the cat might be a deal breaker.

Household staff don't usually come with pets. Is there no one who can take her?"

My back stiffens. "She's *my* cat. I'm not getting rid of her for anyone."

Her heavy sigh fills my ear. "Okay. I'll be in touch."

Satisfied I've laid down the law regarding Glee, I make breakfast. Glee comes over, weaving around my feet. She gives me a loving meow and purrs, as if thanking me for speaking up for her. Or does she only want breakfast? I pour her a bowl of chow and water. She pounces on the chow immediately. That bit of necessity done, I warm a cup of cold coffee in the microwave while waiting for my toast to pop up in the toaster. When it does, I snoop in the refrigerator for butter and jam. My heart stills at the sight of a jar of marmalade.

The doorbell rings, and the bottom drops out of my stomach. I know who it is. How did he find me?

CONFESSIONS

A GLANCE THROUGH THE peephole confirms my suspicions. It is Kent. His features are haggard. There's gray circles under his puffy red eyes, and his hair is messed as though ravaged by a windstorm. Despite this, he looks amazing in jeans and a T-shirt, both of which appear molded to his body.

"Please open up. I need to explain," he pleads.

My eyes close, and I lean back against the door. A lump blocks my throat, and my heart pounds erratically in my chest. When he begs again, I unhook the chain and open the door. I anchor my hands on either side of the door frame. Whatever he has to say can be said on the doorstep. "Say it."

Seeing his way blocked, he steps back as though he doesn't want to push me. "I'm sorry I didn't forewarn you, but I'm not sorry about what I did."

Bile rises to my throat. His words strike me like a punch to my heart. This man, this man I've trusted with the secrets of my life, has totally failed me. And he isn't sorry? It seems incredulous after the last six months we've spent in each other's company. Especially after that kiss in Sutton Lake, the dinner of a lifetime in Paris, and the necklace he gave me. My spine straightens, and I hold my head high. "It doesn't matter. You've made your wishes known. I've moved out and I'm moving on."

"No! That's not what I want!" he explodes, advancing on me. "Please let me in so we can sit down. I have some important things to tell you. Things that will make you see what is truly going on here."

He reaches out to take my hand, but I brush it away. "I'll give you five minutes."

I step away from the door, letting Kent pass into the room.

His clothing looks as though he's slept in it. He sits on the couch and pats the spot beside him.

I need to sit elsewhere, where he can't touch me. I don't want my body to overrule my head. I hate what he did, but my heart still aches for him. Aches to love him instead of fight with him. Even so, I steel myself for some bombastic explanation. I settle into the rocking chair beside the fireplace.

Glee comes into the room, meowing. She looks at me, then at Kent, as if choosing sides. When she makes up her mind, she nuzzles Kent's leg. A semi-grin breaks out on Kent's face as he bends to stroke the cat's fur.

Ingrate! So much for the one who saved her and fed her from her abandoned kitten state. I cross my arms over my chest, further angered by Kent's intrusion and Glee's treason.

I tap my fingers against the wooden arm of the rocking chair and start rocking at a good clip. I glare at the two of them, the man and the cat. "Well, I'm waiting for your explanation," I glance at the time on my phone, "and your time is running out."

Kent continues to pat the cat, who settles in his lap. "I need to explain a few things that happened months ago to make this all make sense. Starting back at the dinner party with Franco Cartoni."

My rocking continues at an agitated pace. "Go on."

"That evening, Franco told me he didn't have long to live. Mere weeks, actually. He also told me that if I wished, he'd put in a good word for me to replace him at the Venetian symphony. Chances were slim. They'd likely prefer to give it to another Italian conductor, but I figured what could it hurt?" He shrugs in a *come what may* gesture.

My chair slows a little. Glee is belly up in Kent's lap, his hand rubbing the soft fur there. My teeth clench. Glee has never done that for me. Every time I've tried rubbing her belly, she's lashed me with her claws and twisted out of my reach.

"At the funeral, I was approached by the chairman of the Venetian symphony's board of directors. Mr. Enrico de Luca. He asked if I wanted to be considered for the job. I figured, why not see what they have to offer and what I can offer them in return? I couldn't stay longer due to commitments here, so we made plans to meet again during the European tour in July." He pauses as the cat jumps down from his lap. "We met up in Geneva. If you recall, I snuck away for two hours. He and I discussed the prospects."

Glee jumps up on my lap. I stop rocking and stroke her feather-like fur as she nuzzles my chin.

Meanwhile, Kent continues his story, "When we got to Cologne, I teleconferenced with him and the rest of his board. By the time we reached Paris, I had an offer and a contract waiting. I signed it in Paris. I start there on October 1st."

My eyes bulge open. I can't believe he's leaving. Leaving Baymont's symphony, leaving Baymont, and leaving me behind. The gall of this guy, to up and leave everything he's worked so hard for over the last ten years. While I didn't understand his motive for doing this, a tiny part of me knows he hasn't been exactly happy in Baymont. Especially after the Cynthia and Malcolm fiasco.

"Why leave now? What's the hurry?"

He sighs and runs his fingers through his disheveled hair. "Before the tour, the board offered me a new contract. There were some unacceptable changes in it...no more livery car, no more assistant conductor, no more stage tuxedoes, no more tours to other countries, and no raise."

I blink rapidly. "But why?"

Kent shrugs with a heavy sigh. "Malcolm's a control freak. He doesn't like the fact that I knew about his tidy affair with Cynthia. He broke it off with her, perhaps he was afraid I'd out his affair to the rest of the board. I believe the dismal contract offer the board just gave me is meant to get me to leave. Retaliatory, perhaps, but it worked."

I ponder his explanation. "Well, I guess congratulations are required." Glee goes belly up in my lap. I oblige and stroke it. She closes her eyes and purrs. "That's why you fired me. You're moving to Venice, Italy."

"Yes, and I don't have much time. But you didn't have to move out so abruptly. It will be a few more weeks before the townhouse goes up for sale. I told the board and the musicians yesterday, and handed in my notice. They've already posted my position.

"Hmm." It all sounds too neat. "You didn't tell me."

"No. I didn't have time. I called the agency and told them I was moving to Europe. It seems they promptly called you. I should have told you first. I'm so sorry you found out in such an insensitive manner."

I close my eyes, listening to my heart shatter like windshield glass into a million chunky pieces. I struggle to my feet, sending Glee flying. She lands on the carpet, gives me a well-deserved hiss, and walks away. "Well. Thank you for the explanation. I appreciate it." I march to the door.

"I'm not finished," Kent says, remaining seated comfortably on the couch.

"I am. You don't have to explain anything else."

He rises and grasps my hand, holding on while I try to pull it away. "I want you to come with me."

My insides freeze. He can't be serious. A loud voice in my head asks, Why not? What's keeping you here? I glare at him. "I'm supposed to leave everything behind to go to Venice to be your housekeeper?"

His gaze holds mine. "No." He slips down onto one knee beside the couch. "I'm hoping you'll go with me as my wife."

I can't breathe again. Is he serious? He strokes the back of my hand, turns my palm over, and kisses it. His lips graze each of my fingertips. I'm shaking like an earthquake. "S-seriously?"

"Of course, I'm serious. I've been fighting my attraction to you since the day you walked into my office for an interview." He raises his index finger and adds, "Even though you fell asleep during my performance."

He slowly shakes his head. "I've tried to keep my distance. You are my employee. It could be a fiasco if you and I...and yet, I couldn't help kissing you in Sutton Lake. I thought your reaction and your dismissal were because of your husband."

"It was then. But...my feelings changed incrementally." Tears well in my eyes, my thoughts racing. "All this time...all this time I've been fighting my attraction to you, you've been doing the same?" Fat, happy tears slide down my cheeks.

Kent stands and pulls me into his arms. "Yes. I knew, I could sense your feelings. But I couldn't act on them until I was sure. After that kiss...well, let's say I felt rejected. I questioned if I'd got things all wrong...that you didn't like me as anything more than a friend. Our time together on the tour told me I was right the first time. I chose to trust my gut."

"I'm sorry for all that. I—"

"It doesn't matter now."

When he pulls me against his chest, I let him. The heavy thud of his heart matches my own.

"So, Abigail...will you come with me to live in Venice as my wife?"

At that instant, Glee meows crazily, weaving herself between our legs.

Somewhere during all my blubbering, I say, "Only if we can bring Glee."

He flashes me a lopsided grin. "I've already checked. We can."

Kent's soft lips brush mine. My control crumbles, and I kiss him back like I'm devouring him. I feel the vibrations of love, and passion and safety passing between us. Our lips pressed together again. Kent says, "Say it."

He kisses me harder, opening my mouth against his and slipping his tongue inside to twine with mine. Our bodies meld together like this is where I've always meant to be. Like I was indeed made for the maestro.

I break free for a nanosecond. "Yes."

• • • •

EPILOGUE AVAILABLE free at https://getmybook.com/ djul3z76d6

Acknowledgments

Thanks to Valerie Lynne and the Connecticut Chapter
of Romance Writers of America for critiquing the
manuscript at various stages of its development.
Kudos to Marion and Tabitha, my beta-readers,
for providing insight into the readers perspective.
My editor, Lynne Pearson, from allthatediting.com
...It's *always* a pleasure working with you!
Extra special thanks to a conductor who wishes
to remain anonymous, for his help understanding
what and how a conductor does his/her job.

Coming next! Title TBA: Chapter One

CATHERINE GALAN BREEZED into her favorite restaurant, her gaze bobbing to acknowledge the greetings and smiles of the restaurant patrons. Some diners held out their hands to grasp hers, while others rose to kiss her soft, pale cheek.

One woman, a cousin by marriage, insisted, "Lady Catherine, we must get together soon! We have so much to talk about."

Catherine graciously smiled and patted her cousin's arm. "Amelia, I'll give you a call this week to arrange our date," she said before retreating to the private table in the back corner of the room.

Her shopping bags dropped to the marble floor with a light thud as she sat down across from Keith Duncan. "I'm so sorry I'm late. The fitting took far longer than I anticipated." Her fingers touched the silverware, adjusting each piece to suit her OCD fancy.

"Cat, you could have texted me." Keith's grimace flashed, his jaw stiff, and his back rigid. "Besides, it looks as though you did some shopping on the way here." His chin jerked in the direction of her pile of bags. Bags from shops just three doors down from the restaurant.

She forced a smile on her face. "Grace Lily and Ink & Pink had sales going and today is the last day." Catherine coyly shrugged one shoulder. "I don't think you'll mind once you see the lingerie I selected for our wedding night." She ignored his clenched teeth. "Come, now. Let's have our dinner." She gestured for the waiter who stood a distance away, waiting to take their order.

As the waiter approached, Keith growled. "Still, you could have warned me. I've been sitting here, waiting, for over a half hour, Catherine."

On hearing his snip, the waiter reversed direction and retreated to the kitchen.

Catherine reached out her left hand, her long elegant fingers, the gelled nails painted a pale pink, her engagement ring sparkling in the dim light. "I'm sorry, darling. It won't happen again, I swear."

Keith picked his napkin off his lap and threw it down on his empty plate. "That's what you said last time, and the time before that. All the times before that." He glared hard at her. "Tell me why I should stay?"

The bottom of Catherine's stomach dropped. She had told him that, so many times before she couldn't count them all. "Because you love me." She quickly added, "And I love you." She flashed him a sympathetic dazzling white smile. "Let me tell you about the few changes the wedding planner and I have made. I know you're going to love them!"

He crossed his arms over his broad chest. "What is it this time?" His eyebrows bunched as his glare deepened.

Dread curled in her stomach this time. She had promised him there wouldn't be any more changes. "I'm going to arrive at the kirk on Mars, my newest Arabian horse. You're going to meet me at the kirk door and escort me down the aisle to the minister." She tried to ignore the hardening in his eyes, but it accelerated the furious pounding in her chest. "Once we're married, Ross will escort Mars down the aisle. We'll mount him and ride out of the kirk together." She couldn't help the cracking of her voice even though an amused look shown on Keith's face.

Keith burst with laughter so loud the other diners stopped speaking and stared at them. When he caught his breath, he asked, "Did you clear this with Reverand Barry?"

Catherine's hands shook out her napkin and placed it on her lap. "Well, not just yet. But he's an old friend of my father's. I'm sure he will allow it."

His eyelids closed and he slouched back in his chair. "Catherine. Why does this need to be such a circus. It's a wedding. A private one at that. Can't we just have a quiet service?"

Catherine gasped. The audacity of him to suggest they do something so banal on their wedding day. "Keith, we've known each other all our lives. When have I ever done things half-baked?"

"Now's the perfect time to start. We won't be living so high flung when we're married."

Throwing her shoulders back, she said, "I have standards I must adhere to. I'm a daughter of a Lord."

"That shouldn't matter." He ran his fingers into his blond hair, then gripped the lot of it as if he were going to tear it out. "Let's just elope. There's no need for a huge production."

Ripples of horror caught in her throat. "B-but we should do this up royally..."

"You are not royal, damnit."

She blinked rapidly, trying to force her tears out. "Still, I deserve...better."

Keith groaned and shook his head. "Don't try those manipulative fake tears on me. They won't work this time."

· · · ·

KEITH PRESSED HIS LIPS together. He was so tired of fighting with her about her folly for extravagance. It's no use. She couldn't...wouldn't understand he lived a simple life. A life he preferred over her more aristocratic ways, and craved to maintain despite the different social status levels between them.

Somehow she'd got it in her head that marrying him, she'd bring him up to her level in society. When he'd wanted just the opposite. A quiet, private wedding. A sedate life living at his house in the village. He closed his eyes knowing he hadn't even broached the topic of where they would live. Her new job at the soon-to-be-open art gallery in town would keep her in Nairn, but that didn't mean they'd live at the castle. It finally, irrevocably dawned on him, she wasn't going to change.

He held out his hand across the table. "Give me your left hand."

Catherine smiled her beautiful smile, probably thinking she'd won this argument as she had all the rest. Her delicate hand, her long slim fingers caressed his open palm.

"Catherine. I'm reneging my proposal." He pulled his mother's engagement ring off her finger.

Also by Diana Rock

Fulton River Falls Series
Melt My Heart
Proof Of Love
Bloomin' In Love
First Christmas Ornament
Quest For Love

Colby County Veterinary Series
Bid To Love
Courting Choices
Tulsi's Flame

Standalones
Hollywood Hotshot
Havilland's Highland Destimy
Little Bit of Wait
Maid For The Maestro

Don't miss out!

Visit the website below and you can sign up to receive emails whenever Diana Rock publishes a new book. There's no charge and no obligation.

https://books2read.com/r/B-A-YUKN-QLTFG

BOOKS 2 READ

Connecting independent readers to independent writers.

About the Author

Diana lives in eastern Connecticut with her tall, dark and handsome hero and two mischievous felines. Diana likes puttering about the yard, baking and cooking, hiking, fly-fishing, and Scottish Country Dancing. Sign up for Diana's newsletter at DianaRock.com to receive special news, blog posts and free books and bonus chapters.

Read more at DianaRock.com.

www.ingramcontent.com/pod-product-compliance
Lightning Source LLC
Chambersburg PA
CBHW020319200626
46814CB00006BA/2321